TRAVELLING LIGHT

TRAVELLING
LIGHT

PETER BEHRENS

This edition published in 2013 by
House of Anansi Press Inc.
110 Spadina Avenue, Suite 801
Toronto, ON, M5V 2K4
Tel. 416-363-4343
Fax 416-363-1017
www.houseofanansi.com

Distributed in Canada by
HarperCollins Canada Ltd.
1995 Markham Road
Scarborough, ON, M1B 5M8
Toll free tel. 1-800-387-0117

House of Anansi Press is committed to protecting our natural environment. As part of our efforts, the interior of this book is printed on paper that contains 100% post-consumer recycled fibres, is acid-free, and is processed chlorine-free.

17 16 15 14 13   1 2 3 4 5

Library and Archives Canada Cataloguing in Publication

Behrens, Peter, 1954–
Travelling light / Peter Behrens.

Issued also in electronic format.
ISBN 978-0-88784-827-8

I. Title.

PS8553.E3985T72 2013   C813'.54   C2012-906737-7

Cover design: Alysia Shewchuk
Cover photograph: Jarrod McCabe
Text design and typesetting: Alysia Shewchuk

 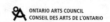

We acknowledge for their financial support of our publishing program the Canada Council for the Arts, the Ontario Arts Council, and the Government of Canada through the Canada Book Fund.

Printed and bound in Canada

For Mary Behrens and Aidan O'Neill

And the girls I tried to talk to after class
Sailed by, then each night lay enthroned in my bed,
With nothing on but the jewels of their embarrassment.
Eyes, lips, dreams. No one. The sky & the road.

A life like that? It seemed to go on forever—

—from "The Poet at Seventeen" by Larry Levis

BOY'S LIFE

CIVIL WARS

Civil War

We used to fight race wars in Montreal. Think of us in our snow boots, ski jackets, and woollen tuques. The wars began with each side — French and English — building its snow fort and packing snowballs, then venturing out to attack the enemy.

The violence — fraying, hysteric — escalated with each assault wave. Screams were our language. We had icicles for spears; when our supply of snowballs was exhausted, we hurled chunks of ice. We fought hand-to-mittened-hand, floundering in fresh snow, spitting and clawing at each other's numb, freezing faces.

From a certain distance — given the thinness of our northern air, the pellucid quality of our sunlight, the crisp shadows cast by spruce, maples, elms — our warfare may not have appeared as vicious as it was. War's beauty often deceives. Flesh was sensitive in subzero January afternoons; every blow ached, wounds bruised yellow. Drops of blood plummeted through deep, crystalline snow, and by the time we disengaged, most were crying, tears glueing our eyelashes.

What troubled me was the disloyalty of Frances, my older sister, who always fought alongside the French kids. Her alienation from us was essential, like a code sculpted on a gene. The sheer strength of her; the way she slashed and thrust with the icicle in her hands. Both of us screeching, me trying to punch her in the belly, land a good solid one, fell her.

Teeth

Our city was studded with churches like pieces of costume jewellery, too massive to be valuable. The power of the Church was weakening, though when a bus drove past a church, most men tipped their hats and many passengers made a Sign of the Cross.

In sermons wedged between Mass rituals we were told that sin was native and natural and confession the cleansing, the only virtue. Year after year we genuflected on cue, then roused ourselves to stroll up the aisle and receive a Holy Communion wafer. Returning to our pew, kneeling, I sucked the pulpy host from my teeth, swallowed it, then slipped my teeth around the back of the pew in front of me and bit hard, compressing the dead cellulose, tasting the salt and the varnish. *That* was hard and real, and bitterly satisfying.

The Structure

Montreal was as close to home as my father ever got. There was a middle-class Jewish neighbourhood at one end of Queen Mary Road, and two miles away, at the intersection of what had become Boul. Reine-Marie and Côte-des-Neiges, a French-Canadian neighbourhood had mushroomed from a farming village to gather itself defensively around the Université de Montreal, whose space-age campus sprawled up the mountainside. Most restaurants in the city were owned by Greeks. Lower Outremont was occupied by Hasidic Jews and once-Yiddish streets east of Park Avenue were Portuguese. There were tattoo parlours for sailors on St. Lawrence Main, and across the Lachine Canal, the oldest industrial district, where the *Scotch*—not the Scots—made nineteenth-century fortunes importing molasses from the West Indies, refining sugar, milling wheat, and manufacturing rope and shoes. Irish Griffintown was cut up with new highways and concrete overpasses, but a black stone marked the grave pit where victims of famine and ship fever were buried.

He took us on long drives through districts no one else we knew had ever visited. Always east: to the locomotive shops, Molson's Brewery, Maisonneuve Ward. Street after street lined with three-storey walk-ups and steep iron outside staircases. He steered us down boulevards crowded with factory workers after the factory whistles blew at noon on Saturday. He took us to a Sunday Mass in a Hungarian church, a Portuguese church. He bought salami at a Czech delicatessen on the Main and black bread from a Russian crone in a bakery in Park Extension, but my sisters and I would not eat it. In the back seat of the Buick we were restless, bored, unsettled by the exotic feel of whatever it was that attracted him.

Tenants

We lived in an apartment, not a house. In the summers he rented us a beach house in Maine or borrowed a cottage in the Laurentians from his rich friends. His early life had included unhousement, internment, deportation. Success in business wasn't enough to restore what was taken away in August 1914, on the Isle of Wight, when his German father—suddenly an "enemy alien"—was arrested and removed and imprisoned for four years. After the armistice they were immediately deported to Germany. My father and his Irish mother did not speak German. He learned to. He came of age in the Weimar Republic. After Hitler was appointed chancellor, my father made plans to go to Shanghai, but when that city was suddenly occupied by the Japanese army, he went to Canada instead, travelling on his British passport.

His suits and shoes were made in London. He sent his children to expensive schools and stayed in the best hotels whenever he travelled, but he would not, could not imagine himself as a homeowner. Which word was more alien to his flighty sense of himself: *home* or *owner*? He never possessed any part of the security granted as birthright to other families we knew. He invested in life insurance policies and we lived as tenants and people in borrowed houses.

The French Kids

Their names were Daniel and Yvon; they had moved into a flat across the street; their building had the best driveway for playing baseball. Their mother was a producer at Radio-Canada and a separatist; they didn't have a father. We fought them for years, also played hockey, soccer, and baseball with them. In a driveway between two apartment buildings I watched a baseball fly upward and bounce on the roof of the building across the street, and sometimes this was our language, but the relationship was unstable, the peace always fragile, and we were prepared to resume hostilities at any moment.

They would not speak English and we did not speak French. Nonetheless, one summer, working together, we built a race car from scavenged lumber, a rain barrel, and a set of lawn-mower wheels. We dragged it to the top of our steep street and took turns hurtling down the hill, past barking dogs in what felt like a movie about fear, speed, and collapsing time.

The Janitor

He came from the country up north. Tall, with a dark complexion and strong cheekbones, *comme un Huron*, people said. He seemed ferocious stalking up the street, pulling a cart with his tools, the knot of keys jangling at his belt. He swept snow from the walks using a broom of twigs bound to a broken hockey stick. In the spring he slung storm windows down to the street on a rope and hauled up copper mesh screens, old and stiff, streaked with green.

The building stood somnolent in midsummer, panting in the heat. When we tried to play handball in the cool, earth-smelling garage, the janitor shooed us outside, to gum-soft asphalt soaked in hot light. But the afternoons sometimes broke open with thunderstorms, sudden slabs of rain, trees swaying like hula dancers, the steep street a black torrent, nervous drivers pulling over to the curbs, glints of yellow light, and everything shining for a while.

Sacred Heart Convent

Frances passionately loves the nuns and will stay late to help

arrange folding chairs in the auditorium or stuff packets of
biscuits into gift boxes to be sent to the mission in Uganda.
On Saturdays she chaperones rich Central American board-
ers on shopping expeditions downtown, and is always on call
to help decorate the chapel. Even my parents are jealous of
her devotion. When our sister Jean is enrolled as a day girl,
Frances spins a narrative that permeates the school. According
to Frances, Jean has been a terror ever since the day she was
adopted. Jean bit a doctor's hand deep enough that blue cords
of glistening muscle were exposed. Arrested for shoplifting
at age seven, Jean still wets her bed savagely. Denied *The
Monkees*, she seizes the television set and pours it out the window. It explodes hitting the sidewalk, and shards of picture
tube zinging through surprised air kill a dog. None of the
stories are true. Maybe Frances is describing her dreams. But
she is captain of the basketball team and president of Student
Council, and Jean, the new girl, is shunned. At the gymnas-
tics exhibition before Christmas break we sit in folding chairs
and watch Frances launch off a springboard and fly over a
wood-and-leather horse. She soars up, up beyond the suppli-
cant hands of spotters, her back arched and arms spread in a
perfect flying angel, face tranquil and pale like the face of a
saint upheld to the light.

Saturday Midwinter
Saturday mornings he wore suede oxfords, a tattersall shirt
from L. L. Bean, and a pair of old grey flannels. He visited the
public library, borrowed history books, diaries of statesmen
and soldiers, and detective novels. He took us on long, desultory drives through distant parts of the city, neighbourhoods

no one else ever visited. Now I understand he was trying to attach himself to something. He took a glass of beer with his lunch and a small piece of bitter European chocolate. Afterwards he fell asleep on the sofa in the living room while listening to the Metropolitan Opera broadcast from New York. The steam radiators were scalding to touch, the air brutally dry, dust motes spun in shafts of winter sunlight. By four thirty it would be dark outside. Someone brought him his tea. Window glass was stinging cold. There were heaps of snow in the street below, isolated yelps from the few·children still out playing.

The Café

On Wednesday nights they always ate dinner at Café Martin on Mountain Street. He had been a regular since his bachelor days. Mountain Street was named after Bishop Mountain, first Anglican prelate of Montreal, but by the seventies its name had been changed to Rue de la Montagne. We admired their lives, the scent of her perfume, her sheath dresses, the burnish on his beautiful shoes glowing from somewhere inside the leather, and tried hard not be angry when they left us behind with a sitter, but anger, like electric current, can deliver lethal shocks, or illuminate cities, and it never just disappears.

The School

The headmaster chain-smoked and was a pioneer in the field of sex education. The school was trying to soldier its way through the sixties. We endured warning lectures from psychologists and policemen, drug raids in the locker room, bomb threats from separatists. When the fire alarm sounded, we streamed out to Royal Avenue and formed ranks patrolled by prefects. We were caned for infractions and learned to live in the shadow of fear, mostly fear of humiliation. In the hallways ancient chalk dust mingled with the scent of watery soup from the dining hall. Hallways, museums of doomed youth, were lined with sepia-tinted team photographs of a generation of Old Boys slaughtered in the trenches. They wore their hair parted in the middle, ferociously slicked down. The rolled necks of their woollen hockey jerseys caused them to lift their chins, which gave them a tautness, a wariness as they gazed at the camera, as though they were aware of the history awaiting them.

Europe

On birthdays our grandmother sent five-pound notes and English children's books in brown paper parcels tied with brown string, the knots lumped with scarlet clots of sealing wax. Before the First World War she had been an Irish governess in Saxony, where she met our German grandfather, whom she called "Bobs" and who was dead. When she came to Montreal, she attempted to school us in the manners and style of the Edwardians, or perhaps the gentry of pre-war Saxony. She spoke German badly and no French. Her boyfriend, the Count, had been in a cavalry charge and lived in the same seaside boarding house at Bournemouth. She could describe her parents being pelted with garbage on their wedding day, at Sligo. She had walked out of Frankfurt's rubble in 1945 to barter silver picture frames for potatoes in black fields. Montreal was less real for her than Europe, and at the dinner table on Sunday evening she liked to draw our father,

her son, into arguments about politics and history, Germany and England and Ireland, and my sisters and I escaped as soon as we could and headed for the TV room, where Fred MacMurray was starring in *My Three Sons*.

Operating Instructions

You understand that everything we tell you about ourselves and everything we say about the others is partly a lie, partly a dream, and not to be trusted.

Autoroute

My parents did not trust the French to run things fairly and were always annoyed with the government. They did not speak French themselves. In Montreal you could get by without it but in the country it was more difficult. One Friday afternoon we were headed north on the Laurentian autoroute when our car was pulled over by a Sûreté du Québec cruiser. My father said *bonjour* but the cop did not reply, only held out his hand for licence and registration, then returned to his grey and yellow police car with the documents while my father muttered about *storm troopers*. When the cop came back and wordlessly handed over the ticket, I felt compressed between my father's irritation and the cop's silence. People sharing a country but not a language come together clumsily and dangerously, like jealous armies.

The Fall of New France

Through our mother we were descendants of an Irish officer who sailed up the St. Lawrence with General Wolfe's army and camped all summer on Île d'Orléans while the artillery pounded Quebec. On a September night the British crossed from the island on boats and the soldiers filed up a narrow trail at Anse au Foulon. They had nearly gained the heights when one alert sentry challenged, *"Qui vive?"* Our ancestor, educated at the Catholic universities of Louvain and Paris, replied *"Vive le Roi!"* his delightful accent causing the sentry a few seconds hesitation, during which his throat was cut. The remaining pickets were overcome and the British regiments formed in line of battle on a wheat field just outside the town walls. In the foggy morning General Montcalm attended Mass at the Ursulines Convent, then sortied his troops through St. Louis Gate to give battle on the field. He was shot in the breast, his army broke and ran, and Quebec fell to the British, all on account of our ancestor. Wolfe died too.

The Game

The French had been calling themselves *Canadiens* when we were still British. By the time we were Canadian they had become *Québécois,* our histories chasing each other, jealous, intolerant, never quite letting up. *Le club de hockey Canadien* was also known as the Habs — *les habitants*, pioneers of New France. They were slight, tough, wiry; deft stick-handlers. Their best skaters could stop on a dime and leave you nine cents change, people said.

When the referee who had ejected Rocket Richard from a playoff game in Boston the week before dared appear on Forum ice with his chrome whistle attached to his finger like a wedding band, people threw smoke bombs, then ransacked St. Catherine Street, the biggest riot since the Legislative Assembly was burnt down in the eighteen forties.

The night in 1965 when the Canadiens played the Chicago Black Hawks for the Cup, you were in the stands because your parents were in Europe and the housekeeper's daughter, Bridget, had won a pair of tickets in an office pool and by some miracle of grace flowering from her lonely young spinsterhood had invited you, age ten, to accompany her. You travelled down Côte-des-Neiges on the 65 bus, then walked west along St. Catherine Street in the thickness of an anxious, well-dressed crowd and squeezed into the Forum to find your seats high in the blues. Charlie Hodge and Glenn Hall were goalkeepers and Claude Provost shadowed Bobby Hull—the Golden Jet—so closely he hardly got a shot on goal. And when Beliveau, captain of the Canadiens, skated his victory lap, Cup hoisted high, sweat soaking his red jersey black, how you cried and cried.

He Died

He died in a hospital room in Montreal believing he was in Frankfurt and it was 1939. He had returned that summer hoping to persuade his Catholic but hopelessly cosmopolitan parents to quit Germany for England or Canada. He was unsuccessful. He managed to squeeze aboard the last train for Rotterdam with his British passport, hours before England declared war. He was stranded at Rotterdam for three weeks before he got passage to New York. From there he caught the train up to Montreal, where half a century later he sits up in his hospital bed commanding me to fetch his suitcase from the closet, we have to get to the *Bahnhof,* catch the last train, the Dutch frontier will be closing and he'll be trapped in a country gone insane. Quickly. Hurry. Hurry!

Intersection

Frances has a partner at last and pays the fertilization clinic and they have a baby girl and Frances loves their baby but the partner will sometimes remark, almost casually, that the baby is, after all, *her* baby, not *their* baby. The partner threatens to take the baby and move back to Russia or to Toronto and we see how difficult this is for Frances to hear, how vulnerable she is, how hard she works to support her little family, and we resent her partner for being cold, ungrateful, and more than a little crazy. A few days before the baby's first birthday Frances is on a business trip to Chicago. It's raining. The car she's a passenger in runs a red light and gets T-boned by a truck. Frances is killed. What does her life feel like to her, approaching that intersection in the rain? Does it have a texture and a shape? Is it something she can nearly hold in her arms, like a baby?

But Frances lives within herself—then she doesn't—and what she knows she never tells.

French Kids (II)

My father was dead and I finally persuaded Mother to leave the flat, which had become too large and empty after years of being too small and crowded. Five or six different landlords had owned the building during the past few years. The heating machinery was breaking down. The janitor had died and there was no one to shovel the snow from the steps. I found her an apartment in a modern building with a doorman, just down the street from the church where she was married. On the last day of the move I was putting a last carton of odds and ends into the trunk of my rented car when I saw Daniel, one of the French kids, across the street. I had not spoken to him in twenty-five years, except once when I helped him and his brother push a car out of a snowbank. Now Daniel was also loading cardboard cartons into the trunk of a car, a Toyota, the same model my mother owned, except blue, not grey. I crossed the street and we shook hands. For years I had been taking French lessons in California; at last we spoke the same language. He said his mother was leaving the neighbourhood as well, going back to Victoriaville, where she had grown up. He was a mathematician, his brother Yvon a sound engineer. It was like an encounter with a friendly stranger, also with someone you are afraid knows you too well. I don't know why children who share a street, a neighbourhood, prefer to ignore history until it shrivels and carries no weight and finally melts away like snow does eventually, even in Montreal, but that was what we had done and it was too late to do anything about all that now.

YELLOW DRESS

This time Dr. and Mrs. Ormonde had been invited to a conference in Moscow and another in Helsinki. Every time they went away routines were broken, food tasted differently, the house itself felt foreign. Silver-framed family photographs on the hall table seemed like portraits of strangers, and Ross felt he and his sister Anna were living the lives of different people, not the children who'd once lived at their address.

To make it worse, their housekeeper, Marie-Ange, had gone back to the Gaspé after her brother was killed in a fire. She had not returned, and a new woman, Mrs. O'Brien, had arrived in a taxi with her suitcase only one hour before the Ormondes left for the airport.

Ross and Anna watched from the living room window as she got out of the cab. "Ugly old hag!" Anna whispered.

The first Sunday their parents were away, Mrs. O'Brien took them to Mass at her own parish in Verdun instead of their church, the Ascension of Our Lord, in Westmount. "I've a daughter whom I have to keep an eye on," Mrs. O'Brien explained.

It took three buses to get to Verdun from Westmount. On the steps outside the church after nine o'clock Mass, they were introduced to Mrs. O'Brien's daughter, Joan. Ross thought she looked too old to be anyone's daughter. Her hair was orange and black. She was clutching a handbag, and a missal.

"So these are the Ormondes!" Joan said. "Aren't they sweet?"

People were already going into the church for the ten o'clock Mass. Joan dropped the missal into her purse and took out cigarettes and matches. Her slip showed beneath the hem of her dress. A button dangled from the front of her coat.

"Ah, Joan, can't you make the effort, at least?" said Mrs. O'Brien, plucking off the loose button and nodding at two old people entering the church.

"Look at you," she said, turning back to Joan, who had lit a cigarette.

"What's wrong with me?" Joan said.

Cigarette ash dribbled onto her coat and her mother swiped at it, leaving a streak of grey on the cloth.

"Did you go out last night?" said Mrs. O'Brien. "Were you alone? Did you have company?"

"No, I was watching the game. Were you?" Joan said, looking at Ross.

"Sure," he answered. He always watched the Saturday night game. The Canadiens were the greatest hockey team in the world, and Beliveau was the best player.

"I thought Monsieur Tremblay might call," Joan said to her mother.

"He didn't though, did he. Get him out of your silly head, my girl!" said Mrs. O'Brien. "Come, I don't like this smoking in front of church."

They trooped down the steps and began walking to the O'Briens' flat. Ross had never been in Verdun before. The rows of three-decker houses were made of brick the colour of dried blood. In a few of the small, square front yards, crocuses were poking up through crusts of snow.

Mrs. O'Brien went into a corner shop and Joan turned to Ross. "Don't you miss your parents?"

He did. He worried a lot about them. They might never return. There could be a plane crash.

"They *have* to go away," said Anna sharply. "Daddy *has* to go to conferences."

Joan laughed.

Mrs. O'Brien came out of the shop with a big bottle of ginger ale. Anna walked on ahead with the housekeeper and Joan and Ross followed a few steps behind.

"I'll tell you," Joan said, "I didn't like it either. I used to hate her for going away to look after other kids. I was put with neighbours and they were not very nice."

They had to climb a steep outside staircase. The O'Briens' flat was on the third floor. It was dark inside, warm, and smelled of linoleum. There was a green velvet sofa in the living room, an old-fashioned radio, and a tinted photograph of Pope Pius XI.

"Sit here and I'll bring your ginger ale," said Mrs. O'Brien.

Joan took off her coat, sat down, and patted the space beside her on the sofa. "Come sit. Don't be shy!" she said.

Anna ignored her and sat down in an armchair. Ross sat on the sofa. Joan's perfume smelled like lemons. Her red nail polish was chipped. She wore a yellow dress with short sleeves. The dress needed cleaning and a seam at the shoulder was a little torn.

Joan lit a cigarette. "Who's your favourite player?"

"Beliveau!"

She laughed. "Monsieur Tremblay says Beliveau is even better than the Rocket. How'd you like to go to the Forum? I won a pair of tickets for the fifth game. I might as well take you."

"Who's Monsieur Tremblay?" said Anna.

"My fiancé."

"How come you don't go to the game with him?" said Anna.

Joan didn't answer. She stabbed out her cigarette and picked up the newspaper from the floor, snapping it open and hiding behind it. All they could see were her chipped red fingernails gripping the edge of the page. Looking at Ross, Anna raised her eyebrows.

Ross heard the icebox being opened and shut and ice cubes rattling. The flat was so small he could hear the bottle being opened and ginger ale fizzing into the glasses.

"You know what?" Joan spoke from behind the newspaper. "Don't you wish it were summer? I wish the snow was all gone and I didn't have to wear a coat."

Catching Ross's eye, Anna pointed her finger at her head and twirled it around. She thought Joan was crazy. Mrs. O'Brien came in with four glasses of ginger ale on a tray.

"Joan! Put down the paper. I thought you said you weren't going to wear that awful dress anymore."

"Joan invited my brother to a hockey game," said Anna primly.

"We'll see about that," Mrs. O'Brien said. "Why won't you go with your precious monsieur?"

Joan was silent. Ross felt sorry for her. If she felt like taking him to a hockey game instead of Monsieur Tremblay, what was so bad about that?

Mrs. O'Brien, Ross, and Anna drank their ginger ale. Joan stayed hiding behind her newspaper.

"We're leaving now, Joan. Mind, I don't want to see things going on like this," Mrs. O'Brien said. "Drink up, children."

Mrs. O'Brien collected her heating pad, her iron pills, and an orange-juice squeezer and put everything in a shopping bag. Joan put the newspaper aside and followed them to the door. She grabbed Ross's hand and said, "I was only joking. Monsieur Tremblay isn't my fiancé. He's married to someone else."

"Come, children, we'll miss our bus." Mrs. O'Brien herded Ross and Anna out the door.

"Goodbye, goodbye," Joan called gaily, as they descended the steep iron staircase.

Dr. and Mrs. Ormonde had been gone a week when Mrs. O'Brien put Anna's red skirt into the washing machine with her white blouse. The red dye ran out, ruining the blouse. Anna was furious. "You'll pay for it!" she yelled. When Mrs. O'Brien told her to calm down, Anna stamped around the kitchen. "Stupid old bitch! Stupid old bitch!" she screamed. When Mrs. O'Brien said to hold her tongue, Anna picked up her wet blouse and whipped it at the housekeeper. Mrs. O'Brien leapt forward and slapped her, and Anna grabbed the old woman's hand, digging into the flesh with her fingernails. Mrs. O'Brien screamed. Anna ran down the hallway and slammed the door of her room.

Mrs. O'Brien leaned against the sink, wearily. Her eyes were very pale blue.

"She always has a big fight with someone when they go away," said Ross.

"Why?"

Why did their parents have to go away? He knew Anna shared his anxiety, but neither of them wanted to talk about it because talking about it made the possibility of their parents not ever coming home seem more real.

When she came home from school the next afternoon, Anna apologized to Mrs. O'Brien and the housekeeper made cinnamon rolls for their tea. They were sitting at the kitchen table when the doorbell rang.

Ross went to the door and found Joan already turning away, as if she hadn't really expected anyone to answer the bell.

It had been raining all day. The snow was gone and rainwater was sluicing through the gutters. "Is my mother here?" Joan whispered, unbuttoning her raincoat. Her stockings were spattered with mud. A plastic rain bonnet was tied under her chin.

"Joan?" said Mrs. O'Brien, coming down the hall. "What do you think you're doing here?"

"Oh, don't worry, I'll only stay a while." Joan pulled off her raincoat and was about to drape it over a chair when her mother seized it.

"Not on the furniture!"

Mrs. O'Brien opened the hall closet and placed the coat on a hanger.

Joan took off her rain bonnet. She was wearing the yellow dress. She picked up the photograph of Ross's mother in its silver frame and gazed at it.

"Leave things be, Joan," said Mrs. O'Brien.

"She's like someone in a magazine," Joan said, "with those beautiful pearls around her neck."

Mrs. O'Brien took the picture and set it back down on the table as the kettle whistled on the stove. "You may stay for tea, Joan, but then you'll have to take the bus home."

As Mrs. O'Brien hurried back to the kitchen Joan stuck out her tongue. Then she winked at Ross. Standing before the hall mirror, she touched her hair. "How are you all getting along?"

"Okay."

"No squabbles?"

"Not really."

He followed her into the dining room. Inside the dining room cabinet, next to the salt bowls and pepper shakers, was an envelope that had been in there as long as Ross could remember. *To Whom It May Concern* was written on it in his father's handwriting. Folded inside was a sheet of paper with a typed list of phone numbers, bank accounts, names of lawyers and doctors and relatives. The envelope was to be opened if their parents did not come back.

Joan gazed at her reflection in the polished dinner table, then wandered into the living room. Taking a handful of cigarettes from a silver cigarette box, she bundled them into a tissue and placed them in her purse. "You know what? Where Monsieur Tremblay lives must be like this. If I lived here, I'd never go away."

"They're coming home in ten days."

"Well, they'll go away again," she said. "That's the kind of people they are."

He followed her to the kitchen, where the housekeeper was pouring tea. Joan sat down and stirred two spoonfuls of sugar into her cup. As she spread jam on a cinnamon roll, a blob of the jam fell onto her yellow dress.

"Oh, Joan," said Mrs. O'Brien. "Take your dress off and let me rinse it."

Joan scraped at the blob with her knife.

"Let me have it," said Mrs. O'Brien. She stood up. "Go into the bedroom and put on my robe."

"I'll wash it myself." Joan sat back and lifted her teacup. She eyed her mother lazily.

"It has to be done now, otherwise the dress will be ruined."

Ross could see spots and stains all over the dress. It hadn't been washed for a long time.

"Raspberry jam is the *worst*," said Anna.

Joan put down her teacup and laid both hands flat on the table. She was smiling.

"Take off the dress," said Mrs. O'Brien.

"You'll ruin it otherwise," said Anna.

Joan walked down the hall towards the bedroom. She didn't come out, and when they had finished their tea, Mrs. O'Brien sent Ross and Anna outside to play.

It had stopped raining. There were puddles everywhere, water dripping from bare branches of trees. They got on their bikes and rode through the neighbourhood for the first time since autumn. The gardens all smelled of mud and the roads were strewn with wet sand left over from winter.

Anna began pedalling faster and faster, pulling ahead of him. Finally she skidded to a stop and stood waiting, astride her bike.

"They won't come back," she said as he rode up. "There's nothing you can do. You can wish for them all you want but it won't matter."

She pedalled away and he stood gripping his handlebars. He felt helpless. He started for home. As he rode up their street he saw that everything was exactly the way it had been before: the branches bare, the smell of mud. He put his bike in the garage then found Joan sitting on a stool in the kitchen wearing a green dressing gown and reading *National Geographic*. She did not look up. Mrs. O'Brien was washing dishes in the sink. The damp yellow dress was spread out over the radiator. It looked like a petal from a huge flower brought down by the rain.

Joan came to dinner two nights later, still wearing the yellow dress. This time she brought two bottles of Black Horse ale, which she and her mother drank with their meal. Joan said she had won the pair of hockey tickets in an office pool, and Mrs. O'Brien finally agreed that she could take Ross to the Forum. But after supper he stood outside the kitchen door and heard them arguing.

"I wish you'd sold those tickets," Mrs. O'Brien was saying. "You could do twenty-five dollars for the pair and get yourself a new dress. I'm surprised they haven't sacked you already, going to work in rags. You're not brushing your hair," Mrs. O'Brien said, her voice rising. "They'll have you in an institution before long."

When the Ormondes were away they sent postcards. Ross received a card showing the onion domes of the Kremlin lit up at night. Then there was a postcard of their hotel: his mother had marked their room with a little X. Ross studied the cards, kept them for a few days, then tore them both into tiny pieces, which he threw out his window at night.

Next afternoon he came out of school and saw Joan O'Brien waiting at the entrance to the schoolyard. He slipped away from his friends and warily approached her.

"I was on my way home from the office," Joan said. "To tell you the truth, I got fired a couple of weeks back, but they were still holding my hockey tickets for me." She looked at him sternly. "Don't go telling my mother I was fired, now. That's our secret. All right?"

"All right," said Ross.

She took a pair of red-white-and-blue tickets from her purse and showed them to Ross. "Now let's go get a Coke."

Down on Sherbrooke Street his schoolmates were waiting at the bus stops. He followed Joan into a greasy spoon where the tables smelled of harsh cleaning fluid. They sat in a booth and Joan removed her gloves. A waitress brought their Cokes in bulbous glasses stuffed with ice. Joan took the bundle of cigarettes wrapped in the tissue from her purse and lit one.

"How come you always wear the same dress?"

"Who says I do?"

"Every time I see you, you do."

"Don't you like it?"

"Well, it's okay."

"I bought this dress at Holt Renfrew," Joan said. She puffed hard on her cigarette and the ashes fell off, dropping onto the table. "One lunchtime I went in to buy mascara. I had a few minutes so I went up to the third floor. Mother says I waste money, but what's wasted if it makes you feel good? The first day I wore this dress Monsieur Tremblay stopped and picked me up at the bus stop when I was waiting for the bus home. He was driving his car, and he gave me a lift. We were going along St. Patrick Street and he says, 'Joan, what a pretty new dress you have on today.'

"He drove me right home. We talked about the Canadiens. I hoped he'd pick me up again but he never has. I tried to see him at work but he's not in my department and he's always busy. I tried phoning him at home but his wife answered. I think she's someone beautiful, like your mother with her pearls."

That night Ross wrote his parents by flashlight, using red ink. He described Anna's fight with the housekeeper. He told them about Monsieur Tremblay, Joan, and the yellow dress. He told them Joan would be taking him to a hockey game. He said he was looking forward to going to the Forum and watching Beliveau score goals.

Joan arrived at the house on Saturday evening wearing her overcoat with the button missing. Underneath she was wearing the yellow dress. Mrs. O'Brien said if she couldn't look decent she couldn't take Ross to the game. But it was too late for her to go home to change. Mrs. O'Brien took Dr. Ormonde's clothes brush and made Joan stand in the hall while she brushed the overcoat ferociously. "You're the one that needs a brushing!" she said. "If I was strong enough I'd take the back of this to you!"

Finally she let them go, and Ross and Joan hurried to the bus stop at the corner. The evening was cool and shiny and the sidewalks crackled with leftover grit. They caught a bus heading down Côte-des-Neiges and Joan sat with her purse on her lap, smiling and not talking. When the bus began its long swoop down the mountainside, she grabbed Ross's hand and gave a hard squeeze. They got off at St. Catherine Street and joined the crowd streaming towards the Forum. There were policemen on horses, and the hooves made a bright, clapping sound on the road.

Inside the main door of the Forum they handed their tickets to an usher and were swept by the crowd down a passageway. As they came out into the arena, Joan took off her coat and carried it over her arm. They asked another usher for directions and were pointed towards their seats. People turned their heads to watch Joan go by. When they reached the correct row, people stood to let them pass. One or two said hello or *bonsoir* and Joan nodded regally and smiled.

"You promised you wouldn't wear that thing!" said a chubby blonde woman sitting directly above them.

"Ross, this is Molly," Joan said to Ross. "She was my best friend at the office."

"You promised you'd turn yourself out tonight," Molly complained, "and here you are wearing that thing. They'll never take you back. They're running an office, Joan, not a circus where people can wear any old thing."

No players were on the ice yet but the stands were filling up and the arena felt alive with excitement. The ice gleamed and the air smelled of smoke and steam. Molly introduced her husband, Frank, sitting next to her. Frank worked for the Canadian Pacific Railway. He had binoculars on a strap around his neck.

"Let me see those, please," Joan said.

Frank passed her the binoculars and she began scanning the rows of seats below them. Ross saw the two teams step onto the ice from opposite ends of the rink. The goalies skated slowly, like grandmothers, towards their respective nets. Beliveau was the last of the Canadiens to step on the ice, and the crowd roared.

Molly leaned over, tapped Joan's shoulder, and pointed to a couple climbing the stairs. The man wore a dark blue suit and a double-breasted camel-hair coat, and he carried a fedora. The woman wore a mink stole. Ross guessed it was Monsieur Tremblay and his wife. Joan stared through the binoculars. When play was about to start, Frank tapped Joan's shoulder. He wanted his binoculars. Joan handed them over reluctantly.

Beliveau won the face-off and scooped the puck to Yvan Cournoyer, who immediately rushed in on goal. "Shoot! Shoot!" Joan screamed. Cournoyer slapped a shot but the Boston goalie trapped it casually and held on for the whistle.

Halfway through the period there was still no score, and Joan asked Frank for his binoculars. The Tremblays were seated six or seven rows below, next to a skinny little man whom Molly said was vice-president of the company.

Molly leaned over and whispered in Joan's ear.

"I'm not going to do anything," Joan said. She pressed the binoculars to her eyes. Tonight she smelled of warm wax, Ross thought, like candles being extinguished. Every time the Canadiens had control of the puck and pressed the Boston goal, people around them stood up. Joan stood up too but she kept the binoculars pressed to her eyes.

At the end of the period Boston was ahead by one goal. The Tremblays rose from their seats.

"Want a Coke? Want a hot dog?" Joan asked Ross.

They went downstairs and behind the stands, where the concessions and restrooms were. The cement floor was strewn with litter that had been flattened by thousands of pairs of shoes. Ross noticed the Tremblays in front of one of the booths, sipping drinks from plastic cups. Monsieur wore his camel-hair overcoat draped elegantly across his shoulders, like a cloak.

"Why did he have to bring her?" Joan said. "What am I supposed to do now?"

"Want a Coke?" said Ross. "I'll buy you one. I have money."

Then Molly appeared out of the crowd and took Joan's elbow. Molly began steering her towards the ladies' room. "We'll see you back at the seats," Molly told Ross. "Can you find your own way?"

"Sure."

Ross joined the line at a concession stand and bought two Cokes in plastic cups. The Tremblays were a few feet away, talking with another well-dressed couple.

A buzzer sounded and people began pressing into the passageway that led to the arena. The second period was about to start. Ross found himself squeezed right behind the Tremblays, close enough to catch a whiff of Madame Tremblay's perfume, the same as his mother's: Chanel No. 5.

The crowd was eager to see the face-off and he was being pushed right up against Monsieur Tremblay. The two cups of Coke were very full. He hadn't had time to snap the lids on and the first time he spilled some, it was an accident. The puck was dropped and the crowd roared and he couldn't see a thing. Then he spilled another splash of Coke onto Monsieur's camel-hair coat. He did it deliberately, not thinking why he was doing it, and not caring if he was caught. It soaked into the camel-hair coat which was the colour of butter, almost. Little brown drops dripped from the hem. But Monsieur didn't turn around—he hadn't felt a thing. Ross knew all about spilled Coke—it was sticky. It made a mess. He kept sloshing Coke out as they started up the steep arena stairs. He was right behind the Tremblays but they didn't turn around; like everyone else they were in a hurry to get back to their seats and enjoy the rest of the game. He had splashed out half of the Coke in both cups before the Tremblays reached their row and people started standing up to allow the couple to get to their seats.

What was left of the Coke he dumped into one cup, dropping the empty on the stairs. When he reached his seat he handed the Coke to Joan and she immediately asked for a straw, which he had forgotten to get, but she drank it anyway, and her eyes kept shifting back and forth, back and forth between the action on the ice and the Tremblays.

In the intermission between the second and third periods the Tremblays stayed in their seats. Frank brought hot dogs for Ross and Joan and Molly. Joan kept the binoculars pressed so hard to her face that they left red rings around her eyes.

"You look like a bird," said Molly. "A flamingo or something, like in Florida."

At the beginning of the third period the Canadiens scored

two quick goals. Boston came back and tied the game. With two minutes of play left, Ross watched Beliveau charge down the ice, nuzzling the puck on his stick. Beliveau lured the Boston goalie from his crease, shouldered aside a defence-man, and made a deke that had the goalie sprawling on the ice. Then Beliveau flipped the puck over the goalie's prone body into the net.

Everyone was on their feet cheering. Seven rows below, Monsieur Tremblay was hugging his wife. On the ice the Canadiens were dancing on their skate blades and touching Beliveau with the tips of their sticks, hoping for a piece of his magic.

With one minute left in the game, the Tremblays left their seats and began moving towards the exit. Monsieur had a cigar in his mouth; his wife was holding his arm. That was when Joan called, "Hello, Monsieur Tremblay! Hello!"

Monsieur Tremblay glanced over his shoulder. He smiled and waved vaguely in their direction and kept going down the stairs.

"He didn't see me," Joan said. "He didn't know it was me." She stood up quickly but Molly and Frank grabbed one of her arms each and pulled her back into her seat as the crowd began chanting, counting down the last few seconds on the clock.

The siren sounded and the Boston players left the ice and fled down a passageway to their dressing room. The Canadiens clustered in front of their bench, hugging their goalie, slap-ping each other's pads, congratulating each other. People were chanting, "Bel-i-veau! Bel-i-veau!" Joan was the only person in the whole Forum still in her seat. Her coat had fallen on the floor. Ross picked it up and Molly took it from him.

The crowd roared even louder as Beliveau was pushed out from the knot of teammates and started skating a slow victory lap around the rink with long, effortless strides. Beliveau dipped his head from time to time, acknowledging the cheering, and Ross, who couldn't take his eyes from the team captain, felt love sweeping through his body, like wind fluttering a banner.

VOODOO STARFIGHTERS

I know that she's not crazy. She hears secret messages. Not really secret, but I'm too young to hear them. When the fighters cut across the summer sky — Sabres, Voodoo jets, CF-Starfighters — they split the air like thunder, and my mother goes into her bedroom and hooks shut her door.

Messages come from out on the muskeg late at night, when my father is away on base. Base is sixty miles from our house. I have never seen it. I was born in Montreal and then we went to Germany, but the muskeg swamp is the only home I remember.

When she hears messages, she comes into my room, her feet scraping on the floor. She lights the lamp and wakes me. I know what to do. I kneel and pull the shotgun out from underneath the bed. There are shells in the pine armoire but I don't need them; she doesn't make me take them anymore.

She waits in the room while I go down the stairs and across the kitchen, carrying the 410. Things that once frightened me — the shape of the stove, a kettle hanging from a nail on the wall, a jacket thrown over a chair—are familiar now in moonlight. I unhook the screen door and step out onto the porch. There is the smell of creek water, and sometimes I hear a loon or a beaver tail slapping. I stand for a minute or two with the gun barrel pointed at my toes. I know the Dipper, Orion, the Dog Star. My father says sentries on the base stay awake at night by sorting through the constellations.

I go back inside and upstairs. If she is asleep in my bed, I touch her shoulder to awaken her. After she has gone back to her own room, I slip the gun beneath the bed and put out the lamp.

She and I have always lived at Rockingham. There is no town, only pulpwood loggers, fishing guides, and farmers. The closest town is Saint-Viateur, twenty miles away. On Friday nights my father drives in from base, his car loaded with groceries. He stays two or three days, sometimes longer. He was a pilot in the war. He knows they're watching him at the base, and he hates the checkups the base medical officer puts him through four times a year. Any month, he says, may be his last on the flight list. In the meantime he is still a pilot. Voodoos and Starfighters are his ships.

In the summer mornings I watch the flight break from the western hills and scream down over the swamp. After the planes disappear, the air rings like a plucked wire until the tension breaks with a loud *boom*. Sometimes they sweep around again in formation and come down on a strafing run over the Rockingham–Saint-Viateur highway, checking their airspeed so that six miles away I can hear the howl of the engines.

My father plants the garden on Victoria Day, always black-fly season. We wear hats draped with netting and elastic bands around our sleeves and cuffs. He fertilizes the soil with manure from Maguire's barn, and swamp muck wheeled up the road in a barrow. I construct fences to stop the porcupines, using scraps of wood, chicken wire, mothballs. Our basement is lined with jars and tins of preserves, labelled by year. There is a tin casket for potatoes. We have a chicken house. In the autumn we'll hunt down a moose, haul it home in Maguire's truck, and butcher it in the yard. We have a smokehouse, and my father buys casings from a sheep farmer in Saint-Viateur to make sausage.

When he's on base, I take my mother out in the canoe to gather water lilies. Every year the creek changes course, but the scenery is always the same, with the same gaunt trees lining the banks. She trails her hands in the water. The dead trees are full of nests. Once a bird attacked us and kept attacking us until I stood up in the boat and fought it off with the blade of my paddle.

He drives us to Mass at Saint-Viateur on Sunday. I once lived for four days with the priest when I made my First Communion. At confession before Mass my mother goes into the booth before me and I hear her whispering in French. She never speaks French to my father or me, only to the priest, and sometimes to Maguire or Maguire's wife. After confession she kneels at the altar rail and says penance while the church fills up. When I go into the dark booth, it smells of perfume, and the leather pad is warm and creased where she has been kneeling.

The priest talks in English. "Alexander," he says, "wouldn't you like to come here to school with us?"

"I can't."

My father has told the priest I attend school at the base. At the base he tells them I go to school in Saint-Viateur.

"Why can't you?" the priest says.

"I go to school at the base. I'm learning to be a pilot," I tell him. "They're teaching me Voodoo and Starfighter."

"I will speak again to your father," the priest says. Then he coughs, the signal to begin confession. Later, when he says Mass, he wears gold and green robes and the church fills with incense. When it's over and we come out, our car is parked at the curb and my father is eating bakery rolls, drinking coffee from a cardboard cup, and reading a Montreal newspaper spread out over the steering wheel. His black hair is flecked with grey and brushed back against the sides of his head. He wears old khaki trousers and a flannel shirt rolled up at the sleeves. One of his forearms is marked with white blotches the size of dimes, shrapnel scars from when his ship was shot down over Germany. There are other scars scattered like coins across his back and shoulders.

He folds the paper and tosses it into the back seat when my mother and I get into the car. "Well, Lucie, did you enjoy yourself?" he says.

"The priest was asking about the schools."

"Screw the schools," my father says, starting the car. "He should read the newspaper. Berlin, Cuba—do you know we have bombers in the sky twenty-four hours a day? So do they. School or no school. Missiles everywhere. Underneath the ocean."

The priest, standing on the steps outside the church, is surrounded by old women. His robes look less wonderful in the sunlight. I can see the cuffs of his ordinary black pants. He is blessing the women one by one, but he's looking at us when we drive away.

"Maybe he's right about the schools," my mother says.

"You know there's nothing there but lying and catechism. I'd rather have him go to school on the other side. No hocus-pocus in Russia. Maybe later, in Germany, there'll be good schools."

There is talk on the base of the squadron's being transferred back to Germany.

"It's all so frightful," my mother says.

"Not to worry. We'll take care of you, won't we, Alex?"

We are heading down Rue Principale towards the gravel highway, passing people walking home from church.

"Can we stop at Pierre Cid's? I need some more shells. I want fishing line and candy. It's Sunday."

"What shells do you need?"

"One box, twenty gauge."

"Get any bunnies this week?"

"Two."

Cid's *magasin général* is at the end of the village. A group of old farmers with pipes sit on the bench in front of the store. A tin thermometer nailed beside the door says BUVEZ 7 UP and ÇA RAVIGOTE. I go in with my father and take what I need from the shelves.

"Well, Captain," says Pierre, punching at the register, trying to get the cash drawer to slide open. "Do you think there will be the war?"

"Without a doubt," my father says in French. "Always."

"You're right." The old man struggles with the drawer. He

is no good at operating the register and his wife shouts at him when he makes mistakes.

"If it doesn't start over Cuba," my father says, "it'll start over Berlin. Or Turkey. Laos. Those Chinese islands. If it doesn't start this month it could start next month, or next year."

"You're right!" The old machine makes a *ting* and the cash drawer slides open.

"Can I get some toffee?" I ask my father.

"One box of Mackintosh, Pierre."

Mackintosh toffee comes in a cardboard box with the honey-coloured slab of candy wrapped in wax paper. On the drive back to Rockingham I break the slab into small, sweet shards. My mother accepts a single piece but my father hates candy. I put a piece in my mouth and suck the flavour of burnt sugar. If you put your lips over the end of the empty box and blow, it swells up and makes a hoarse, moaning sound. A moose makes that sound when he's been shot — a good shot with a powerful rifle like my father's .30-06 — when he's going down and blood is in his lungs.

The gravel road from Saint-Viateur to Rockingham goes out past woodlots and a sawmill that isn't working. The road is oiled and graded three times a summer. The only traffic we pass is a stake truck hauling pulpwood and two Jeeps from the base. My father drives at sixty. My mother has rolled down her window and put out her arm, and her palm is swooping and diving in the breeze. Gravel spews from the tires and cuts into the bush, snapping and whistling through the leaves.

The turn for our road is at Maguire's. The Maguires are poor and dirty and they say my mother is crazy, they are the ones. Maguire has a boy, Pardieu, who speaks English and French at the same time. He and I sometimes go into the muskeg to kill beavers that dam the culverts beneath our road. Last year Pardieu came with us when we hunted moose. Old Maguire was a soldier in the old, old war; he was gassed and gets money. Last winter he killed a black bear and stretched out the skin on the door of his barn. He said he would take the skin to the base one day to sell it.

Pardieu has only nine fingers. The mother is fat and smells of vinegar. Old Man Maguire smells better, of smoke in the woods. In the springtime they make syrup up in the stand where the maples are. In the winter they cut pulpwood.

When Maguire was nailing up the bearskin, his wife pointed to me and said to her sister from Saint-Viateur, standing on the porch beside her, *"C'est le petit gars là*, the boy in the bush with the crazy woman."*

Maguire's skinny cows are out in the road. My father slows and honks his horn. I lean from the window, put my lips around the Mackintosh box, and blow. "Stop it!" says my mother, putting her hands over her ears.

From Maguire's it is another three miles in to our house. Before we are there our dogs have heard us and are out, dancing in the road. The great thing, my father says, is to be able to anticipate an attack. One war may be over, he says, but other wars always begin.

We spend the afternoon working in the garden. When he's ready to leave, he puts on his uniform and kisses us goodbye. After he has driven down the road my mother brings a chair out to the porch and sits for hours, watching the skeletons of trees against the red evening sky.

My father zips into his sky-blue flight suit and walks out to his ship.

Pardieu comes up the road. We pick up the canoe and carry it to the landing.

My father settles into the cockpit and locks down the canopy. He runs through a check in twenty-five seconds, then ignition.

Pardieu and I lay shotguns in the bottom of the canoe and start paddling. The canoe slides through brackish water. The muskeg smells of animals, birds, rotting pine.

My father has clipped on his oxygen mask and is starting to boost, tapping the throttle stick with the heel of his hand.

We've stopped paddling. We've loaded our guns and are trying hard to listen. The canoe rocks gently on the water.

My father streaks above us all, screaming.

SMELL OF SMOKE

Green remembers failing sunlight when he last saw her. Four o'clock in the afternoon and shadows of the arborvitae hedge and the maples, firs, and birches were already stealing across the lawn towards the swimming pool. It was still summer and it was almost over.

His mother and a couple of his aunts were reclining on chaise longues. The women had been sunbathing and were just starting to notice the freshness in the air. Maggie had disappeared into the cabana, wearing a two-piece bathing suit. She came out rubbing her wet hair with a towel, dressed in blue and white striped bellbottoms, a wide leather belt with a brass buckle, a T-shirt, and sandals. She was tanned from days of sailing on Green's little pram, the *Nutshell*.

He was stretched out on a chaise on the same side of the pool as the women, but separate from them. Turquoise water glinted between him and Maggie. He was still wet. They had raced twenty-five lengths and he had won. His skin stank of chlorine. He was shivering.

When Maggie called goodbye across the pool, his mother and aunts waved. As far as they were concerned, it was only the beginning of the end of another summer, and Maggie was only returning to Boston, where she took studio classes at the Museum of Fine Arts School—the "Museum of Fine Rats" she called it. Green watched her walk down the gravel path carrying her bathing suit and towel, pass through the gate, get into the white sports car, and drive away down Bord-du-Lac Road.

Maggie's parents' house was one of the oldest on the Lakeshore. In the days of New France it had been a manor house and a fur-trading post, and there were gun slits in the basement, where the *seigneur* and his family and servants barricaded themselves when the Iroquois and the New Englanders—*les bostonnaises*—raided up and down the St. Lawrence. The fieldstone-and-rubble walls were three feet thick. The gun slits were stuffed with pink insulation fibre.

People called it the Lakeshore, but the lake was really just a widening in the St. Lawrence River. The water had current, it had a flow.

The restless youngsters of New France and the fanatic Jesuits in their black robes used to set off from there, paddling upstream, plunging into the Ohio country, then down the Mississippi, baptizing Indians and claiming an endless *Louisiane* for the kings of France.

Now the Lakeshore was merely a Montreal suburb where businessmen built comfortable houses, paid yacht club dues, and took the train into the city five days a week. There were Indians in a village on the other side of the golf course, but they kept to themselves.

Blood and furs, fortune hunting, holy anointing oil, the transportation of faith—all that had been forgotten.

The Harrisons had no roots in Montreal. Maggie was born on an airbase in Labrador and her parents were from out west. Mrs. Harrison wore turquoise eyeshadow and a matching hair band. Maggie's father was an Air Canada pilot, flying DC-9s across the Atlantic every week. He drank rye and played golf. According to Maggie, he grew up on a ranch in Alberta, and he walked the fairways with a bowlegged strut.

Maggie and her parents spoke to each other in language so spare, so cleansed of inflection, Green thought they might as well have transmitted their communications using semaphore flags.

One afternoon when Green accompanied Maggie home, she left him in the kitchen with her mother, who, without asking if he was hungry, fixed him a peanut butter and jelly sandwich. Mrs. Harrison always fed Green, who was too unsettled in her presence to feel much of an appetite. Maggie reappeared a couple of minutes later carrying a compact vinyl suitcase, the type that was called a train case.

"Let's go," she said.

Green was standing in front of the dishwasher attempting to swallow the sandwich, which was sticking in his throat.

Mrs. Harrison said, "Where?"

"Green's for the weekend."

"Well. Take care."

The next thing Green knew, he and Maggie were out of the house, spinning along Bord-du-Lac Road in her white sports car.

Green's real name was Robert Greenaway Metternich.

Maggie was the only one who called him Green. The nickname was a joke, of course, but because it was hers exclusively, it had the click of intimacy to it. She used *Green* all summer, in public, around the yacht club. Green had no pet names for her. *Maggie* felt private enough, intimate enough.

Green wondered if anyone knew what they were doing. The unusual thing about their romance was the difference in their ages. Maggie was twenty-one that summer. Green was fourteen.

His parents occasionally questioned him, but they really had no idea how he spent his days, or what he thought about. There would be long spells with no questions whatsoever, then one morning his father would fire a volley across the breakfast table. "Are you sailing today?" "Did you read the editorial in the *Star*?" "Who are your friends at the club?"

Green did not give out more information than was absolutely required. He tried to emulate Maggie's laconic interchanges with her parents. The Harrisons' western Canadian accents were terse. Perhaps the brutal winds that came out of there — the Alberta Clippers — had taught them to shape words closely and to slip them out between barely parted lips, afraid that if they opened wider the cold would penetrate their mouths, freeze their tongues, crack their teeth.

Maggie's house and Green's were three-quarters of a mile apart on Bord-du-Lac Road. Both houses were quiet almost all the time, but Green decided hers was quieter. From just inside the front door he could hear the clock on the electric range ticking, though the kitchen was at the other end of the house. Perhaps the purity of the silence was also a western thing.

Early one midsummer morning Green was getting dressed

in a kind of stupor. Pulling on his shorts very slowly, tying the laces of his sneakers, looking out over the lawn at the silver maples and watching cars go by on Bord-du-Lac Road. He heard the words inside his head, then repeated them aloud. "I am in love with you, Maggie Harrison." He kept his voice low. He was an only child in a big house, so it wasn't likely anyone had overheard. The house was so solidly built that it ate sound.

"I love you, Maggie, and I want to marry you."

Saying the words made him dizzy. He thought he must be leaving his childhood, shedding it like a carapace. And suddenly he felt so open, so soft and unprotected, that he had to sit down on the edge of his bed.

He never repeated the words to Maggie. He cannot remember many of their conversations, but certainly he did not. He did not use the vocabulary of longing, because there was nothing unrequited in their relationship. Nothing unconsummated. He had everything he wanted before he knew what that was.

She did once say, "Green, if you were twenty-one, I would marry you."

She was peeing when she said it, in the pink bathroom attached to her bedroom, in the fur-trade house. Her parents were in Laguna Beach, California — they flew everywhere for free. Maggie and Green had just had sex in the basement and she had shown him the gun slits. Green pulled out handfuls of pink insulation fibre and peered through a narrow opening between the stones. It was dark, so he could not see the lake very well, but he could smell the water. He pressed his mouth and nose right up against the slit so that his cheekbones were touching cold, sharp rubble, and he breathed in the darkness and moisture, the scent of Indians, muskets, and fur.

He could imagine himself inside her skin, feeling what she felt, and so he understood how to touch her. How roughly, how softly, with what rhythm, and for how long.

It did not seem strange that she should pee in front of him, so unembarrassed, with her underwear crumpled in a ball beside the sink. It did not seem strange to be so intimate with a twenty-one-year-old woman.

And when she said that she would have married him if he were twenty-one, he understood she was not being serious. Marriage was as unlikely as a visit to Mars or a walk on the moon.

He used to have a Polaroid snapshot that showed half a dozen young people sitting on a diving board at the club. Maggie and Green were both in the Polaroid, but not sitting together, and no one seeing the photo would ever think of them as a couple. Green was just a boy, sunburnt and squinting, Maggie a wry, pretty young woman. Nothing in the photo connected them, but that was the night it had started, in the parking lot on the lake side of the road.

He doesn't know why she chose him, what role he was playing in her life that summer, if he was standing in for someone else or representing something, or if she was just a girl who got excited breaking rules. Screwing one of the older boys around the club would have been breaking the rules, but a pretty ordinary infraction. Screwing Green was more dangerous, though it was difficult for Green to see himself in those terms. At fourteen he was shy and polite—"well brought up," people at the club would say.

Perhaps she was looking for danger, but in a regulated dose. Danger that she knew she could handle. That was Green. She could handle him perfectly.

She did try to get him to dance at the club, but he would not, afraid of looking ridiculous. Not that the club dances were extravagant or formal, as they had been in his mother's era. On the Lakeshore in 1968, barefoot girls and boys in madras shorts hopped and shook to the call of a record player set up on the concrete patio by the club pool. There were bowls of potato chips, hamburgers on a grill, ice chests of Cokes, and Green, who was neither young enough nor old enough to feel at his ease.

Just the summer before he had built a diorama of the Normandy invasion on the Ping-Pong table in the basement, meticulously hand-painting hundreds of miniature troops and constructing the cliffs of Normandy from bricks, screen mesh, and plaster of Paris. He used matchboxes for German pillboxes and more plaster of Paris for the ocean. He painstakingly assembled, painted, and decaled plastic Messerschmitts and Spitfires, suspending the tiny planes on nylon thread with puffs of cotton wool to simulate an anti-aircraft barrage. He stole fine white sand from the sandboxes in Pointe Claire Park for his invasion beaches.

He had not anticipated the power of sex, the authority it would exercise over his happiness.

Whenever they slept together, his self-consciousness eased. He felt closer to a line of balance, almost graceful. He had grown four inches during the previous year and was so unaccustomed to his height that he could trip and fall over while walking on a smoothly clipped lawn. Maggie made him feel powerful. When they were sleeping together, she made him feel he had radiance in the world.

"Sleeping together" — they did not sleep much. During sex he was always hyper-awake. Afterwards they usually couldn't fall asleep without the risk of getting caught. Sleeping happened only on those weekends when both sets of parents were away.

The first time he slept with her in his bedroom he awoke before dawn, startled to feel her presence. She wore one of his shirts, nothing else. It had been a warm night and the sheets were bunched at the foot of the bed. She lay on her back. Her heat impressed him. He found himself studying the patch of fur between her legs. His own pubic hair was sparse; hers was thick. In the moonlight he could not tell its colour, but it gleamed. It could almost be blue, he thought. He ran his fingertips lightly through her bush and she stirred but did not awaken, and he fell back to sleep with his hand cupping her there. In the morning they had sex again, then she showed him how to make coffee using his mother's percolator.

At the end of summer Maggie went back to Boston and the School of Fine Rats, and a couple of months later her father was transferred from Montreal to Vancouver. The house with the gun slits in the basement went up for sale. Green got the news in a letter from Boston that he reread a dozen times and eventually lost; he was still too young to be able to hold on to such things, to value scraps of paper. One afternoon in October, on his way home from school, he went by the Harrisons' house and peered in through a window and saw the rooms were bare. A realtor's sign was plunged into the lawn. The Harrisons had already moved on.

Maggie had first brought him back to the fur-trade house after a Friday night dance by the club pool, when her parents were in La Jolla, or Santa Barbara, or Phoenix.

It was dark and she had tripped over a sprinkler while crossing the lawn. He remembers her small, fierce shout, like an animal snagged in a leg trap. He knelt down beside her on the grass. She was rubbing her big toe. There was a pungent aroma of chemical fertilizer and pine needles composting. She had placed her hand over his heart and looked straight at him, unsmiling. He was unaccustomed to such focused attention from anyone and it was hard not to look away. There was intensity in her gaze that he had never encountered before, also a coolness. She was looking at him, and seeing him.

For about a minute they stayed like that on the lawn, motionless. Then she got up without a word and he followed her inside.

About five months after Green last saw Maggie, he and his father were driving through an unfamiliar section of Montreal on a Saturday afternoon in January. Green's father was searching for a yard he had heard about that still sold bags of fireplace coal. Cordwood was available everywhere, and cheap, but Green's father had a nostalgic longing for the resiny aroma of coal smoke and the hissing, clinking noise of coals glowing in a grate.

But coal was hard to find. They had already tried two or three yards where split hardwood was selling for only

eleven dollars per cord, delivered, but at each yard the fore-
man claimed they hadn't sold coal for years. *"Depuis dix ans,
peut-être!"*

But Green's father was determined to find coal. It was a
very bright, very cold winter day, ten degrees below zero at
noon, white smoke licking from furnace pipes, snow in heaps.
The sky was electric blue, the river had frozen. They kept
driving through the unfamiliar part of the city, looking for a
coal yard—Green's father had been told about a place somewhere off Upper Lachine Road, or maybe Boulevard Saint-
Jacques. They heard on the radio news that a pack of wolves
had crossed the river and were frisking on the runways at the
international airport.

"Anything you want to talk to me about?" When he said
this, Green's father was leaning over the steering wheel, scanning unfamiliar street signs. "Anything at all?"

Green said there wasn't.

Then his father asked him to check to see if there was a city
map in the glovebox. Green unfolded the map and they kept
searching for the coal yard without finding it. Then Green's
father nosed the car into a parking space burrowed out of a
snowbank in front of a workingmen's tavern on Saint-Antoine
Street and asked Green if he would like to have a beer.

Green had never been inside a tavern before. There was
a slag of orange sawdust on the hardwood floor and men sat
alone at small tables, reading tabloid newspapers and sipping
slender glasses of beer. The television screen mounted in one
corner showed a blank green eye. It would be switched on for
the Saturday night hockey game, nothing else.

In those days, in the province of Quebec, women by law

were not allowed into taverns. His father ordered them each a glass of beer and showed Green how to sprinkle salt on the beer, to bring up the head. Green wondered if the entire outing had been carefully planned, if his father had been looking forward all week to this first glass of beer with his son, this little ceremony of masculine initiation.

Green understood he was supposed to put away the summer, forget it. That made sense. But he knew he wouldn't be able to.

In her only letter, Maggie had written *I wish we could do the things we used to do and I hope your mama doesn't read this. I'm going to Europe next summer. I'm going to wear sandals & smoke Gauloises & sip absinthe & be lonely.*

After they finished their glasses of beer, Green and his father got back into the car and kept driving up and down streets lined with three-storey tenements and steep iron staircases plastered with ice and snow. They finally found the coal yard in what had been the stable yard of an ancient farmhouse, now tucked between the concrete piers of an elevated expressway. While the roar of traffic stroked the air like a rasp, Green's father purchased six fifty-pound sacks of coal, which fitted neatly into the trunk of his Pontiac.

Green never heard another word or read another line from Maggie. Other lines in his life have crossed, occasionally sparking, blowing fuses, but she stays apart from all that. Her ghost is pure, and savage.

She's like the scent of burning coal. These days, when Green, on his travels, smells burning coal—it might be on a winter's day in Cork—the scent seems to enter him, not as an ordinary sensation, pleasant or unpleasant, but as love enters the body, or stringent loneliness, or awareness of being lost without bearings. The scent of burning coal *possesses* him, for a few seconds at least, and everything mixes together, past and future, but mostly past, and in those few seconds, it all comes at him, all at once — he feels it squeezing his lungs, but he has learned to keep breathing.

RICH KID

They used to meet beneath the electric crucifix on Mount Royal. She sold roses and carnations from table to table at sidewalk cafés on Rue Saint-Denis, and she would tell the boy, "Meet me *sous la croix*. Bring a blanket and something nice to drink." In those summer nights he trusted her more than he would later, but not enough so that he didn't say, *Promise me you'll be there?*

Near the crucifix were many secret spots where they would lie on tufted grass that grew between outcrops of grey limestone and crumbling rivulets of shale, the underbrush littered with discarded cigarette packs and worse. She liked strawberries and he'd buy a basket of berries at the Atwater Market and carry them up to her, in a paper sack stained with juice. Lying in darkness, they could hear wheels rattling on the carriage road and the patter of drivers pointing out the sights of the city to tourists. The crucifix, lit up to be seen from the villages twenty miles around, made a wild electric sputtering. She had been thrown out of her last apartment.

She was staying with a girlfriend, she said, in a room on Carré Saint-Louis. She smelled tart and untended, like an old, neglected orchard.

The bed they slept in, come autumn, when she found a place of her own in Saint-Henri, was a narrow army cot with blankets abrasive as sharks' hides. Cats possessed her neighbourhood that fall, stalking the alleys at night; he could hear them scratching at the cardboard he had taped across broken panes in her kitchen window.

The previous winter she'd shared an apartment with a gay biker, Serge. She claimed Serge had killed a Russian sailor with a baseball bat in an alley behind the Iroquois Hotel. The only time the boy met the biker was just after Christmas, when he came by to collect a bag of tools stored under her kitchen sink. The three of them sat in her kitchen smoking hashish, and when she told him she was still planning to paint his portrait, Serge got up and kissed her. In February she met a United States Air Force sergeant in a bar on Crescent Street. One weekend in March the airman took her down to New York State and married her in front of a justice of the peace, but she was back in Montreal by Thursday with a black eye, driving a Mustang with orange New York plates.

Late afternoon in the kitchen, she boiled water for tea. Light had long since left the streets that side of the Ville-Marie Expressway, and Saint-Henri seemed a dead zone, its streets rusting and stealthy. They lay in the narrow bed, clothes piled on the cold floor, cats scratching and nibbling on their toes. Naked, she was small-breasted and clumsy. He could hear the clock on the kitchen stove ticking. He wondered if the airman might show up.

A few days later she drove down to Plattsburgh, New York, in the Mustang. But three weeks later she was back in Montreal again.

Encouraged by his parents, the boy left the city that spring, went out west and found work on a cattle ranch, making hay, castrating. He steered a swather through hayfields, then a buck rake, then a baler, cutting the grass, curing it, and squeezing it into dead blocks of feed. Working with a small surgical knife and disinfectant, he performed his first castrations quickly, but then there would be another and another and his wrists would grow tired as the pearly testicles piled up in the thrashed mud.

In November he returned to Montreal without informing his parents and called her early one Sunday morning from a phone booth on Peel Street.

Her telephone rings and rings until the receiver is knocked off the cradle and clatters on the floor and a male voice swears dimly in Québécois. The boy asks to speak with her. The man calls out her name and the boy hears her shout, "Tell that *maudit* kid to leave me alone!"

The first snow of the season is hustling and blowing at the corner of Peel Street and Rue Sainte-Catherine like salt thrown across a city that's barely alive. The boy's hands are pale from the cold, jittery from caffeine. He hangs up the phone, but in another day or two he'll go to her apartment down in Saint-Henri, he'll try to see her.

TO THE DEAD GIRL

...because her body was gold and the ticking of her heart was smooth, joyful, and inexpensive, like the best of the counterfeit watches, the knockoff Pateks and Rolexes, on display that winter morning in the window of Meyerowitz Bijoutier, corner of Sainte-Catherine and the Main, Montreal, 1978.

Though her body waited all night (so the newspaper said) trapped against a bridge pier by a slab of pack ice and twenty feet of ancient, sodden telephone pole, both of which had been rollicking downstream before they were snagged on the icebreaker piers of the Pont-Victoria.

How cold was the current sliding below the bridge? Five degrees Celsius? And how many ships laden with soybeans, wheat, venereal disease, were slipping through the Seaway channel that morning, ice marled thick on their bows?

If they had left you a while longer the current might have swept you off again, and you, the slab of ice, and the telephone pole would have continued your journey downstream. Instead, three boys walking across the bridge on a dare happened to notice you. At first they thought you were waving, but it was only the current rocking you, I suppose. And they thought they heard you screaming, but it must have been ice grinding against the bridge pier.

The way you used to sway and argue, the siren-and-light-bar nights of your youth and glory, with talent bookers for the nightclubs of La Tuque, Rouyn-Noranda, and Schefferville. With your boyfriends the *camionneurs,* the CEGEP instructors, the shop stewards. And the poetics you learned. And those beautiful *haïtienne* hookers, your companions-in-arms. The way six of you would crowd into one booth in the front window at Mr. Steer Steakhouse on Rue Sainte-Catherine.

But you are dead, dead ten years. They fished you out of the river and it wasn't until after they had hauled you aboard the police launch that someone noticed the bullet hole in your neck, beneath the soggy fall of your hair.

They ran your convent school photograph (obtained from your brother in Témiscamingue) on the front page of the *Journal de Montreal.*

And months later they happened to arrest your murderer, after picking him up for something else — possession of drugs, or stolen goods. Suffering heroin withdrawal in a cell on Drolet Street, he blubbered your story to his cellmate, who belonged to a car-stealing crew out of Saint-Leonard and needed someone to dime out.

Now hardly anyone remembers your name or that of the man who killed you in a motel room after sharing a takeout order from Chalet Bar-B-Q, the *"repas familial"*: one whole barbecued chicken, coleslaw, French fries, extra sauce, and four dinner rolls. A few hours later he lifted you from the trunk of his 1974 Chevrolet Monte Carlo and dumped you into the ri—

Enough. Tell me what you remember of your life, not your death. What will become of us? I can hear our St. Lawrence River rushing down to the sea. I don't want to forget you and know that I will.

THE SERVANTS' WAY

Mr. Heaney had been dreaming again about World War I and the battle of Vimy Ridge. His father, a young lieutenant, had died there, in the Flanders mud, when Mr. Heaney was two years old.

He had been having the same dream since he was a little boy. The dream was always in a sepia tint, and it flickered, the way old World War I newsreels did. When he grew older, past the age his father had been when killed, in the dream he was his father. He had been dreaming the war for such a long time that it handled in his daytime mind more like a set of actual memories than a dream. Jackhammering in the street reminded him of machine-gun fire. Woods in late autumn recalled a ruined forest after an artillery barrage—wrecked stumps, shattered limbs, mad swirls of green leaves shaken down by artillery concussion. He had never actually seen that ruined forest, though he'd spent college summers in the woods, working as a logger. But the memory felt authentic.

Last night's dream had been pungent and Mr. Heaney lay in bed soaked by dread. He could still hear whistles screaming up and down the line, to signal the start of the big offensive. He could smell the gun oil and wet woollen uniforms. Soldiers huddled at the bottom of a trench still lurked at the edge of his vision.

He rose from bed without disturbing his wife, Alix. The stillness of early morning—once the dream cleared—was his purest, most blessed time of day. As soon as he was up on his feet World War I started fading, as it always did, and by the time he'd pulled on his dressing gown, it had disappeared.

Heading to the bathroom, he passed his children's bedrooms. Clare was pregnant and married to a resident in cardiac surgery at Stanford. Jean was at the University of Toronto working on her PhD. His first son, Bobby, had died in a skiing accident. The only child left at home was Michael, eighteen, and Mike was leaving in a couple of hours, driving out west in his new old car, headed for a summer job on Vancouver Island.

In one corner of the bathroom there was a scale and a set of small dumbbells. Six months after his heart attack Mr. Heaney had resumed his morning exercises. The sound of his own breathing was a comfort, the sense of his heart knitting together, nourished by exercise.

After stretching, he showered, shaved, then walked down the hallway towards Mike's bedroom, pressing footprints onto the lush carpet. Pausing at his son's door, he pushed it open a few inches and peered inside.

The room was slightly less of a disaster than usual. Most of Michael's gear was already packed in his car. The bed was unmade, of course. Mr. Heaney walked across the room to look out the window. The night had been chilly and clear with a full moon, and there was a beard of frost on the grass. The milkman's truck had already gone by. The morning newspaper lay out on the driveway.

He had lived in Westmount all his life. In 1939 wearing his militia uniform he had stood at attention at the corner of this very street watching King George VI and Queen Elizabeth being driven by in a Packard. When the Second War came, he hadn't been allowed to join the overseas army because of what the doctors called a heart murmur, though his heart didn't give him any trouble for another thirty-five years.

Pinned to the wall above Mike's bed was a road map with three thousand miles of Trans-Canada Highway, from Montreal to Vancouver Island, traced in red Scripto ink. Mr. Heaney had fixed up a summer job for Mike at a sawmill on the island.

"Won't it be dangerous?" Alix had said.

Mr. Heaney traced the red line with his fingertip. He wasn't going to leave for the office until after Michael was gone and he knew for certain that Alix was going to be all right.

He went back to his own room and started dressing.

Mike Heaney ran along the road circling Westmount Summit. He nodded at other runners and they nodded back. Running wouldn't be the same if you had to talk to people.

It was a beautiful day to travel. Road sand left over from winter gritted beneath his shoes, and cool, fresh air made his head ache a little. The road around the summit still made him think of Hilda, his girlfriend until she'd dumped him on the first day of spring. They used to go for walks around the mountain on the coldest, bluest January after-noons, then eat supper at her parents' house, then watch television, then make out on the living room sofa while the trees made weird groaning noises with the cold. And back in September, in the earliest days of the relationship, they spent evenings on a blanket in the summit woods, smok-ing pot and looking out across the urban valley of Côte-des-Neiges and the thousands of headstones in the Catholic and Protestant cemeteries.

What had really hurt his parents, what they hadn't been able to overcome, was not being able to bury Bobby. His brother had been heli-skiing in the Monashee Mountains in British Columbia when he disappeared into a crevasse of a glacier. The guide and the other skiers saw it happen but were afraid to go too near, and within minutes of the accident it started snowing heavily and the helicopter pilot insisted on lifting them all off the mountain. It snowed for ten days: five or six feet of fresh powder. When the weather cleared, a search-and-recovery team from Banff was landed by helicop-ter, but almost immediately an avalanche buried two of the team. They were dug out unharmed but the helicopter pilot insisted on taking everyone off the mountain. An assistant head warden of Banff National Park and a geologist explained to the Heaneys that glaciers were unstable, that fissures opened up and closed again, that they might not be able to recover Bobby's body even in the spring. And they were right. They never did recover him.

Yesterday, without telling his parents, Mike had retrieved some of his brother's camping gear from the attic. He hadn't told his parents that he planned a visit to the glaciers on his way out to the Coast. And he hadn't told them that he had no intention of returning to Montreal in September, or going back to university. He needed to start his real life, and out west seemed the best place to do that.

Before getting out of bed that morning he had been listening to Mr. Dylan on headphones. The songs had all taken on new meaning since his decision to go out west. They were like the voice of his own feelings and memory, Dylan whispering, *I shall be released.*

Alix Heaney glanced at her husband while he sipped coffee and studied the architect's plans. For two years she had wanted to get the kitchen redone and now they were finally going ahead with it.

Her husband sighed. "Do we really need all this, Alix? The kitchen seems fine to me."

An estimate had been included with the plans, and she had been shocked by the figure, but she did not want to grow old with everything getting old around her. Her parents had died in a house full of 1920s furniture. She wanted everything modern and well designed, the most functional and beautiful appliances, the best lighting and tile.

"The kitchen seems fine to you because you spend absolutely no time here except when you're eating breakfast," she said. "I don't think you've ever actually used the toaster, let alone the stove or the dishwasher."

Mr. Heaney smiled and laid the architect's plan aside. "I guess you're right."

"Of course I'm right. Are you ready for more coffee?"

She'd had a terrible sleep, finally dropping off just before dawn. In the dream she was at their summer cottage in Maine. She was leaning across the old iron range and polishing the tiny kitchen windowpanes when the contractions stuck in her throat like a piece of meat. She went to the crank telephone on the wall and tried calling old Mrs. Snow, who lived in the farmhouse on the main road. The phone rang and rang and no one answered. Ocean light poured in, gleaming on floorboards she had just finished painting with shiny boat enamel. She grabbed her red coat and headed to the car. Crouching over the wheel of the DeSoto she drove fast for the main road. The sandy little track was littered with yellow leaves. The car startled a doe and fawn, and the deer went bounding into the spruce woods. The pain was terrible. She leaned forward and bit the steering wheel, clamping her teeth around the plastic and biting down as hard as she could. Then the baby started coming out of her. Then, before she reached the Snows', the dream stopped and she awoke.

Standing in her kitchen in Westmount, Alix lifted a softboiled egg from a pot and put it in a silver cup, which she set in front of her husband. She could still feel the steering wheel's dense pressure on her teeth, the neutral taste of hard plastic.

"I had a peep in Mike's room," Mr. Heaney said. "What an unholy mess."

He tapped open his egg and began to eat it with a spoon.

Alix began washing dishes. There weren't many—her own juice glass, a marmalade knife, a plate with crumbs of toast and butter—but she filled the sink and swirled hot, soapy water in the glass.

"Leave that for the dishwasher, why don't you," said Mr. Heaney. "Come and sit down."

She watched him scooping his egg. She'd always loved his hands, the strong knuckles, well-shaped fingers, neatly pared nails. He was a fastidious man.

The fresh morning—trees out in new leaf, the smell of wet grass drifting through the kitchen window, the sharp sunshine—reminded her of the *Life* magazine story about the wives of the astronauts and those brilliant Florida mornings when their men rocketed into space leaving behind game, pretty, utterly bereft wives.

In another hour or so Mike would be blasting off. Alix looked at her own hands. They seemed a pair of sad, tired things, birds in a cage.

She heard her son on the back porch, knocking sand from his shoes. Mr. Heaney folded his newspaper as Mike came inside. He was wearing grey sweats, the sleeves too short for his long arms. His cheeks were flushed from exercise. He shut the door and kicked off his shoes.

"How many miles?" said Mr. Heaney.

"Six," said Mike. "Up to the summit and twice around." He dropped into a chair and Mr. Heaney reached across the table to give his son's biceps a squeeze.

"What will you have?" said Alix. "Let me scramble some eggs."

"You're going to have to put on weight, Mike," his father said. "I was skinny until I started rowing. That's when I put on some good, hard weight."

"I got these pains in my side."

"Did you stretch?"

"Nope."

"You have to stretch."

Alix broke eggs into a bowl, added milk, stirred, and poured them into a pan.

"Are you all packed up?" Mr. Heaney said. "Remember what I said about driving after dark. Better to get a good start, quit at sunset, and find a good place to camp. After dark is when all the nut-jobs are out on the road."

Alix put bread into the toaster. "How far will you get tonight, Mike?"

"Maybe Sault Ste. Marie?"

"Will you please phone us from wherever you are," Alix said.

Mike looked at his father and shrugged. "Sure."

The day they heard about Bobby, Mike's father was waiting in the living room when he got home from school. After he'd been told he wanted to go someplace to be alone, someplace he wouldn't have to believe Bobby was dead, but his father held him close and wouldn't even let him go up to his room until he promised that he understood. He had promised, but even then his father kept hugging him and wouldn't let him go, and then Mike realized his father was crying, and then he had really felt scared.

Mr. Heaney shook open the *Gazette* to the financial section. "Wasn't Clare going to call?" he asked.

Alix dished Mike's scrambled eggs onto a plate. Their oldest daughter had promised to call before Mike left, even though it was awfully early in California. Alix took a sip of coffee and summoned a mental picture of Clare in her bedroom in the purple darkness that must still be covering the Pacific coast.

Jean, their younger daughter, was most likely still in bed in her little apartment in Toronto, probably with her latest bearded boyfriend.

Since Bobby, Alix had always been aware that her children, separated from the house, might cease to exist, and if it happened she wouldn't even know until someone—some stranger—called to tell her.

For a long time after his death she'd had nightmares of her son trapped in a burrow in the millions of tons of ice and glacial till that had consumed him. The glaciers were melting, shrinking by inches every year. Six years after Bobby's accident there was an item on the CBC News about a hiker who'd fallen into a crevasse in the 1920s and been rescued but left his knapsack and skis behind. Half a century later the knapsack turned up at the foot of a retreating glacier, and the sandwiches inside were still frozen, perfectly preserved.

"Dome Petroleum's down, Alix," Mr. Heaney said. "I wish we'd sold those shares of yours last month."

Many times in the years since Bobby's death they had reassured themselves they were doing all they could for their surviving children. They'd always wanted children in their own image of themselves—magnetic, wilful, tough—but Alix wondered if they had been fooling themselves and all that they'd had to offer as parents had been taken from them and not replaced. She needed to hold Clare, Jean, and Mike close, not because she loved them but because she was terrified of losing them. Terror took up space that should have been filled with love, just love, pure and simple. She did love them, but it was never simple and direct, the way it had been with Bobby.

Mike finished breakfast and went upstairs. Alix was washing dishes in the sink and Mr. Heaney was sipping a third cup of coffee when their daughter finally telephoned.

"Mike's still in the shower," Alix said over the phone, "but Daddy is right here and he's not leaving for the office until Mike's gone."

"Let me speak to her," Mr. Heaney said.

Alix handed him the receiver and went back to the stove and tried to adjust the flame beneath the coffee pot. The pilot had gone out. As she struck a match and held it to the pilot she noticed her hands were trembling.

Mr. Heaney covered the receiver and said, "Give Mike a shout, would you? He must be out of the shower by now."

Alix walked slowly to the front of the house. She glanced into the living room, which had been redecorated over the winter. She had studied hundreds of fabric swatches and paint chips, determined to get the room exactly as she had always wanted it. Walls and carpets were pale grey and the furniture was upholstered in heavy Irish linen. She could hardly remember what it had looked like before the renovation. On the ninth anniversary of Bobby's death her husband had suffered his heart attack lying on the old sofa. She'd knelt beside him, loosened his collar, and kissed his hands. Her gesture had frightened him and he'd pulled his hands away.

Michael heard the phone ringing as he stepped from the shower. Towelling his hair, he went to his bedroom and started getting dressed. From the window he could see his car out in the driveway. He studied it for a moment, pleased with the way the paint gleamed, then he sat down on the corner of his bed. In the shower it had occurred to him that maybe he was being born now, this morning, this actual hour. He let the feeling soak in further as he sat on the bed. How great — if he could only believe in it. If only he could trust that it was, in some sense, true.

His mother knocked on the door. "California on the phone!"

"Okay," he said. "I'll take it in your room."

As he passed his mother he deftly kissed her cheek. In his parents' bedroom he picked up the bedside phone. He intended to tell his sister about his plan to visit the glaciers but before he could mention it their father was back on the line. He began asking Clare about her pregnancy. Mike said goodbye and went back to his own room.

It had once been Bobby's room and, in some indefinable way, still was. Anyway, it had never felt to him like *his* room.

Sometimes he wondered if his brother would have been as large a presence in their lives if he were still alive. Bobby had become something more than a person, but no one could give a name to what he actually was.

Gathering up a few last things, he stuffed them into a small backpack. He had already decided to skip the goodbyes if he could get away without them. He would spare his parents all the emotion and just slide away. That would be easiest on everyone, especially his mother.

He silently went down the hallway carrying his shoes, then down a set of back stairs they called the servants' way, though they'd never had servants, except burly old Mme Poliquin, who came once a week to clean the house. His sisters used to sneak up the servants' way coming home late from a date. Maybe Bobby had too—Mike couldn't remember. The stairs led down to the basement and a door that opened to the driveway. As he was going down the stairs he could hear his father on the kitchen phone still talking to California.

It was early enough so that the driveway was still shaded and the air almost blue. He'd polished and waxed his car and in the morning light it shone the same blood red as the tulips in the flowerbeds.

He unlocked the driver's door, eased it open. Tossing in his shoes and backpack, he slid behind the wheel. Then he released the parking brake and pushed out the clutch and the car started rolling silently towards the street. A neighbour getting into his own car across the street waved and Mike waved back. The neighbour looked surprised.

Michael turned the key and the engine fired. He suddenly felt an urge to roll down the window and yell to his parents, or to the house—yell something spirited, and reassuring, but he couldn't think what. He could smell fresh exhaust jetting from his tailpipes, moist and sweet and promising, and he let in the clutch and drove away.

That night Mike slept on the ground beside a lake in northern Ontario. He'd meant to phone home from a gas station but forgot about it while paying for the gas and only remembered as he was unrolling his sleeping bag and swatting mosquitoes. And by then the last payphone was probably twenty miles back.

Alix finally went to bed at midnight and dreamed the house was destroyed and nothing was left but a pile of empty glass bottles.

And Mr. Heaney sat in the kitchen with a shining glass of whisky, neat, wondering if his dead father and himself and his dead son were in some ways the same person. The dead were joined to the living. They would always be powerfully connected. Or was that just hocus-pocus?

His throat narrowed and for a few seconds he felt very close to tears. But instead of giving in, which would have been weak and pointless, he sat up straight, poured another finger of golden whisky, then raised his glass and took a sip.

AWAY

INTERSTATE HEAVEN

"I hate this stuff," said Olsen, the younger of the brothers, maybe nineteen.

I was in a coffee shop at Elko, Nevada, with two brothers who had picked me up out in the desert. On the table between us was a bowl with little plastic tubs of coffee creamer, and Olsen was reading the label on one of the tubs.

"'Non-dairy product,' that's what it says. Cancer for sure."

"Quit your complaining," said Timothy. He was maybe twenty-one.

"Would you drink this stuff, professor?" Olsen said.

"I have in the past," I told him. "But no, I don't think so."

Olsen was looking around for the waitress. "Where's the bitch?"

"Leave her be," said Timothy. He stirred his coffee and began scribbling lines on a napkin. He had told me he was a poet. While he jotted what could have been verses, his pencil point kept making gashes in the soft, fibrous paper. He tore the lid off a creamer and a jet of the milky white gunk hit his brother on the chin.

"Bastard!" Olsen jerked a napkin from the steel container and wiped himself furiously. He needed a shave, and the paper made a rasping sound.

"Sorry," said Timothy, laughing. "But hey, it was an accident."

The manager, behind the cash, squinted at us. The waitress with green eyes came over to stand by our table, her hip cocked, balancing a tray and a plastic coffee pot.

"Refill?"

"Yes," I said. "Please."

"Fuck you, toots," Olsen said, crumpling the napkin and throwing it at her feet.

"Shut your mouth," said Timothy.

"What did he say?" she asked.

"Don't tell me to shut up, big brother," said Olsen, clutching his mug. I noticed the star-shaped earring in his left ear.

"I'd be happy to shut it for you," said Timothy.

They had been working in the oilfields of Wyoming and were headed home to California, they said. I could imagine the brawls Timothy had fought and won in the oilfields over the writing of poetry. His writing, he said, was all about young women. He wrote at night and made Olsen sleep in a tent outside their trailer.

Timothy suddenly broke the pencil in half and dropped both halves into his brother's coffee mug. Olsen shoved the mug across the table and it slid off the edge and broke on the floor. I could see the manager coming around from behind the cash. Timothy reached over and wrapped his hands around his brother's throat. The manager pushed the green-eyed waitress out of the way and pointed a pistol at my heart.

"Get out of my place," he said. "Get out right now."

"Let's get out of here," I told the brothers. "I'll pay for the coffee."

I laid money on the table and followed them towards the door. The manager trailed me, occasionally poking my shoulder with the pistol. Looking back, I saw the waitress starting to clear off the table. I was about to wave to her but knew the gesture might be misread, so I just followed the brothers out into the colourless daylight. As soon as we were outside Olsen kicked over the USA Today vending machine. The manager rapped on the plate-glass window with his pistol. Olsen whirled around and ripped open his shirt. The buttons went skittering. "Do it to me then, big man!" he screamed, thrusting out his bare white chest.

From the other side of the glass the manager just stared.

Olsen cackled. "What a chickenshit, what a big fat slice of bird pie!"

A lot of the desert was military test range. As we walked towards the brothers' white Falcon, a flock of fighters came in quickly, dropping from the sky like stones. "F-16s!" Timothy shouted. The brothers began shouting and waving as the jets swept overhead. Timothy aimed both index fingers and made machine-gunning noises and Olsen whooped like an epileptic Comanche, pulling pins from imaginary hand grenades and lobbing them skywards. The jets swiftly disappeared, leaving contrails like white claw marks on the sky. The noise faded until it was lost in the pell of traffic from the interstate.

Timothy held open the driver's-side door and I scrambled into the back seat. Timothy got behind the wheel. Olsen stood on the passenger side, drumming his fingers on the roof.

"You want to walk to California?" Timothy said.

Olsen leaned down to address his brother through the open window. "Your wife's a whore. The only home you'll ever have is a trailer at Rock Springs."

Timothy hardened as if a piece of wire had been inserted into his body. His neck became stiff and his head cocked aggressively, like a large fist.

"Your mind's a slave," Olsen said.

Timothy jumped out, walked around quickly, and threw open the trunk. He lifted something out and slammed the lid. I saw him holding a canvas seabag. Olsen stopped his drumming on the roof. Timothy whirled the bag around his head a few times, then flung it as far as he could. It landed on the asphalt twenty yards away. Jingling keys, Timothy got behind the wheel, slammed his door, and fired up the engine. Olsen reached in through the window and pulled an automatic pistol from under the passenger seat. I saw his earring sparkle. Timothy reached over, rolled up the passenger window, and locked the door. Olsen started banging on the window with the pistol butt. He began moving around the car, striking the fenders with the pistol.

"Let's get out of here," I said.

"Hold your horses, professor." Timothy shifted into reverse and the Falcon rocked backwards, grazing Olsen, who barely had time to skip out of the way. We began chasing him across the parking lot. He dodged and twisted like a matador. He managed to get behind the car and break the taillights. Timothy went into reverse again and backed up over the seabag. Olsen leapt onto the hood and started banging on the windshield with his pistol. Timothy jerked and swerved, trying to shake him off the car, but he held on by clutching the stem of a windshield wiper. Timothy slammed on the brakes and he tumbled off, landing on hands and knees on the asphalt.

We started driving away. I looked back and saw Olsen scrambling to his feet. He crouched and took aim, gripping the pistol with both hands just like a policeman in a movie. I saw the pistol buck and flame but didn't hear the shots. Timothy hit the gas and we went screeching out of the parking lot, bouncing over the curb and thrusting into the hectic traffic on the boulevard.

I could see the big green sign for the I-80 but at the last moment Timothy changed his mind, and instead of joining the entrance lane we stayed on the overpass. On the other side of the interstate the boulevard was immediately narrower and dustier, lined with furniture stores, auto-supply stores, churches, gun shops. At the first big intersection Timothy made a U-turn, and I knew we were heading back to the parking lot and Olsen. Timothy said now I would have something to write about. I imagined him in the library of a great university, poring over all the wrong books, noting their wrongheaded anti-wisdom in a ledger he'd keep tucked inside his shirt.

We passed over the interstate once again. Up ahead I saw Olsen hiking alongside the road, seabag on his shoulder, pausing only to stick out his thumb. We passed him and made a U-turn, then passed him again, then pulled over. As Olsen approached the car Timothy reached over and unlocked the passenger door.

Olsen got in.

"Don't ever put a fucking piece in my car without telling me," said Timothy.

"Yeah, yeah, yeah," said his brother, twisting around to drop his seabag on the back seat beside me. "Let's get out of here."

"I mean it."

"I heard you the first time," said Olsen.

Between Winnemucca and Reno the Falcon blew a front tire. Timothy wrestled the car to the shoulder and we all got out. Timothy opened the trunk and dragged out the jack and the spare. They both took off their shirts. The same eagle tattoo was scribed on both their backs. They knew how to use tools and worked fast, wrenching off the shredded tire. While they were fitting on the spare I saw my backpack nestled in the trunk. I decided I would grab it, dash across the interstate, and try hitching another ride. It didn't matter if I was going in the wrong direction: I needed to get away from these two. Olsen was torquing lug nuts. Timothy was cranking down the jack.

As I reached for my pack I heard a rustling. Looking up, I saw a pair of needle-shaped fighters. As I watched they launched missiles from their wings, and I watched the missiles trace incisions on the sky.

LYLE

Jerry watched his father dashing his horse around in the corral muck, cutting out the animals he wanted, running them through the gate Jerry held open.

At noon Jerry's mother called them in for dinner. He ate lentil soup while his parents listened to the livestock report on CKRD Red Deer. His parents loved listening to the radio. His mother had it on in the house all day and his father kept a Japanese transistor radio in the barn. They loved rock and roll. They had met at a high school dance in Caroline and married a week after graduation. Late at night they sometimes danced with each other in the kitchen. They liked to jitterbug. His father whirled his mother around until she gave a little scream. Then he would release her and let her spin away, catching her hand at the last second. He'd pull her towards him and lift her off the floor while Jerry watched, feeling curious, and embarrassed.

The soup had a burnt flavour, a bit like the smell at branding but not nearly so strong. "Hell smells like branding,"

Lyle had once said.

Jerry picked up his bowl and was about to drink the rest of his soup when his mother noticed. "Jaroslaw! I don't make soup so you can drink it like Coca-Cola!"

Jerry picked up his spoon and at the same instant heard the sound of a car turning into the yard. "Cunninghams are here," he announced.

His father, a compact, wiry man with dirty blond hair and sideburns—his nickname in high school had been Jimmy, short for Jimmy Dean—went to peer out the window.

Jack Cunningham was an old rodeo cowboy who came in spring to help with branding and stayed on for the summer work. He had a wife and four kids. They stayed from May through October in a cabin on the riverbank quarter. Lyle, Jack's son, claimed that they wintered in the Rockies, camping with Indians on the Kootenay Plains. He said that Indians had taught him to change himself into an animal and that once he'd been a timber wolf, dragging kids and hunters back to his cave.

Jerry's father took his hat and stiff new jacket from the peg and reached outside for his boots.

"She'll want to come in and use the flush toilet," said his mother, wiping her hands on her apron. "Tell her she can use the privy behind the barn."

"Coming, Jerry?" said his father.

Jerry leapt up from the table and grabbed his jacket.

"I don't want him making friends with that Lyle again," his mother said. "And wait! Hold your horses, mister. Finish your soup."

The car was stopped in front of the corrals. It seemed to be riding low on its springs. Jack Cunningham leaned against one fender. The car was streaked with mud and the windows were rolled up tight. Mrs. Cunningham sat in the front seat, wearing a kerchief over her hair and a red nylon windbreaker. She rapped on the windshield and Jerry's father tipped his hat.

While the men lit cigarettes Jerry peered into the back seat. The twins, Sheryl and Sharlene, were sitting next to the windows, big, waxy-looking blonde girls wearing eyeshadow. One of them made a face at him. Lyle and Wayne were squeezed between their sisters, sitting very still. Both boys were small for their ages, and small-boned. Lyle held a yellow mongrel pup on his knee and pretended not to notice Jerry. Both boys' heads had been shaved.

The year before, Lyle had tried walking a perfectly straight line across the ranch: across the pastures, over the fences, through the plowed fields. He made Jerry follow him and wouldn't allow them any detours. If a tree stood in their path they'd have to climb up and over it rather than step aside a few inches. He'd insisted they climb straight over the barbed-wire fences instead of looking for a good spot to crawl under. Jerry had torn his jeans and cut his hands painfully trying to get over a stretch of tight, taut wire.

Wayne's eyes followed Jerry but Lyle was still pretending not to see him. Their fathers' voices droned on. The dog nosed up to lick Lyle's chin and Lyle began scratching its ears. One of the girls grabbed his wrist and tried to press it back on the seat. They struggled for a moment, then Lyle punched her thigh. The dog started yapping and Mrs. Cunningham twisted around in the front seat and slapped the girl, catching her on the side of the head.

"When my mother was a girl in Pincher," Lyle had said, "at the beer parlour, she just about killed a soldier. Nearly broke his head with a beer bottle."

Lyle sat back in the seat, hugging the dog and grinning.

Jerry stepped away and went to stand behind his father, who had one foot on the bumper. He and Jack were looking out across the corrals to the cattle grazing in the home quarter.

"Find any work over the winter?" his father was saying.

"Packers in Calgary. Then we went to her brother's at Pincher."

"How is Mrs. Cunningham feeling these days?"

Jack licked his lips and tossed the butt of his cigarette into the mud.

"She's fine. Everything's all right with her."

"I'll come down later and bring you some things."

"We'll need a cash advance."

"That's all right," said Jerry's father. "What were you doing down at Pincher?"

"Breaking horses. Almost broke me."

His father laughed. "You're an old cowboy—you've just about broke it all anyway. Go down to the cabin, clean it up, get settled. I'd like to start branding tomorrow."

Jerry and his father watched the car slowly turn around, then drive cautiously out of the yard, riding low on its flattened springs. His father always said Jack was no good at operating machinery—the swather, a grain truck, even his own old beater car. Jack Cunningham was a horseman pure and simple, Jerry's father said, an old Alberta cowboy, last of the breed.

For supper that night Jerry's mother served them tongue, mashed potatoes, and beets, and rhubarb pie for dessert. There was nothing on the radio but classical music. Jerry's father, drumming his fingers on the table, said, "I might take a little run to the cabin and see if they're settling in. Want to come along?"

"No, thank you very much," his mother replied. "It always depresses me."

"Jack's not so bad," said his father, "but she gets worse every year. I don't know how they'd keep going if they didn't come here."

After a moment his mother said, "You'll bring them some food and blankets. Jaroslaw should go along with you and help."

The idea of going to the Cunninghams' in the dark made Jerry nervous but if he said he wanted to stay at home his mother might think he was feeling sick and make him take a dose of medicine.

When the dishes were cleared, she began packing boxes with canned food and frozen bread. "One week's wages advance, but not more," she told his father. "They'll only spend it at the beer parlour in Caroline."

Jerry's father loved to drive his new red pickup with his left wrist hung over the wheel and his right arm across the seat back. The truck still had the sweet smell of new but it rattled on the washboard road. There was a full moon in the sky. Jerry's father suddenly reached down and switched off the headlights. They both laughed and Jerry watched the truck's moonshadow skipping along the roadside.

The old log cabin was surrounded by big spruce trees and defunct machinery—a buck rake, a Cockshutt thresher, a flywheel John Deere tractor—all of it junk. The summer before, Lyle had told Jerry he'd seen the devil sitting like an old farmer on top of the Cockshutt. The belts had been whirring, the knives clattering, the pickup teeth going round and round.

Jerry's father honked and in a moment Lyle stepped out onto the sagging porch.

"We've brought some supplies," Jerry's father called. "Come down and give us a hand."

Lyle helped them lift the cardboard boxes out of the truck.

"Where's your dad?" Jerry's father said.

"Went into town."

They carried the boxes inside. Mrs. Cunningham was sitting at the table in the kitchen. She was younger and smaller than Jerry's mother, with green eyes set wide apart. Her hair was messy.

"Well, aren't we glad to see you!" she said.

"Where's Jack?" said his father. "Where are the girls?"

"Gone to town. We nearly didn't make it this year. That car was making such a noise we didn't think it'd do the trip."

Jerry disliked the sweet, dirty air inside the cabin. There was no electricity. His father's skin looked mustard yellow in the light of the kerosene lamps.

"Where's your other boy?"

"Wayne's sick. We put him to bed early. He's asleep. He's my baby," said Mrs. Cunningham.

She stood up and fetched two Cokes from the icebox. Jerry's mother did not allow Cokes. "You take these and go play somewhere," Mrs. Cunningham told Lyle. "Go play in the barn. Be nice to your guest." She reached to tousle Jerry's hair, then turned to his father. "You sit right down here for a visit. Give me a cigarette."

"You can sit in the truck and play the radio," his father told Jerry, "while I visit with Mrs. Cunningham."

"I want to go home," he whined, putting down his Coke. The dirty light threw their shadows on the wall, which made the room seem even more crowded.

"You go outside like I said."

Mrs. Cunningham took a cigarette from his father's pack. "You're not afraid of the dark, are you?"

His father struck a match for her. Lyle held the screen door open. Jerry picked up his Coke and walked out and Lyle followed him and let the door flap shut with a bang.

"Lyle, be nice," Mrs. Cunningham called.

The spruce trees were whispering in the breeze. Even the white moon looked hot. The old machines in the yard, with their rotted rubber belts and smell of rust, looked like ghosts of themselves, or huge insects.

"Why don't we sit in my dad's truck?" Jerry said as Lyle walked towards the barn. "Keys are inside. We can listen to the radio."

Lyle ignored him. Finishing his Coke, he flipped the bottle into tall grass that hid rusty coils of barbed wire and some old tires. Pulling a flashlight from his pocket, Lyle tugged the barn door open and shone the beam inside and upwards. A criss-cross of rafters and cables threw shadows on the roof, which was stuttered with holes large and small. Inside the barn smelled of old straw. Tools that hadn't been used for years—baling hooks, scythes, branding irons—hung on one wall.

Lyle pulled the barn door closed behind them. Playing the beam against a wall, he closed his fingers slowly over it so that it looked like a black giant's hand reaching down to get them. It was something Jerry had done with his own flashlight, plenty of times. Lyle put the light in his mouth and his cheeks glowed red. Then he took it out. "I got this flashlight off a kid at Pincher."

"Probably robbed it," Jerry said.

Lyle played the beam around the barn. "Want to go fishing tomorrow? I can get us a million worms."

"Tomorrow's Sunday. We go to church."

Lyle switched off the flashlight.

"Put it on," said Jerry.

"Come fishing."

"Nope," said Jerry. "Turn on the light."

Instead he could see Lyle stick the flashlight into his pocket. Clapping his hands, he took a step closer to Jerry. "You're a little puss, aren't you. What happens if I pull your tail?"

"You're crazy," Jerry said.

Lyle froze, then cocked his head as if he'd heard something. "Shh. Listen."

"What?"

Lyle raised both arms and started walking like a robot,

holding his arms out stiffly, making a whirring noise. He stopped when his knuckles bumped into the wall. His fingernails scratched at the wood. He took hold of the shaft of a branding iron and lifted it from the wall. Turning around, he started staggering towards Jerry, like a sleepwalker, like a robot, like a vampire. He was holding the branding iron like a war club. Jerry took one step backwards, then another. Lyle kept tottering towards him. Jerry hurriedly slid the door open and went outside. Guided by the moon and the yellow light from the cabin windows, he headed for his father's truck. He was nearly there when the cabin door opened, throwing a splash of yellow light across the yard, and his father stepped out.

"What's the matter, seen a ghost?" His father looked at Jerry, then held open his arms, and Jerry ran to him and let his father pick him up.

Mrs. Cunningham's voice called from inside, "Don't you think I'm any good?"

His father told Jerry, "I shouldn't have brought you here." His father set him down, then held his hand as they walked towards the truck.

"Don't you think I'm worth it?" the woman yelled.

"Don't pay no attention, Jer."

His father had him climb in first, then he got in and shut the door. She was still yelling as they backed out to the road.

"Don't say nothing to your ma, chief," Jerry's father said. "No need to get her upset."

His mother was afraid of germs the Cunninghams brought from Pincher and the stockyards. She phoned the school to make sure Lyle and his sisters would be scrubbed, deloused, and vaccinated by the school nurse, but none of them turned up at school. On Saturday Jerry's father drove to town and came back with a rifle, a single-shot .22, which he presented to Jerry along with a box of ammunition. The little bullets were cold and greasy, the size of gumdrops, and when Jerry shook them, he heard grains of powder rattling inside the brass cartridges.

After lunch Jerry took his rifle and went off hunting gophers in the meadow. An hour later Lyle appeared. He said the Alberta Stockmen's Association paid a nickel apiece for gopher tails and offered to help collect the bounty by clipping off the tails.

"I don't need help," said Jerry. He held the rifle casually over his shoulder, the way he'd seen his father and other ranchers hold their rifles. He and Lyle were standing in the meadow. Wind was blowing waves through the high grass.

Lyle disappeared and returned half an hour later with a pair of rusty shears and a brown paper grocery sack. "You can do all the killing," he promised. "I'll just cut off the tails."

In the afternoon's dry green heat they moved through the meadows. Jerry did all the shooting. The little bullets slithered through the high grass. By mid-afternoon they had six gopher tails in the paper sack, which was seeping rust-coloured gopher blood. They were down to the last five bullets.

Lyle said he knew a new game to play but they needed

Wayne, who was back at the cabin, tied to a rope so he wouldn't wander.

"What kind of game?" Jerry asked suspiciously.

"Wait here, I'll go get him," said Lyle. He started off towards the cabin and Jerry sat down on a log by the river-bank. After half an hour Lyle hadn't returned and Jerry began firing at the river. He skipped four bullets off the water's surface and was loading the fifth when he saw Lyle leading Wayne through the high grass. Lyle carried a spade over his shoulder.

"Don't waste ammo," Lyle yelled. He came to where Jerry was sitting and grabbed the rifle before Jerry could stop him.

"Follow me," Lyle commanded, sliding down the bank and wading out into the river without taking off his boots.

Jerry and Wayne followed, fording together, Jerry holding the little boy's hand. They struggled up the slippery bank, which had been muddied by cattle, and followed Lyle into a stand of aspens on the other side. Lyle was carrying the rifle and the spade and shouting, "Hup-two-three-four, hup-two-three!" The high grass was thickened with wild roses, corn silk, devil's paintbrush.

Lyle yelled, "Halt!" and propped the rifle against a tree. "First we'll make him dig his grave. Wayne, start digging!"

Wayne squatted down and began scratching at the ground with his fingers.

"You give him a hand," Lyle said to Jerry, holding out the spade. When Jerry didn't move, Lyle slung the rifle over his shoulder and started kicking the spade himself, breaking up grassy clods, shovelling out gravelly soil underneath and piling it alongside the hole.

"Give me my rifle," Jerry said.

"Not when I'm under orders. I'm a soldier. I got to do what they say."

The hole was four feet long, not much more than a foot wide, and a foot deep. The earth was mounded neatly beside. Lyle threw down the shovel, pulled off his belt, and used it to tie Wayne to the trunk of an aspen tree. Taking a bandana from his pocket, he tied a blindfold over his brother's eyes.

"What are you doing?" said Jerry.

"Executing the prisoner." Lyle worked the rifle bolt, pushing in the last cartridge, and began stepping backwards, counting off his steps.

Wayne giggled and whispered, "Lyle? Lyle?"

Lyle wrapped the sling tight around his forearm, settled the butt into his shoulder, and lay his cheek against the stock. "Ready," he called. "Aim."

It was happening so fast Jerry felt dizzy. It didn't seem real. It was like watching a cartoon.

"Fire!"

The shot cracked out. A splinter of wood sparked off the tree trunk a couple of inches above Wayne's head. Lyle worked back the bolt, ejecting the spent .22 cartridge. Jerry could smell gunpowder. He walked up to the tree and untied the little boy, then pulled the blindfold off. Wayne grinned and blinked. There was a white scar on the tree where the bullet had torn off a scrap of bark. There was a white gob of spit in the corner of Wayne's mouth.

Lyle grabbed his brother by the arm. Jerry seized hold of the rifle barrel and, after a moment of silent contest, Lyle relinquished it. He led Wayne over to the hole and made him lie down in it. Wayne lay still while Lyle spilled some handfuls of dirt over him. Wayne giggled, happy he was still included in the game. Then Lyle began scooping dirt in a frenzy, using both hands, like a dog burying a bone. Wayne shut his eyes and still didn't try to get up. He was still smiling.

"Give me a hand!" Lyle said.

"Stop it," Jerry said weakly.

Lyle picked up the shovel and scraped in more dirt. The little boy was being buried but he didn't say anything or try to stand up.

"You can carry the rifle," Jerry said, "but you better stop."

Lyle ignored him.

Not knowing what else to do, Jerry started walking away through the quaking aspens. He soon came to the river. He could still hear the shovel at work. He hesitated, looked back, then, wading into the river, started splashing across. After pulling himself up the slippery bank he kept going across the hayfield. After stumbling through the deep ditch, he climbed up onto the graded gravel section road. He could see the cluster of dark spruce around the Cunninghams' cabin and started walking in that direction. His boots and socks were wet and felt squishy.

As he approached the cabin he could hear music from a radio inside. It sounded like a transistor, not a house radio. The rope Wayne had been tied to lay in the yard. His father's red pickup was parked alongside the old rusty machines.

Jerry thought he could hear his father's voice inside the cabin, mingling with the woman's. Were they singing? What were they doing? Instead of going nearer he stayed out on the road and kept walking, even though he was headed not in the direction of home but the other way. He walked as fast as he could, the road ahead of him so white and straight and pointed like a needle to the line where everything disappears.

VULCAN

Out there jobs were easy to come by. I quit the rigs in August that year. The grain harvest was coming in and I knew there would be a shortage of hands. The Manpower office in Calgary found me a job, trucking, at a grain farm down at Vulcan, Alberta. I took a locker in the Greyhound depot, stored my gear, and bought a ticket on the next bus south.

The farmer met me at the café where the bus stopped. His name was Steve. We drove out to his farm, nine miles from town on the provincial highway. In the fields swathers were laying down the wheat and barley, and on some fields the threshing had started. The air was full of dust and chaff and the highway was streaked with yellow grain slopped from trucks rushing to the elevators in town.

As we drove into the yard I saw a combine and two trucks with grain boxes parked in front of the barn. The house was set on one side of the yard and on the other side an ATCO trailer was set up on blocks. There was an old Ford half-ton in front of the trailer, its hood propped open with a broken hockey stick. A man and a boy were peering at the engine.

"That's the hand I hired yesterday," Steve said. "He done nothing yet but poke around in the piece of junk that brought him here. Little fellow's my boy, Pete."

Steve shut off the engine and opened his door. "Found out what's wrong with her?" he called. "I think your old beater may have given up the ghost."

The hired hand stepped back and pulled away the hockey stick so that the hood dropped with a heavy iron *clang*.

"Rings," said the kid.

"No," said the hand. "Plugs need cleaning, like I told you."

He sounded irritated at being told something by a twelve-year-old. He looked about nineteen himself, a lowlife, just the type you always find out there.

"There's a bunk for you in the ATCO," Steve told me. "My wife laid out bedding for you. I set up the shower for you boys behind the barn. Go easy on the hot water." He started walking towards the house. "Supper in an hour," he called back.

The kid offered his hand. "I'm Pete. He's Duane. You and him drive the grainers. Duane's already took the Dodge so you get the International."

Duane had slid behind the wheel of his pickup and was trying to start it. It was turning over but it wasn't firing.

"He'll never get it running right the way it is. Duane, what we ought to do is pull the plugs and check compression."

The trucker spat onto the ground. "That's what you think. It's the plugs are old, that's all."

"No way."

"Yes! What do you know about trucks?"

"More than you," the little boy said calmly. "I wouldn't have bought this piece of junk."

"Need a tune-up, that's all. Anybody could do it."

"Not you. You don't have any tools."

I left them arguing. The truck was no good, anyone could see. I got my duffel and went up the steps of the trailer. Inside were two bunks. One was neatly made up with army blankets and flannel sheets, the other was a mess.

I sat down on the fresh bunk. My people were miners and fishermen in Cape Breton, Nova Scotia, but there was none of that by the time I came around. I've been back home a couple of times but I can't stay. Things aren't the same in Nova Scotia as out here—if you get a job there, you hold onto it for dear life. And the pay is nothing. In three months up on the rigs I earn more than my father would have made in a year of fishing and collecting unemployment.

An outfit in Edmonton leases ATCO trailers. You see them everywhere. Leave one job for another, and six months later and five hundred miles away you find yourself sleeping in the very same trailer. Men scratch their names on the walls. They write dates, and the names of places that now sound to me like prisons—Fort St. John, Grande Prairie, Fort McMurray, Alsask.

Duane pulled open the screen door and stepped inside.

"Why don't you take your boots off," I said. "This place is bad enough."

He muttered something but he knew I wasn't fooling around. I'd drop him in about three seconds if he didn't come to heel. He kicked his boots into one corner and fell down on his bunk.

"Next time leave them outside," I said.

He was a lowlife and I didn't like the idea of sharing that damn ATCO with him for however long it took us to bring in the crop. For a moment I had the idea to just pick up my gear, sling it over my shoulder, and walk out of that trailer into the sunlight, across the shit-smelling yard and down the section road. Just get down to the highway and hitch a ride away from it all. I thought of my father's house on Cape Breton, which was white and shining and perfectly clean, and of meadows that slant down to the sea. When I left there, I left the world of people who dwell in houses, and since then I have always lived in trailers or motels.

"That kid don't know nothing about trucks," Duane said.

You can't do anything about trash except ignore it. I want a ranch of my own, land I can afford, maybe in south Saskatchewan. I'll get my brothers out from Cape Breton and we'll raise horses.

A woman's voice was calling us for supper. Duane pulled on his boots and I got up from my bunk and we left the trailer and walked across to the house.

It was clear to me Steve and his wife, Donna, did not trust Duane. They were afraid he couldn't do the job and his mistakes would cost money.

"The thought of that boy operating a thirty-thousand-dollar grainer is making my hair grey," Donna said.

The three of us were having coffee in the kitchen. Supper was over. Duane and Pete had gone back outside to work on Duane's pickup.

"It's hard to find hands," Steve said. "We get crazy people

from the city or boys like Duane without a brain between their ears. How the hell are we supposed to bring a crop in?"

"Government does not think of the hard-working farmer these days," said Donna.

"The men we used to have are all getting rich up on the rigs," said Steve.

"Or on unemployment insurance, hanging around the beer parlours in Calgary," said Donna.

"Pipeline, tar sands," said Steve. "That's where the money is now. We're stuck with the likes of him. He says he paid two thousand for that half-ton in Prince Albert. Whoever sold it to him ought to be arrested. The thing's not safe to put on a road."

"Where does he come from?" I asked.

"He says he was washing cars in P.A. He's been a harvest hand before. I drove around with him in the Dodge and he knows how to split-shift, anyhow. He says he wants to go up on the rigs."

"That'll be the day."

"God help us if he smashes into the combine," said Donna.

"Pete's going to ride around with him. Pete can help him out. They get along okay. Pete's quite a mechanic—he's got more tools than I do. Maybe Pete can even get his pickup running."

"I don't want our son spending a lot of time with him," Donna said. She stood up to get the coffee pot from the stove. "How old are you?" she asked me.

"Twenty-five."

"You look older." She poured coffee for Steve, then me. "You look like one of the men we used to have around here. You look like a worker."

"Why did you leave Nova Scotia?" Steve asked.

"What is it you're all after, coming out west?" Donna said.

"Jobs. Money."

I sipped coffee. I like kitchen coffee they make on the farms. I like old houses with curtains on the windows and kids' drawings posted on the fridge. I like looking through the window to the row of windbreak poplars out on the road. I like the taste of that coffee. On the rigs, in the dining halls you get your coffee from a steel urn, with twenty men in front of you and twenty more lined up behind.

Steve said, "You'll keep an eye on that Duane, will you."

"Sure."

"I hate having to depend on someone like that. If Pete was old enough we'd only need to hire one man."

By ten the next morning the dew was off the crop and the threshing began. Steve and his father drove the combines. The machines never stopped moving—when a hopper was full, one of the grainers would draw up alongside then move down the row in tandem while grain spewed into the box. As soon as it had a full load the truck pulled away, bouncing across the stubble towards a break in the fence, then speeding down the section road to the granary bins or to the elevator in town.

We ate food brought in glass dishes from the house and served from the back of a station wagon. We sat on folding chairs around a card table set up on the wheat stubble. If Pete was around, he and Duane bickered about Duane's old pickup. When Pete wasn't around, Duane didn't have much to say. Once he asked me about the rigs. "You been up there, ain't you?" he said.

"Yes, I have."

"Well, I'm going next year. What's it like?"

When I first came out west, my big idea was getting rich on the rigs. I worked along the Saskatchewan border and up on the Beaufort. Sooner or later I always quit to try something else, but sooner or later I always go back to the rigs. That is where the real money is.

"I want to make real money," Duane said. "I want to fix up my truck. Pete says I need to rebuild the engine but I'd like to put some mag wheels on her is what I'd like."

I knew he could never get work on the rigs. He was too dumb and too scrawny. The work would kill him. They'd take one look at him and turn him down. They are hard men up there, none harder than some of the Cape Bretoners. Duane wouldn't last a week. I tried telling him, but of course he didn't understand.

Every now and then we'd shut down early and get a night off. I'd borrow Steve's pickup and go into town. I met a girl one night at the beer parlour and got a thing going with her. She was blonde and pretty and just out of high school. We never had trouble. I hated the beer parlour, with all the harvest hands drunk and getting into fights. All the lowlife. A couple of glasses of beer, then I'd take this girl and we'd go down to the river.

This was not the way I was meant to be. I never thought of myself living this kind of life. I don't know what I expected.

People on the rigs have money and you can get all the things you think you want—trucks, powerboats, trips to Hawaii. They need the workers, they pay you well, and when you're working, you can't spend it anywhere but the beer parlour or the lottery. When a job is over, there's no reason to stay, so you head to another job; you sign up for six months on a seismic crew or road construction so you don't have to think about where you're going—which is nowhere. In small towns people won't talk to you. You're a transient. You get into fights.

I think, *I will save money and get back to Nova Scotia.* But I've been out here too long and don't believe I could ever go back to stay. I remember the things I hated about it—the dead quiet of those towns on a Sunday, the church with no one inside but old people. Everyone on Cape Breton seemed to be just waiting to die.

I'll buy an old ranch in southwest Saskatchewan, east of the Cypress Hills, and breed horses. It's ghost towns down there. Too dry even for wheat. Land is cheap. I don't know a lot about horses but I could learn. I'll get my brothers out there. We'd all be happier than on the rigs.

Duane I don't think owned more than the clothes he wore, plus a cowboy hat kept hanging on a peg, and his old half-ton. Sometimes I would ask him, "You want to come into town?" because I pitied him and not because I wanted him around, but he never wanted to come. The only person he had any time for was the kid, Pete. When we came in from the fields, the two of them would get to work under the hood of Duane's half-ton, as long as there was light to see by, or until Pete's mother called him in to bed.

Half the time the piece of junk wouldn't even start. Pete fiddled around with pliers and a screwdriver while Duane sat pounding the wheel. Then Pete would yell, "Give 'er!" and Duane would grind the starter, smacking the dash with his palm and cursing. Pete and I would have to laugh. The motor would finally catch and the whole truck would be shaking and coughing blue smoke. Duane gunned it until it warmed up, then Pete jumped in and the two of them would head out on a test drive. Sometimes they'd stall in the middle of the road and Pete would prop up the hood and start fixing the problem while Duane just hunkered down and pitched gravel at cattle in the pasture.

I asked Pete about Duane's truck.

"It's crap," Pete said. "Compression's no good. He hasn't really let me drive but I can tell the front end's wobbly, so the ball joints are probably shot."

"Why bother working on it?"

"It's fun. I like old trucks. You learn a lot. You know what Duane's doing with his harvest wages?"

"What?"

"Paint job. Two thousand bucks. In Red Deer."

"Maybe you should talk him out of it."

"He's nuts," Pete said. "You can't talk him out of anything."

One night I went to town but my friend wasn't there. I had a couple of beers and came back to the farm. We were going to finish threshing in another few days if the weather held. We'd been working eighty hours a week and we were all tired.

Driving down the section road I was thinking about where I'd go when the crop was in and we got paid. Half a mile before the farm, I passed Duane's heap coming in the other direction. Duane was in the passenger seat and Pete was driving. He waved as I drove past.

I was lying on my bunk when Duane came in an hour later. I heard him pull off his boots outside and then the squeak of the springs when he lay down. He always slept in his clothes. He turned on one of the overhead bulbs and picked up a skin magazine. I could hear moths crashing into the screen.

I was nearly asleep when the door smacked open. I sat up in a hurry. Steve DiCesare took two steps over to Duane's bunk, grabbed him by the shirt, and hauled him to his feet. The magazine Duane had been looking at fluttered away.

"They ought to hang people like you!" Steve shouted. "They ought to cut off your balls!"

He punched Duane in the face and you could hear his nose crack. Steve slapped his head from one side to the other and Duane's blood sprayed on the plywood wall.

"What's he done?" I said.

"You stay out of this. He went after my boy. I'll teach him."

I got in between them and began pushing Steve back.

"Keep out of this!" he said.

He tried to get around me but I kept shoving him back.

"You're as bad as he is!"

"You'd kill him—you don't want to do that. Go back to the house. I'll get him out of here."

I pushed Steve outside. The trailer's flimsy door had been

pulled right off its hinges. Behind me Duane was snorting through his busted nose. Steve was about ready to take a swing at me, I could tell. There was a light in the upstairs window of the house. I could see Donna standing there.

"She said get rid of him! But I wanted to make my crop!" Steve was practically crying.

"Go back inside."

"Get him out of here before I kill him!"

"I'll get rid of him for you."

"Get him off my land. Now! Tonight! Now! Don't wait till morning!" He was retreating towards the house. "If I see him again I'll kill him."

I waited until Steve was inside. Then I went back inside the ATCO. Duane was on his bunk, snorting. Sheets and blankets and the wall were spotted with his blood.

I made him sit up and started pulling his cowboy boots on his feet. I took his hat from the peg and jammed it over his ears. He didn't have a duffel, just a grocery sack, and I threw in whatever I could grab of his stuff. I gave him a T-shirt to try to stop the blood. He wasn't talking or making sense, he was just bleeding and whimpering the way people do after they've been whipped. I went through all his pockets and found the key to the half-ton.

I helped him outside and put him into his truck, then I got behind the wheel, got it started and drove out through the yard smoking oil like a bastard, front end shaking like it was going to fall apart.

At the little hospital a nurse sat behind the reception window in the ER. There was no one else around. She didn't look glad to see us. Duane was holding the bloody T-shirt to his nose — I never seen anyone bleed so much, it was all over the truck. Both eyes had swollen almost shut.

"Looks like someone's been in a fight," the nurse said.

"I found him behind the beer parlour," I said. "Someone's punched him out."

"Well," the nurse said. "Are you harvest hands?"

"I don't know who he is."

"Do the RCMP know anything about this?" She started tapping her keyboard. "Does he have his Alberta Health card?"

"Lady, I don't know, I just found him."

"He must be working on one of the farms."

"Why don't you just help him?"

"And where are you employed?"

I had to get along. We'd be threshing in the morning. I leaned Duane against the wall and let go of him.

"Come back here!" the nurse called.

No way. I went out and across the parking lot and started walking quickly through the town, knowing if the Mounties saw me they would stop me as a suspicious character, there on the streets past midnight. I crossed the train tracks. I walked past a row of grain elevators looming over that town like ocean ships tied to a wharf. After I got out to the highway I had to walk a few miles before I was able to hitch a ride the rest of the way to the farm.

I got paid five days later when the crop was made. They wanted me to stay on for fall plowing but I headed back to Calgary then signed up for a seismic survey crew. We're in the bush, working ninety days straight, nowhere to spend wages. The money piles up. When this job's over I'll probably go to Hawaii for a couple months. Maybe Thailand. I don't know. Somewhere with girls and a beach.

Back home I'd be just another poor fisherman, wouldn't I?

NIGHT IN A VILLAGE

They told us to look for a metal scow and a man who would paddle us across the river. The Rio Grande was low and we could have forded it carrying our clothes, but they said it was the custom to take the scow. Strangers were not welcome in the village otherwise.

When we came down to the river, there were men on the opposite bank, fishing. The boatman saw us and paddled across. When the scow bumped the bank, he laid down his paddle. He told us for five dollars he would take us to the other side.

He folded the money I gave him and slipped it into a plastic purse. Then we sat down and he brought us across. We stepped out of the boat and one of the fishermen set down his line and approached us. He wore a cap with a Budweiser logo, and plaid golf pants cinched with a piece of frayed nylon rope. In Spanish he told us his name was Ramón. He told us he would guide us to the village.

We followed Ramón along a path through the tule reeds.

The path was black and moist and the pale reeds were dense and tangled. After a few minutes we broke clear and stood at the edge of the desert again. It was like being inside a photograph; there was no wind, nothing moving. A ridge of dry mountains rimmed the horizon, cool and detailed in the pink light.

I opened a can of beer as we walked. The only sound was our shoes scraping the dry, fissured ground. I passed Calisha the beer and she offered it to Ramón.

"Miller time!" he said. His skin was copper-coloured, and beneath the cap his face was all planes: flat forehead, creased cheeks, and small, triangular eyes. He tilted his head and drained the can as he walked. His teeth were black stumps and there was a strand of moustache on his upper lip. He smacked his lips and pitched away the can.

Calisha wanted to take his photograph, so we stopped and he stood gazing into the camera, thumbs hooked in his belt loops. She took half a dozen photographs and we resumed our journey. Already we could see the little village ahead, a cluster of huts the same tawny colour as the desert.

As Ramón marched us down the main street, the only people we saw were women leaning in the windows of the adobes. In front of one of the huts there was a cement terrace surrounded by an iron railing. Ramón said this was the cantina.

We entered the terrace through a gate and Ramón disappeared inside. I lifted two chairs from a stack in the corner while Calisha stood at the railing taking pictures of the street. Ramón came out followed by a man in a wheelchair, who wore a straw hat pushed back on his head and had a thin cotton blanket spread over his legs. His face was solid and handsome and his mouth was full of metal teeth. He said he was the owner and asked what we would have to eat. We ordered tacos, burritos, and beer. A big woman with long black hair stood in the doorway with her arms crossed, watching. Ramón said something to her in his chirping voice and the woman looked at him scornfully, then turned and went back inside. Ramón followed her and returned with a handful of cans that he set down on the table, keeping one for himself.

The light was fading and there was an early moon in the sky. Calisha leaned back in her chair and took my picture. She was wearing a white dress. The hairs on her arms were golden. "Why do you look so angry?" she said. "Why can't you relax?"

Half a dozen children had gathered on the other side of the railing, staring at us and whispering. When she pointed the camera at them, they shrieked and scattered like a flock of sparrows. The owner said they were afraid of cameras and that they expected to be paid when their photographs were taken. She put down the camera, and in a few moments the children had gathered again. They came closer to the railing and she began asking their names. One little girl began to cry. Two boys with huge, nervous grins stepped forward, poking their hands through the fence, holding out rocks they wanted to sell her. She told them she'd pay them a dollar each if they let her take their pictures. She got up and went out the gate. I drank beer and watched her. The man in the wheelchair said nothing.

The little girl who'd been crying wore a torn red dress. Her hair was almost blonde with dust and sunlight. She stopped crying and accepted money from Calisha. The boys dropped the stones in the dust and crowded in, demanding their pictures be taken. Calisha made them stand aside until she could photograph each of the smaller children. The little girl with the dust-blonde hair clutched hold of Calisha's white dress.

When she ran out of dollar bills, the children lost interest in her and began fighting over the money. Calisha walked across the plaza and took pictures of an old turquoise bus parked there. The name of the village was written in red letters on the bus, and the driver's window was trimmed with feathers and a statue of the Virgin of Guadalupe.

She returned to the terrace, and Ramón and the dark-haired woman served our food. The owner spoke harshly and Ramón scurried off to bring us more beer. The tacos were greasy and the burritos were stuffed with beans instead of meat. We heard the woman in the kitchen slap Ramón. When he came back onto the terrace, his eyes were bright and his cheeks were crammed with food. The owner sat watching us, smoking a cigarette.

When we were almost finished, two girls wearing high heels and frilly party dresses came out onto the terrace and stood beside our table. One carried a school exercise book and a pencil, the other a sheaf of pasteboard tickets. They stood gazing at the tips of their shoes until the owner clapped his hands. Then, without looking up, the girl holding the pencil asked if we would buy tickets for the parish lottery.

"What's the prize?"

The prize hadn't yet been decided, but everyone in the village bought tickets, and whoever sold the most would be crowned *Reina de Primavera*, the Queen of Spring. I gave them money and they instructed me to write my address in the exercise book, so if I won I could get the prize. Ramón began clearing plates and the woman brought us coffee in tin cups. The girls hurried away, heels tapping on the cement floor.

Calisha asked the owner if there was anywhere in the village that had music, dancing.

"I think we should go back," I said, interrupting her.

"You go back if you want to."

"And you'll stay here alone?"

There was another cantina at the other end of the village, the owner said. It was owned by his brother, and if we wanted to go there, Ramón would show us the way.

"Is it all right for women to go there?" I said.

As long as the women were strangers it was all right, he said. It was just a poor, remote country village and things were very quiet. Everyone was related to everyone else. He and Ramón were cousins. The girls who'd sold us tickets were the children of his brother. The boatman who'd ferried us across the river was another cousin.

"Will they mind if I take pictures?" Calisha said.

Instead of answering, the owner stuck a cigarette between his teeth, wheeled over to the adobe wall, and pointed to a fly-specked poster. We went over to examine it. It had a photograph of the owner in his wheelchair, in the back of a pickup truck. Children sat on the tailgate, each child holding a melon. According to the poster, written in English, the owner had been crippled working in the melon fields across the river, and the money he earned in the cantina fed his family. The handbill was six years old.

I paid the bill and Calisha went inside to give something to the woman in the kitchen. Ramón drained the beer cans we'd left on the table, and the owner shouted at him to lead us to the other cantina.

Ramón stumbled, chattering with excitement, as he led us down the dusty street. The cantina was the last adobe. Ramón ducked inside and we followed him into a room lit by a lantern. A wooden bar ran from one end to the other. The bartender wore a flat-crowned Stetson. A boy was polishing glasses. A group of *vaqueros*, Coahuila cowboys wearing boots and spurs, looked up as we came in, then quickly looked away.

We asked for mescal and a dish of lemons. Ramón sat beside Calisha and kept trying to remove the silver bracelets she wore on her wrists. He put his arm around her playfully and she laughed and pushed him away.

When the bartender brought the lemons, Calisha asked if there would be music, and the bartender said there was only one old man with a guitar. He pointed to an accordion hanging on the wall that he himself sometimes took down and played for visitors from across the river.

The boy was sent to fetch the guitarist. Calisha changed film while Ramón begged the bartender for cigarettes. The *vaqueros* glanced at Calisha as if she were a figure in a movie that bored them.

"I wonder if they'll be angry if I start taking pictures," she said.

After twenty minutes the guitarist had not appeared.

We heard shouting in the street and a horse whinnying.

The *vaqueros* took their beers and shot glasses of tequila and moved outside. The bartender came around the bar, wiping his hands on a piece of burlap. "Come out and see," he said.

"What is it?"

"A little show."

Calisha grabbed her camera and we went outside. The only person left at the bar was Ramón, filching cigarettes from a pack of Marlboros.

In the moonlit street a horse was bucking and kicking. When the rider saw Calisha, he whipped off his straw hat and began beating it against the animal's flanks. The *vaqueros* standing against the adobe wall cheered and began pitching beer bottles into the desert, where they shattered on the rocks. The rider spurred the horse harder. All along the street the adobes remained in darkness while the *vaqueros* howled and barked like coyotes and the horse kicked up clouds of dust.

The rider began reining the horse in smaller, tighter circles, digging deep with his spurs. Finally, with an exhausted shiver, the animal stopped bucking. The rider kept spurring but the animal had had enough. The *vaqueros* whistled and yipped. The rider slid off and tied the reins to a bit of fence. I saw how young he was, no more than sixteen. He wore a pink shirt with pearl buttons and jeans tucked into his boots, and a knife in a leather sheath. Calisha took his picture, popping the flash as he brushed past us, heading into the bar.

Ramón was gulping mescal from the bottle on our table. The bartender cuffed him and wiped the bottle. The *vaqueros* were slapping the young rider on the shoulders and tweaking his cheeks. He had high cheekbones and a cat's mouth, small and neat. He took off his hat and pushed a lock of hair away from his eyes. The atmosphere smelled of warm dust and kerosene. I could see bullet holes in the chipped plaster. There was a *Cerveza Superior* calendar with a picture of a heavy-breasted blonde pulling herself out of a swimming pool.

The boy who'd gone to fetch the musician had returned, pushing his way through the crowd of *vaqueros*, leading a frail old man carrying a big guitar case. The bartender told us the man was a famous guitarist of Coahuila who would play for us for ten dollars. The old man took out a twelve-string bari-tone guitar, a *bajo sexto*. When I held out money he ignored me, and I handed the money to the boy. The old man's fingers were shaking and it took him a long time to tune his instru-ment. The *vaqueros* began calling out the names of songs they wanted to hear.

The first song he played was a *norteño* ballad, long and mournful. A man was in flight from soldiers because he had killed the father of Palomita, the girl who was his little dove. In the mountains the hero would grow old alone, his only friends the vultures and the sky. On her hacienda Palomita would ride a grey horse and forget the love she'd once shared, and become cruel and wanton. When the hero came down from the mountains to rescue her, Palomita would kill him with her little knife.

When the song ended, the bartender took down his accor-dion from the wall and started playing dance music with the guitarist. The *vaqueros* started dancing, hands on each other's hips, slamming their heels on the floor and raising fine yellow dust. The young rider, alone at the bar, fingered the knife on his belt and watched Calisha as she photographed the dancers.

The musicians played on furiously, faces concentrated like those of men firing pistols. The music leapt around the room, braying and cackling. There was a scent of lemons from the dish on our table. Calisha finished another roll of film, put down the camera, and took a cigarette from the pack lying on the bar. I saw the young rider offer her a light. He smiled at her and blew smoke through his nostrils.

The boatman was suddenly at my shoulder, tugging my sleeve. "Come, come, it's late. Otherwise you'll have to swim across the river." He waved at the bartender and the music stopped abruptly. The *vaqueros* stood with their arms around each other, still yipping and shouting. The old man immediately put his guitar back into its case.

I took Calisha's arm and led her out to the boatman's truck. There were two children in the front seat, a pop song squawking on the radio. We climbed into the back of the truck and sat on some tires.

We could hear the children singing along with the radio as the truck sped through the village, backfiring. We left the last adobes behind and started bouncing along a mule track towards the river. After a few minutes, I could smell the Rio Grande.

Then we heard screams and hoofbeats, and a pair of riders galloped out of the darkness, spurring their horses, waving their hats. One of them was the young rider from the cantina.

They overtook the truck and began dashing in and out of the beams of its headlights, yipping and howling. Then they dropped back and galloped alongside us, still shouting, hugging the necks of their animals.

Suddenly the truck flew over a ledge and bounced hard,

jolting us. The first horse cleared the ledge but the other one stumbled and went down in a cloud of dust, pitching its rider over its head.

I pounded on the roof and the truck skidded to a stop. Calisha wanted to jump down but I held her arm. We could see the young *vaquero* kneeling on the ground, stunned. He was the one who had put on the show outside the cantina.

His horse struggled to its feet, shook itself, and trotted away.

The boatman got out of the truck, walked up to the young *vaquero*, and began slapping him on the head and shoulders. The other rider, who had pulled up his horse, watched impassively. The young *vaquero* crawled around looking for his hat, trying to dodge the blows. After grabbing his hat he got to his feet and started to brush the dust from his clothes. Ignoring the boatman, who was still slapping him, he limped to the other horse, grabbed the rider's arm, and swung up behind. They wheeled and started back towards the village. The boatman spat on the ground then climbed back into his truck.

The boy who was guarding the boat had caught a string of catfish he wanted to sell but I said I'd spent all my money. We took our seats and the boy shoved us off. There was the sound of the paddle dipping in and out of the river, then a hollow noise as we bumped the other side.

MERMAIDS TOO

Jay was twenty-two and just out of jail when he left for Alberta in a drive-away car with a girl called Betty. They travelled with two suitcases and a valuable 1938 Gibson guitar Betty's great-grandmother had bequeathed her. The country was pure Canadian Shield and Jay set the cruise control for sevety-five miles per hour. There were no towns that weren't mining or pulp towns. There were long stretches of emptiness with gas stations every few hours and narrow side roads leading into fishing camps.

Then, just after dawn, the little red hot light on the instrument panel started blinking. Jay pulled over quickly. Betty woke up as soon as the tires bit gravel.

Dust and coolant steam drifted around them after Jay shut down the engine. The only noise was dripping and hissing. Jay got out, threw open the hood, and let the steam flow. He looked to check if there were any burst hoses. It was all too hot to touch and he could not see what was wrong.

Back inside the car, he found Betty scribbling postcards

to her boys. Kyle was five and Duffy was four. Jay and Betty were the same age exactly, and there wasn't much grounding them except their love for each other and for those boys. Their father was a fisherman who had deserted Betty when she was eighteen and drowned on the Grand Banks the winter before Jay met her.

Jay asked if she wanted him to write something to the boys, but Betty looked at him as though he'd gone crazy. "It would only confuse them," she said.

"Did you even tell them it was me you were travelling with?" he asked. "Don't you think it'd be better if they started getting used to the idea? Just what did you tell them, Betty?"

She took stamps from her purse and applied them to the postcards. The boys had been left with their granny. Betty wanted Kyle to be able to finish his kindergarten in one place, and she didn't want to separate little Duffy from his brother.

Jay and Betty had met at a health club, where he noticed her standing at the juice bar in a blue leotard and looking like a million dollars. He'd been working out on the free weights mostly, plus running four miles in the morning and four more in the afternoon. He had started weight training in jail and was determined to keep it up. It was important to him to feel physically powerful.

"You can't be thinking of yourself as their father—that's just jumping the gun," she said, dropping the postcards into her purse. She yawned and stretched. "I'm wide awake now, and I thought I'd never be wide awake again." She twisted the rear-view mirror so she could examine her face. "Do my eyes look terrible?"

"You look nice."

They had been driving nonstop. And he knew she was right about the boys; they weren't his boys. He also knew he had it in him to love those kids and do well for them, and it seemed to him that with all the risks he and Betty were taking together, travelling west with very little cash, and with the trust they had placed in each other from the very earliest days of their love, he had earned the right to sign one or two postcards. Not that he would have signed *Daddy*.

But they were her kids and she was their loving mother, and he didn't press the point. He just felt a little disappointed as he watched clouds of tiny blackflies batting themselves against the windshield. He hoped the engine would cool down on its own. They were supposed to deliver the car to a used-car dealer in Calgary, who was supposed to refund their security deposit of three hundred dollars.

She began brushing her hair. "I need to get out of these clothes," she said. "They're starting to feel itchy."

As long as they were moving he had been able to put aside and ignore his desire, but now that they were stopped he had to lean over and kiss her. She put down her hairbrush and began rubbing the back of his neck, and he started plucking at the buttons of her shirt.

Someone had carved the silhouette of a beautiful girl on the wall of Jay's cell and written beneath it *mon rêve de tendresse*, my dream of tenderness. Jay had served two months in jail for getting into a traffic accident and a fight. The accident had not been his fault.

"Not here. Let's get out and go into the woods," Betty said. "I want to be with you in nature."

There was bush on either side of the highway, stunted

spruce and birch mostly. Jay took a blanket out of the trunk
and Betty brought along the Thermos of coffee they had filled
up past midnight somewhere. They walked up the highway,
but the small trees were packed so densely it seemed there
was no way into the forest. The blackflies began to cloud
around their faces and hair. Finally they gave up. They began
running to escape the flies, and when they reached the car, he
couldn't find the keys. He asked Betty if she had them.

"I didn't even touch the goddamn keys!" she cried.

Those blackflies were really after them. Then he remembered taking the blanket out of the trunk, and saw the keys
dangling there.

He tried to start the car but it wouldn't. They drank some
coffee. After an hour or so a provincial police cruiser stopped
and the policeman put out a radio call for a tow truck, which
arrived after another hour.

At the garage the mechanic lifted up the hood and told
them they needed a new water pump. They followed him
into the office, where he checked a parts catalogue and said it
would come to $225, ordered from the parts store in Kenora,
delivered on the Greyhound, and installed.

"The Greyhound?"

The mechanic looked at the clock on the wall. "They will
put it on the noon bus. It will be here by three."

Jay looked at Betty. She shrugged and stared out the plate-
glass window. Where they were was not a town, just a few
buildings scattered in a clearing along the highway.

"Before I can place an order for what you need," the mechanic said, not looking at Jay but studying the yellow skin on
his own hands, "I have to have the cash in hand. That's policy."

Jay took out his wallet and counted out ten twenties, two tens, and a five, laying the bills on the desk. The used-car dealer in Calgary was supposed to reimburse the cost of any repairs, but who knew what would really happen.

The mechanic picked up the phone, punched a number, and began talking with whoever it was who answered at the parts store as if they were old fishing buddies and the best of friends, which maybe they were.

Across the highway Jay saw a motel. A sign out front said FISHERMEN WELCOME MERMAIDS TOO. There was a café next to the motel.

The mechanic hung up the phone and leaned back in his squeaking chair, placing his motorcycle boots on the desk. Jay thanked him for locating the part and for being willing to work on the car. The mechanic didn't respond. He was working on a toothpick as if he wasn't even listening, but Jay knew that if he did not abase himself a little, nothing much would get done.

They ate breakfast in the café, then sat on its porch in sunshine, watching cars and trucks pass by. There wasn't much traffic.

A hundred yards farther up the highway, a steel bridge crossed a river. The breeze had picked up. The bugs had disappeared.

"Betty, you ought to get out your guitar and sing a little," he suggested. "This is a good place for it."

"Too tired," she said. She was reading a magazine about trout fishing.

He stepped off the porch and went for a walk up the highway. With the sun out it wasn't such bad-looking country. He stood on the steel bridge and looked down at the river. When an eighteen-wheeler thundered past, he felt the bridge tremble. He was in his heart very anxious over the small amount of cash they had left, and thought it likely they would be stealing gas sooner or later if they were going to make it all the way to Calgary. He didn't like to steal but what else were they going to do—beg for fuel? Once they delivered the car they would get back their deposit plus the $225, and with that, he told himself, they ought to be able to make a clean, fresh start.

He walked back to the café and found Betty sunning herself on the porch.

"Think I'll go fishing," he told her. "Catch supper. Would you like that?"

There was a little store in one corner of the café, with a few shelves of clothes, some rubber boots, tins of food, and cardboard cards stuck with fishing lures. An old woman who looked like an Indian stood watching him.

"Good fishing in the river?"

"Not bad."

For ten dollars plus a twenty-dollar deposit she rented him a rod and some tackle. For another two dollars she sold him a plastic cup of worms. He filled out the form for the fishing licence, then walked down the highway carrying the gear. Betty came with him. They scrambled down the steep bank just below the bridge. He didn't know the first thing about fishing but he was hoping he could haul something good out of that little river. He could see himself pan-frying a nice little brook trout late at night, at a campsite somewhere far to the west. They'd build themselves a little fire, fry their fish in butter, and eat it with their fingers.

He practised casting, then set his sights on a calm eddy behind some white rocks. He jabbed a worm on his hook and cast four or five times before he was able to land the hook in the eddy. He let it float there a while and watched his bobbin. He reeled in line slowly, then cast again. He wondered what it would feel like to get a bite. Betty lay in the grass with her shirt off and her white breasts exposed to the sun as he moved up and down the bank, looking for more calm spots, eddies, fishing still pools behind rocks and stray logs. Occasionally his line snagged in submerged branches but he was always able to tug it free.

When the sun was high in the sky, Betty moved into the shade of big white pine and fell asleep. He hooked and landed four fish, two of them good-sized, and two tiny ones, which he threw back.

When a cloud covered the sun, it got cold again, and Betty woke up and started buttoning her shirt, saying she was hungry. He showed her the fish.

"Beautiful," she said. Kneeling on the grass, she studied them. "They're perfect little beauties. What kind are they?"

"Trout, I guess."

"Trout!"

"We'll cook them up tonight, fry them."

"Yes!" she said.

He used his pocketknife to clean the fish and they tore up handfuls of long grasses to put on newspaper to wrap the fish in.

He heard the bus approaching as they were walking back to the café; it didn't sound quite like a truck. Betty heard it too. They both turned around.

"I don't think he's going to stop," she said.

The bus was still a couple of hundred yards away but it wasn't showing any signs of slowing down. Betty clutched his arm. He waited for the whine of the engine or transmission to change, but it didn't. She was right. The bus wasn't slowing. They began waving frantically but the Greyhound whipped right by them and past the little settlement.

Jay ran the rest of the way to the garage and found the mechanic in the office, eating a hamburger.

"Those bus drivers," the mechanic said.

He was a little, wiry fellow and he reminded Jay of a stern-man who a long time before had been a friend, or acquaintance, of his father. The mechanic had rough, strong-looking hands. He wore blue coveralls, and his steel-capped motorcycle boots were propped up on the desk.

"I'll phone Thunder Bay; they can ship it back this way on the next bus. For tonight just get yourselves a motel room," the mechanic advised.

"When do you think we might get out of here?"

The mechanic stood up, still chewing his hamburger, and kicked open the back door. On a stretch of tarred gravel overgrown with weeds were twenty or so car hulks, streaked and stained with rust. From where he stood Jay could smell rotting rubber and faded paint, mouldy upholstery and old brown engine oil lying in pools.

"Have a look," said the mechanic. "Five years' worth of breakdowns out there, mister."

They had a little tent, but the flies were so bad he knew he couldn't ask Betty to sleep outdoors. He asked at the café if he could store his fish in the refrigerator, and the waitress said he could and took his fish into the kitchen.

After returning the fishing gear he walked over to the motel office and rented the cheapest room available. It cost eighty dollars. Beyond the motel parking lot was a ditch with standing water. The bush began on the other side of the ditch. It looked thick, shaggy, and impossible to penetrate. The ground would be muskeg, sour, spongy, and black.

He went back into the café and asked the waitress to bring him a cup of coffee. Betty was sitting in a booth. Along with a hamburger, she had ordered a glass of tomato juice that cost three dollars.

"We can't afford that," he told her.

"I need my vitamin C."

Her hamburger was half raw and half burnt. The tomato juice came in a plastic cup not much bigger than a thimble.

"You can't take all our money and give us just this," he said to the waitress. "Just because we're stranded here doesn't mean you can treat us this way."

"Aw, be quiet, Jay," Betty said, sprinkling pepper onto her juice.

The waitress went away without pouring him any coffee.

"Why fuss?" Betty said.

When she finished eating, he took out his wallet, counted out money carefully, and put down just enough to cover the check.

"You have to leave a tip," said Betty.

"Why?"

"For God's sake, what's the matter with you?"

"There's nothing the matter with me," he said, "that a *maudite chienne* like you would understand."

Betty sat very still for a few seconds. Then she crumpled

her paper napkin, dropped it on the table, stood up, and walked out of the café.

He sat there breaking toothpicks. He didn't want to chase after her. His wallet was on the table and he started flipping through the cash that was left, studying the face of Sir Wilfrid Laurier. Including pocket change, he had $178.92. He tried to imagine it in terms of a budget: so much per day, so much per mile. He didn't see how it was going to last.

Leaving a two-dollar coin for a tip, he slid from the booth. Nodding at the waitress, he stepped outside. The car was in front of the garage across the highway, and Betty was kneeling beside it and repacking her suitcase. She'd changed into black jeans and a belt with a silver buckle and taken her great-grandmother's guitar from the trunk. The mechanic was just inside the garage bay, placing a tire on a remount machine.

As Jay crossed the highway, Betty snapped her suitcase shut. "Where do you think you're going?" he asked.

"Hitching a ride."

The tire machine made a loud hiss, then a slamming noise.

"Catch!" Betty flipped Jay the car keys, then picked up her suitcase and guitar case and started walking down the highway, heading east. She walked fast on her high heels. He followed but kept twenty paces behind. There was no traffic in either direction. Fury sang in his blood like a dose of hot sauce. He had never felt so angry before, not in any of the fights he'd been in, not even the fight after the traffic accident that got him sent to jail.

"It's not me that's dragging you out west," he called. "It's yourself that wanted to go in the first place."

She turned to face him. "Won't you clear out of the way? Won't you leave me alone?"

"Betty, I can't let you do this."

She shook her head and kept walking. He knew, the moment she put out her thumb, any logging truck, any local teenager, any car full of fishermen from the city would stop for her.

He didn't need her. The water pump would come through on the morning bus from Thunder Bay and the car would be fixed by noon. He could continue without her. He could cross the plains alone, out under a wide sky in perfect freedom. Before him, all the wonders of the world: meals, a job, a place to dream in Calgary.

"Betty," he said. "Betty."

Her suitcase was heavy; so was the guitar. She had left the gravel shoulder and strayed onto the asphalt, where her heels made a brisk tapping. He was thankful for the cold wind keeping the blackflies out of her hair.

He heard an eighteen-wheeler rumble over the bridge behind them. Betty stopped, put down her suitcase and guitar, and turned around. She glared at Jay, then stuck out her thumb.

He heard the truck drop a gear, air belching from the brakes. He gazed at Betty, thinking how proud she was and how beautiful, then he turned around. He could see the trucker leaning over his wheel, checking his mirrors as he applied brakes. The trailer wobbled as the whole rig slowed down violently. More air farted from the brakes.

Jay put his finger to his throat and cut it across. The truck instantly picked up speed and rolled right past them, the trucker pouring it on—Jay could hear him upshifting all the way down the highway, until the truck disappeared.

Betty was rubbing her palms, creased red by the hard plastic handles of her two cases.

"Have you mailed those postcards?" he asked. "Where's your purse?"

She groaned. "Oh shit."

"Where is it?"

Another eighteen-wheeler was rumbling over the bridge but she paid no attention. "I must have left it in the restaurant."

"Let's go back."

She stood, rubbing the red creases on her palms.

"C'mon, Betty." He reached for her cases but she snatched them up and took a couple of steps away from him.

"Betty," he said, "I'm heading back now. Come with me. We have a motel room. We're out of here in the morning. Come with me. Our plans are intact."

For a few seconds they gazed at each other, and then he turned and started walking back. He was wearing only a T-shirt and jeans, shivering a little.

"Stop. Wait a minute. I've broken a heel."

He turned around. She pulled off one shoe and waved it at him.

She might have had second thoughts, she might not have gotten into the truck, but he was glad he had gone after her. She wasn't really the type to back down. She might have climbed into the truck even if she hadn't really wanted to.

He walked up to her and put his arms around her. He held her a second or two so she could feel how strong his arms were and how tenderly they could hold her. He pressed her to his chest so she could feel the flutter of his heart. Then he leaned over, grabbed her behind her knees, and pushed his shoulder into her. She folded over him easily and giggled.

"Got you now, babe," he told her.

"Put me down!"

"Hold on." He picked up her suitcase, jamming it under his arm, then the guitar case.

She pitched her broken shoe into the woods. "Put me down," she cried, laughing, whacking his back and shoulders with her fist.

Why does anyone go out west? To make himself into something better. Go out there with a girl, he can start a family. It's a big test. He has to take it.

After getting out of jail, Jay had lived in a rooming house next to what had once been a paper mill in what had once been the heart of their city. Betty's house was out near the harbour, where the air smelled of tides, where the breeze was sweeter than in other sections of town.

On mornings when he visited, her boys were always gone, the house was always quiet. Of course he visited at other times of the day just to see the boys, taking them to the park or around town, letting them get used to him, as Betty kept saying—but as for love, they would rendezvous in the mornings, when Kyle was at kindergarten and Duffy was with his granny and the house by the harbour was so quiet Jay sometimes felt as if he were there to steal something.

At the motel they cranked open the windows to let in fresh air. Being in a rented room excited them both. They checked the supply of packaged soap and folded towels.

When they lay down on one of the beds and started making love, it was sweeter and better than it had ever been, though he knew he had to make it last as long as he could because when it was over, there was a good chance he'd feel terrible.

They made it last until it was dark, when headlights were flaring through the crisp nylon curtains and the FISHERMEN WELCOME MERMAIDS TOO sign was flashing green and red.

Then, when Betty was in the shower, he felt himself sinking into that feeling afraid.

These were his dreams:

First, to never be in jail again, to never let them take him down.

Second, to value life (lives).

Third, to move a little closer to the heart.

Fourth, to never live without women.

Fifth, to love as he was loved.

Sixth, to banish despondency.

Seventh, to keep looking good.

Eighth, to always be on the lookout for something better.

He could see now, coming down before him, all the mistakes made in his life so far: his love of mistakes, misfortune, incorrect choices. He was going west with a woman he loved, hoping to find a job in Calgary, intending to establish a family, but with no true idea of how it was going to happen.

He tried to tell himself there's nothing wrong with, say, construction, if a man wants to start an honest life. Go down to the hiring hall with two hundred dollars, get a ticket in the labourers' union. In a day or two you'll be riding out to a job. You'll be hauling lumber, jackhammering concrete, tying steel.

The bed rocked. He felt himself falling. He spread his arms on the sheets, clenched his fists, felt his biceps, triceps, and pectoral muscles bunching.

He could hear water drilling against the tin shower stall. Betty was singing. Love had always made her, unlike him, most content.

At the end of that day, he told himself, you shall come home. It shall be summer in Calgary. In the evening the sky cools, the moisture settles; you'll smell timothy and clover in the damp. From an upstairs window the Rocky Mountains will seem purple as the sun goes down. After dark, with the kids asleep, you'll lie in bed with the windows open, breathing good western air, arms around your wife.

He climbed slowly from the bed, feeling like an old, old man. Getting down on his knees, he fell forward onto his hands, dug his toes into the carpet, and started his first push-up. At that moment, Betty, in the shower, started singing one of her great-grandmother's songs—"Conor, my brave, my provider, Conor, my horseman, richest of all"—and it reawakened a small amount of his hope. He lowered himself until his nose was touching the nylon carpet and began pressing with the strength in his upper arms, feeling cords of muscle working in his thighs and lower back, and as he counted "One!" he allowed himself to wonder if it was possible, just possible, that despite his poverty and errors, she was singing to him.

ALMOST CHRISTMAS,
WEST TEXAS

They spent the night in an abandoned farmhouse on the scrublands south of Pecos. They might have stayed in a motel—Jimmy Joe had all sorts of credit cards—but when they passed the farmhouse, Jimmy Joe had insisted Thomas stop and turn around. Jimmy Joe said he'd had a dream about the farmhouse, a vision he called it. He said he knew for a fact Bonnie and Clyde had hid out there from the law. Since leaving New York he had been talking a lot about Bonnie and Clyde and the posse that killed the Texas outlaws one hot, sunny morning as they were riding in their car. "That's the way I'd like it," Jimmy Joe said. "Out of the blue. From the side of the road. *Bang bang bang.* Unexpected."

Now Jimmy Joe was unzipping his sleeping bag and getting up, slowly as an old man. He stumbled to the empty window frame, where Thomas was looking out at the highway, and kissed him on the shoulder.

Jimmy Joe claimed he'd sniffed something snowy and western about Thomas the first time they met, in Sheridan Square. Thomas the runaway, the first-ever punker out of Casper, his head shaved in a mohawk strip, the strip waxed, dyed, coxcombed.

Now Jimmy Joe was peering outside, squinting in the light. "Hmm," he said. "A case of early day, West Texas."

The sun was a half-inch above the horizon, the sky pale blue and stretched flat. The only features in the landscape were derricks, and utility poles and wires along the highway. The morning smelled of gas.

"We're almost at the river," said Thomas. "When we get there, there's a little hot springs I'll take you to."

Jimmy Joe still had a headache. "It's okay so long as I don't move. Not as bad as a migraine."

"We'll get you to the hot springs, you'll feel better." Thomas knelt and began rolling up his sleeping bag.

"West Texas," said Jimmy Joe reflectively. "I could probably make a wonderful, berserk painting of it. Plenty of hard edges for the sky, the way it meets the earth down here with such gosh darned precision—"

"Hey, we going to buy you boots today?" Thomas interrupted.

"You betcha." Jimmy Joe started stretching like an old cat or a minor league ballplayer warming up for a game, loose and restless, almost healthy. Thomas finished rolling his bag and stood up, searching his pockets for cigarettes.

"Yeah," said Jimmy Joe, "I need to prop myself up on that highway stripe. If I had the right materials with me I could render Texas whole, I could make you something better than it is. Those nice hard horizons, the enchiladas, that little señorita in the taquería last night—"

"Aw, come on," said Thomas.

"You think I didn't see? That little *facilona*—and you with the aw-shucks swagger? You think I didn't notice? It's enough to make me sick!"

Thomas lit a cigarette. "Time to get back on the road," he said.

"It stinks here, doesn't it," Jimmy Joe said, sniffing. "So far it's not much cleaner than Brooklyn. The light's all right, but. Boyo, maybe things turn out all right, we'll ride the L train again. Does Wyoming smell this way?"

"Wyoming don't have a smell. Only when they're burning off gas. Sage maybe, after it rains."

"Well, it gives me a headache. No epiphanies for Texas today. Got your stuff? Let's get moving."

They walked out. Frost on the yellow grass. The Buick was concealed in a grove of cottonwoods.

"Christmas in a week," said Thomas. His words came out like smoke in the chill air.

"Ah," said Jimmy Joe. "Sweet sanctity, and the lambs at Bethlehem. Boyo, I could tell you a story." He stumbled trying to keep up with Thomas, striding through the weeds like a Comanche warrior. "Hold on a sec," Jimmy Joe called. "Time for a vision. Let me get my breath."

Thomas halted in the middle of the field—once cotton, once pasture, once Comanche roaming ground.

"Holy birth!" said Jimmy Joe, puffing. "Let me give you a story. It's not set in old Judea or West Texas, where the spicy winds seep up from old Mexico and the air smells of cash.

My little tale is set in upstate New York, way up there in the northeast snows—"

"I was in Buffalo once," said Thomas. "It was on the way coming east. I-90 to Albany out of Chicago."

"I was working on a dairy farm in the town where my parents lived," said Jimmy Joe. "It was calving season and I had a job helping in the sheds. Do you know what a calf-puller is?"

"Kind of a winch."

"Exactly. An assembly of pulleys and small-gauge chain. You harness your obstetrician self into a brace at one end and reach up inside the womb, loop the bloody chain around reluctant calf heels, and start winding the damn thing out." Jimmy Joe shivered. "First calf I ever pulled was stillborn. We were all wearing rubber boots and the shed smelled of cows' breath and wet straw. Outside it was snowing. There were two witnesses: the farmer I worked for and a neighbour who'd stopped around to buy some hay bales."

Thomas dropped his bedroll on the grass and unzipped his black leather jacket. "Cold?" he said. "Want my jacket?" He placed it around Jimmy Joe's shoulders.

"What a hero you are!" said Jimmy Joe. He struggled to get his arms into the sleeves and zip the jacket. "I wish there was a mirror. Oh, I love the clothes of war! Greeks going into battle, you know, wore leather. Where was I?"

"Calving shed," said Thomas. He wore a dirty T-shirt; he'd always been more or less oblivious to cold.

"Yes," said Jimmy Joe. "There were three of us, a trinity of wise men. The door at one end was open and you could see the Adirondacks, the grey air—the snow was falling. The stillborn calf was laid out on pink straw in a mess of afterbirth. I was kneeling over the thing for closer examination. The other two lit cigarettes and there was reflective silence for some moments, except for the mooing. Then my boss softly nudged the wet, dead thing with the toe of his boot and told me to be sure to bury it under rocks so the dogs wouldn't get at it."

There was the sound of traffic humping the highway on the other side of the cottonwoods. One hundred and fifty miles to the Chisos Mountains, then Mexico. Dry yellow grasses sparkled in the sunshine.

"Is that it?" said Thomas. "Are you finished? I don't know, it's kind of a crazy story. What's it supposed to mean?" He picked up his bedroll and started walking towards the car. He opened the door, flipped the bedroll into the back seat. Jimmy Joe ran up and they stared at each other across the metal roof.

"Ever since I got sick," said Jimmy Joe, "I always thought, you know, that it might have been a Jesus."

"Don't be crazy," Thomas said. "We'll get you better down there."

"If you can just stay away from those *facilas*," said Jimmy Joe. "Then we'll both maybe be all right."

They had found the old Buick in Jackson Heights. It had needed two new tires in Louisiana and a rebuilt water pump in Odessa the day before. Thomas eased the car out of the cottonwoods and drove slowly towards the road. Once up on the highway he jumped on the gas pedal. The car accelerating had a tough, lonely sound that reminded him of elks bugling or grizzlies smashing through the woods, even though he had grown up in a housing project near the big mall on the east side of Casper. At exactly the right instant he booted in the clutch and slid the column shift into third.

"Whoo!" said Jimmy Joe. His window was cranked down and his hand out flapping in the breeze.

"Maybe we won't stop when we get to Mexico," Thomas said. "We'll just keep on going—Guatemala, Patagonia, and all."

"I'll be dead by then!" Jimmy Joe screamed out the window. "I'll probably die in Mexico City!"

"Then we won't go to Mexico City," Thomas said. "We'll make a detour."

They stopped for breakfast at Carmen's in Marfa, seat of Presidio County. In *Rio Bravo* John Wayne was sheriff of Presidio County, with Dean Martin for his drunken deputy—but Dean healed himself in the end. Jimmy Joe knew everything there was to know about Westerns, which was, Thomas figured, part of the reason they were making this trip.

The cottonwoods along the creek had come out pale green and Mexico was in the air, stronger than ever. They ordered huevos rancheros and Texas toast. Thomas liked the look of the waitress, her tight Levi 505s, her cowboy boots and braided hair. You couldn't stop the way your mind worked. He glanced at her breasts, small and round under the pockets of her western shirt. He'd been with girls in Wyoming and Brooklyn, and he liked the way it went with them, like a long fall from a high building.

Carmen herself stood by their table and asked where they were headed.

Thomas said, "We're going down to the Rio Grande to camp out there for a while, then head into the Sierra Madre."

"Well," said Carmen, a small woman with grey hair and crinkled face, "I promise you it's wild, wild, *wild* down there."

"Wild," said Jimmy Joe, "is just what we need."

Thomas tried to catch the waitress's eye while she poured coffee but she wouldn't look at him. They finished breakfast and went outside. The old Buick had heated up in the sunshine and smelled of food wrappers, dust, and cigarettes. They drove around the courthouse square and past the Presidio County sheriff's office, where the Duke and Dean had made their stand against the powerful ranchers and Ricky Nelson had strummed a guitar. Headed south on Highland Avenue, they passed a shoe store.

"Hold on!" cried Jimmy Joe. "Stop right here!"

Thomas swung into a parking space. Ever since they had crossed the Verrazano Narrows Bridge, Jimmy Joe had been wanting cowboy boots. They'd checked out a dozen shoe stores and western outfitters from Cajun country to the Permian Basin, but he hadn't found a pair that suited him.

Inside the store Jimmy Joe sprawled in a Naugahyde chair while the salesman knelt in front of him with a stack of boxes. Thomas lit a cigarette and leaned against the wall.

"You'll pardon my saying so," the salesman said to Jimmy Joe, "but never have I seen a haircut like that one your young amigo is wearing. How's he keep it all stuck up in the middle like that, like a rooster?"

"He's a proud one," said Jimmy Joe, smiling at Thomas. "I believe it's pride that makes his hair roil up like that. Pride and special waxes."

"Never seen nothing like it. Is he some kind of star or something? Where you all from?"

"I'm a successful New York artist," said Jimmy Joe primly. "My studio's in a former glove factory in Williamsburg, Brooklyn. I have a number of assistants. I have a dealer, an agent, and a financial planner. I'm quite successful, if I may say so. I have collectors."

The salesman was unwrapping tissue paper from around the stiff new boots. Jimmy Joe took off his high-tops and exposed his chubby pink feet.

"I think you'd better slip on socks before you try these on," the salesman said. "Otherwise you can't judge the fit. Week from now you'd feel a little pinching *here*" — he slapped Jimmy Joe on the heel — "and you'd get a hot spot *here*" — he squeezed the flesh on the ball of the foot — "and you'd think back to me, who sold you a pair of boots that didn't fit. And you'd cuss me, now, wouldn't you?"

"Oh, I suppose. Perhaps."

The salesman was cradling the successful artist's foot as tenderly as a kitten. "I have a pair of handmade boots here that an artist will surely appreciate. Let me fetch you a pair of socks and you try 'em on."

Thomas was leaning against an entire wall of shoeboxes, smoking a cigarette and carefully licking his ashes in an old-fashioned ashtray on a steel stand. The ashtray was filled with clean white sand.

"Whatcha thinkin', boyo?" said Jimmy Joe. "Waitresses? Wonderful girls?"

Thomas blushed because he was thinking of the slender, small-breasted waitress and wondering how he could slip away for a few minutes and hurry back up the street and at least introduce himself.

"Whatcha thinkin'?" repeated Jimmy Joe with a sneer.

Thomas bent down to stub out his cigarette. "I'm thinkin' grains of sand," he said. It was a lie he knew Jimmy Joe would enjoy, and it would probably start him in on something and allow him to forget the reasons they were travelling. "I'm thinking grains of sand. Thinking, who changes the sand? Or do they just screen the garbage out of it to keep it so white and soft and clean? How often do they do it? Has this same sand been here forever?"

"I'm thinking all the towns you've taken me through," said Jimmy Joe happily. "I'm hallucinating Arkansas, I'm Kansas bop-kabala. But don't try and fool me, kiddo. I know what you're really thinking."

The salesman had fetched socks from a drawer. Jimmy Joe slipped them on and whispered to the salesman, "You see, it is the week before Christmas, and we are travelling." He shut his eyes and his voice got dreamy. "My young friend Thomas, Brooklyn warrior, Casper savage, it's all his idea—"

"He needed to get out of the city," Thomas explained.

Jimmy Joe leaned back in the chair. "I'm not really a traveller," he said. "Perhaps you can tell. I love to drink tea in my studio in Williamsburg. I have magnificent light and prefer to work bare-chested."

The salesman was struggling to get the boot onto Jimmy Joe's foot. Jimmy Joe reached down and started tugging.

"Will I walk tall and dreamlike in Texas boots to the crooning of America?" said Jimmy Joe.

The salesman leaned back on his stool. "There! Take a few steps, try 'em out."

"Will the earth tremble at my tread in these fine leather drumsticks?" Jimmy Joe asked.

The clerk smiled and shook his head.

"Maybe down in Mexico," said Thomas.

Thomas paid for the boots using Jimmy Joe's MasterCard and they left the store carrying the high-tops in a paper sack.

They got into the car, but before leaving Marfa they had to wait out a freight train screeching and thundering through the centre of town.

"Damn you, Thomas. You never say anything, but I know what you're thinking."

Once the train had passed they could see the yellow sprawl of grassland, nearly desert. In the distance a rim of blue mountains.

"That there," Thomas said, "is Mexico."

"You know I'm going to die down there, someplace real lonely where you don't have to get involved in anything but can just bury me off the side of the road. Isn't that what'll happen? Isn't that how you have it figured?"

"If it's what you want," said Thomas. "You could have died in Brooklyn. The desert is a clean place. And the air is cool, mornings and evenings. Smells nice. That's the way I remember it."

"You know what I'm thinking, boyo?"

"What?" Thomas stuck a cigarette between Jimmy Joe's lips and lit it for him.

"I'm thinking about the calf."

"I was too."

"I buried it in a pit and piled rocks on so the farm dogs couldn't get at it, drag it out under moonlight, howling. Will you do that much for me?"

"Don't even think of it," Thomas said.

NIGHT DRIVING

I like driving at night. I like everything about it. It's the best.

I was a little girl, Daddy would say, Hop right up here, Face. And I'd skitter across the front seat and squeeze up into his lap. He'd settle back a little into the seat, give me room behind the wheel, and there I'd be. What cars we had! My favourite was the last, a '59 Catalina, Wyoming plates. Big wide white with tail fins. We had the back seat ripped out of her and cut open into the trunk. Daddy fixes her up with plywood and a mattress, and there we both sleep. Plenty of room. With little curtains hung on a string round all the windows so what we do is private. Daddy likes it that way.

We are asleep in California six weeks past when *wham! bam!* on the doors, and deputies are there all of a sudden, like out of your dreams, and arrest Daddy and haul him off to jail. I am in jail too, alone and so lonesome, but they don't hold me for long; they turn me loose, which is worse until I meet Johnboy at the church. He now takes care of me and I take care of him and he tells me, Forget Daddy, put that right out of your mind. But I can't. He says, You are a pore little orphan Vetnamee girl. Pretty little slant-eyes. They send him back to Folsom, Johnboy say, for years. My Daddy.

What I liked best was driving at night, me and Daddy both behind the wheel. On the great black roads out there, somewhere empty, Nebraska, Canada.

This past weekend, finally, month and a half after they take Daddy and stick him in jail, me and Johnboy finally get out on the road together. We go up to Tahoe in his van. We're getting married.

Johnboy says, Ah, little Vetnamee girl, I love your tiny feet! 'Cause I like to ride at night with my shoes off and my feet resting up on the dash. I like to steer too, like I done with my Daddy, but Johnboy won't let me behind the wheel of his van. Not yet, anyways.

After our wedding we spend the weekend up there in the trees and mountains, sleeping at nights in the back of the van. Johnboy keeps saying he's going to go fishing but doesn't. Instead he unfolds the beach chair he bought at Walmart outside Stockton, $19.99, and sits and swallows beer with the tape deck playing Rolling Stones. He says sixties songs all remind him of his tour. For dinner we have no fish but food, store bought, I fry up on the Coleman. At night it is peaceful. But it's not like being out on the road.

The best of our weekend is the drive home Sunday night. We come down alongside the Merced River and all the lupines are in bloom. They are my favourite night-driving flower: you can see 'em by moonlight and by headlight, little reflectors out there in the fields. Such white and spooky little flowers, millions of them, waxy, glowing. I would like to weave a great big chain of them and send them to my Daddy, back suffering prison time in Folsom.

They say to me, policemen judges caseworkers, what will become of you? and I say I have Johnboy to take care of me now. And Johnboy is deacon of the church, vfw chapter VP, auxiliary deputy, and has the preacher as witness. I am legal age now. I am an American just like you. Americans can do what we like.

What I don't tell them is I will just wait for Daddy. I'll stay here with Johnboy, who takes care of me, and be good. I like to sing in church and wax his van, but don't tell me to stop thinking of Daddy. Daddy is the one planted inside of me.

We sleep near roadside always, in the Pontiac; we drive off into some little dark corner of a field about two hours before dawn. Beneath cottonwoods, near riverbanks, is where we like to park. We get out and swim in the river. Daddy tells me stories. We laugh and have jokes. We go to sleep.

I hate to remember them wrestling Daddy away, Daddy yelling while they shove him in their car, No peace for the wicked!

The trail out of Tahoe with Johnboy Sunday night comes from the mountain in steep canyon walls and gorge, winds down the river for miles and miles until the valley flattens it out to a road just like any other. Then the lupines disappear and we have the night smells, manure, crops, irrigation ditches.

I was a little girl, we liked the straight highways, my Daddy and me. Daddy says, On a straight road, Face, we make *time*.

Johnboy is a much softer person than my Daddy. By far. Big and soft and easy, which is why I like him so. He's a lock-smith. I like the little tufts of beard he has grown all along the line of his chin. His hair to me is the colour of honey. And his cheeks, all pink. His mouth happy, especially sucking on a beer. My Daddy will drink too but in a different style. Such as one afternoon, when we were staying in Montana, Daddy working housepainter up in Flathead Valley for the Swede — I remember the Swede well: big, floppy moustache and skin speckled with white paint. Next to him my Daddy looks like a brown stick. What happens is, after a couple of weeks the Swede owes Daddy money and we want to leave. We go looking for the Swede one afternoon. We go to a house to collect but the Swede ain't there. We go to another house — ain't there either. We start in on roadside bars where the Swede likes to drink. I wait in the car. At each bar we stop at my Daddy walks inside, madder and madder, and has a drink, looking for the Swede. Then he gets back in the Pontiac and we race down the highway, still looking. Finally Daddy gets fighting with an Indian near Missoula, after almost sixty miles of bars, and hits the Indian with a bottle out there in the parking lot. Out cold. Jumps into the Pontiac, where I'm waiting, scared, and we take off out of there and drive all the way to Oregon, I think.

In Coeur d'Alene a trucker tries to get me up into his cab while Daddy's in the truck-stop shower. "Little Vetnamee girl, Cambojan, suckee suckee," trucker says. Disgusts me. Daddy comes out, his hair all slicked back, wet and shiny looking, looking so young and handsome in fresh white tee and jeans; you can see the little scar inside his forearm he picked up on R&R, Sydney Australia. He steps up behind the fat trucker and chops him with his bare hand. We roll him over then, take his wallet, go on our way.

Now I know my Johnboy ain't like that. He's more gentle, like a great big, soft bear. He's deacon in the church. When we lie together he pretends to growl. He says he respects me 'cause of all the people in Visalia I am the one who has travelled the most and experienced things.

Most of all I am the one who thinks. Thinking is something I learned from my Daddy; I learned it in my all-night driving. Daddy says, You see, in some ways it is a marvellous and wonderful, rich experience for a child, driving.

When Johnboy and me drive home in the van through the lupine fields and then across the wide, flat, sweet-smelling valley with irrigation hissing from big pipes rolled out in the fields and the sound of things out there growing—why, I am the one most at home and he is the one always has a secret little bit of wishing that he was back at the condo, with beer, hot dogs, tacos, cake, stucco, waterbed, La-Z-Boy. We live in the development outside of Visalia.

When I first met Johnboy that night at the church, I think he's a richie. He wears a tie and jacket to church, jacket powder blue. When he offers me a ride back to the motel, I go with him and we drive around in the van, and then instead of the motel he brings me out to his condo. Outside Visalia. To me it's a castle.

My Daddy raised me without religion. On the trunks of our cars he always paints in big, bright red letters ANYONE CAN READ, FEAR NOT! He would say, We're on the road now, Babyface; we worship wide-open spaces; none of these towns and eyesores is right for us. We get all the Lord Almighty we need driving ourselves into sunset each evening. This way he'd talk when feeling especial good and roll down the window on his side, stick out his head, and yell, Yip, yip, yippee.

Which was right, because things didn't go well for us in the towns. We met in Bakersfield, where I was working in the little Vetnamee store, not even going to school, sweeping up, selling jujubes. Daddy pays 'em just to take me out of there, but even so there's a fight.

Once my Daddy got a job on a sewer crew, Casper Wyoming. We live there five weeks. He's not the same man in the towns. They start him feeling bad. Itchy-twitchy, he calls it. Sundays he's off work and we drive around looking for something, neither of us knows what. We drive to the edge of the town, Casper Wyoming, turn around, drive to the end on the other side, turn around again. We go home watch TV. Monday, Daddy goes back off to work. He says, No one bother you. Tell 'em you're my wife—no one knows the age of Vetnamee girls anyhow. Besides, I love you, he says. I take care of you, Babyface, Sugarpie, Sweetheart.

He never talked this way except when we were in the towns. At night he would cry. I try to cook him dinners when he comes home but he likes better we go up to the highway, eat in one of our truck stops out there on the edge of town. Casper Wyoming. Where we bought the Pontiac.

Driving at night makes me sad, with sadness sweet as honey I can't stop eating. Daddy and me have gone through weather in all sorts of places: Dakota snowstorms, midnight hundred degrees in places like Barstow. I tell Johnboy now, sometimes when I'm feeling blue, just what Daddy used to sometimes say—Baby, let's drive to Texas! I say it this morning just before Johnboy leaves for work.

Johnboy gets all hot. He says, Drive to Texas! Ain't you grateful? I have saved you from your Daddy. I have give you room to grow. I have brought you to the grace of the Lord.

I am not really serious, but still. It wouldn't have to be Texas. Could be anywhere at all.

He just ties on his tool belt and stomps out the door. He loves his job; he's always first on the whole street to leave for work. First in all Visalia maybe. I go out through the sliding glass door onto the little porch where the Hibachi sits, look down and watch him cross the parking lot. It's early day and the sun throws a long shadow cross the cement. Johnboy's the only one out there. No one else goes to work this early; their cars are still scattered all over—vans, Trans Ams, pickups—and bikes and plastic tricycles on the lawns, and flagpoles, and grass hissed at night by the sprinkler or otherwise it gets burnt into prickly little stubs. Sprinkler shuts off a little time before dawn.

Oftentimes me and Daddy roll right through these farm towns, these valley towns at night and pull up curbside or in some driveway. We tug off our clothes and go lie out there on the thick, sweet, wet lawns and let the mist of water soak right through us. We lie there looking up at the stars while the poor ones like Johnboy are in their houses asleep.

What can I say? I stand there on the porch in the morning sun with a mug of coffee, wearing a new nightgown, peek-a-boo, he bought me on Victoria Secret, watching him fiddling with the keys of his van, trying to get the door open. He'll look up at me.

You're a misfit, that's what you are, he'll yell. You make sure to lock up that porch door when you go inside!

I wave and he heaves into the front seat and drives away.

In towns at night, when we were feeling clean and empty, Daddy and me liked to slip into homes on little missions. Roll past a home and Daddy points and says, That one. Lets me out at the corner, all dark and quiet, and tells me what he wants. Sometimes it's something easy: rake from the garden, kitchen knife. Sometimes harder. He'll say, Get me a bar of bathroom soap, little one. Or, Fetch me a bedside clock.

I like to slip into the houses, darkness, stay low on the floor. No one ever wakes. I'm good now but Daddy's the best. Once he comes back with a dog collar, big one too, like a Dobie, something mean; says *Rexie* on the collar. Daddy has a way with animals.

Johnboy has lived in this wonder valley all his life; his mom and pop and sisters live in a deluxe trailer park, other side of the city of Visalia from us, work in a factory, work in a health-care centre. We don't see 'em much. They are backsliders. John's Born Again, and the Church, the Pentecostals, now they are his family.

Last night, Sunday night, we drove down, twisting alongside the Merced River past little meadows and hillsides of shiny lupine. I got my toes curled on the cool edge of the dash like I like; we stop at the store coming out of Yosemite for Fritos and beer. I am listening to the sounds of the night driving, crackling of the cellophane bag, when Johnboy reaches in for another handful, radio noise, wind slipping in through loose corners of shut windows. Johnboy reaches over to pat my feet. I am convinced in these kinds of moments that I have waiting for me a destiny, just like my Daddy said when we first met, Bakersfield; the way he would tell me and make me believe, over campfires we set up in little roadside pull-ins in the Rocky Mountains.

Johnboy always trying to get me to tell about life with Daddy. What did he do with you? What did he like? How old was you when you met up with him?

I liked to lean over the fires when they were almost out so I could smell the smoke and get a little of it in my hair and see the last coals glowing. The red embers looked like cities burning and flickering from a plane up high above.

They let me see Daddy just the once, while he's still at county jail.

Locksmith, he says. Ha ha.

I think of our poor Pontiac parked off somewhere in some sheriff's lot, getting dusty and hungry for the road. Probably sold by now, Johnboy says: auction, convict goods. Daddy says nonetheless he'll come to fetch me. Nonetheless, Babyface. Just be ready.

A destiny is something like the stars you see twinkling in the midnight sky when you are travelling across Wyoming. A destiny is the place where you will end up, says Daddy, all happy, with problems forgot and sorrows eased. It is the place you lie with all your friends around, sipping drinks, with the smell of flowers. There'll be a soft little stream and more flowers floating by.

I feel I am getting closer to it while I am travelling at night. Even with Johnboy. My destiny is a seed that the night and all the trips I've taken with Daddy has planted in me. Even if the destiny dries up and hides whenever we stop, and in the daytime. Even if I can't show it to Johnboy, can't tell him what it is when he asks — he'll never understand, I think sometimes. But I will love and try to teach him like Daddy taught me. Like when we'd stop at gas stations somewhere after midnight — Spearfish, Moline, Shelby, Farmington — they would wipe the windshield of the Pontiac and say to Daddy as he was about to pay, Where you going, mister? and Daddy'd look them straight in the eye and say, Up and beyond now, up and beyond is where I'm headed.

The idea is a precious seed Daddy gave me, and all the night and all the travelling will be sure to land me at the one, the only place.

At night out here, outside Visalia, when Johnboy rolls over and presses me against the wall, snoring, I crawl out from under and go stand at the window just to check that it is off the latch. I can see orange lights out on the highway. I look back at Johnboy's bulk on the bed, asleep in pyjamas, hear slurp and sloshing of the waterbed when he rolls again, and the sound of trucks out on the road. Sleep, baby, sleep, I whisper to him.

FATHER'S SON

When my father had his first heart attack, the winter I was fifteen, I felt relieved. I thought it might weaken him a little, even the scales between us.

He was still in the intensive care unit when a massive snowstorm shut down the city. As his only son, I thought it was my duty to ski across Montreal that night to see him. I felt like a *coureur de bois* traversing our silent, boreal city. Stars sparked above Westmount Mountain. My skis left fresh, frail tracks on buried streets: the Boulevard, Côte-des-Neiges, Pine Avenue.

I found him on a narrow bed in the ICU, wires glued to his chest. A cardiac monitor spat green light in the room. An intravenous feeder was plugged into his forearm, plastic tubing shoved up his nose. He was so glad to see me. I don't think I had ever seen him unshaven before. The white beard rasped my lips when I leaned over to kiss him. At that moment, in his helplessness, I loved him as much as I ever had, or would.

The ICU nurses adored his elegant manners, weird ice-blue eyes, beautiful hands. In a hospital bed my father looked nothing like what he was: an executive in a midsize conglomerate that manufactured industrial chemicals and newsprint. No, he was an old Viking. A *comitatus* elder. An ancient warrior with the North Sea flowing in his veins—along with the IV glop.

He was sprung from ICU at the end of the week, briskly dealing with office paperwork from his private room in the Royal Victoria Hospital. He bounced back fitter, twenty pounds lighter, and I came to understand that I had to get away or he was going to eat my life. Nothing grisly, only a kind of painless ingestion. Afterwards I might be spat out at business school, law school. If I was not sharp enough for the practice of law, I would doubtless prove capable of some position requiring a well-tailored suit. Something respectable, reliable, and offering total security. A job that didn't really exist, outside my father's imagination.

The ranch was where my life started. Everything before that felt like someone else's history.

On my first morning I was introduced to the top hand. A loose-limbed, sun-flayed man name of Rick Bean. The first cowboy I ever met. I had expected a big hat, tooled leather boots, spurs. Rick Bean wore spurs, but they were strapped on over Canadian Tire rubber boots. Instead of a Stetson, a nylon mesh cap from a farm equipment dealership in Red Deer.

He stood beside the corral, rolling a cigarette. We solemnly shook hands. His posture was awkward, tentative, as though he had broken bones that had never quite knitted together. His hand felt big, bony, and dry. He hadn't shaved, and his chin was covered with silver stubble. He licked the cigarette and stuck it between his lips. I struck him a match. He asked to keep the matchbook, from a Montreal bar—Sweet Mama's, on Mackay Street. He wanted it to show to his kids.

Everything he did superbly was done from horseback. Rick Bean, I learned, had no feel for machinery. He distrusted loud noises and gearshifts. Brake levers and starter buttons never seemed to work for him. In the operator's seat of a swather, the machine buzzing and clattering like a giant insect, his eyes narrowed to worried slits. His brown face wrinkled in all its creases.

He had been a rodeo cowboy, had raced chuckwagons at the Calgary Stampede. He had won many events, taken some bad spills, and married a waitress met in the Stampede beer tent. She bore six children, not all of them his.

The Beans wintered at Pincher Creek and came up to the ranch every spring. They arrived in a smoking Plymouth Belvedere crowded with skinny children, towing a horse trailer, car and trailer crusted with pale grey mud. They settled into an old squared-timber cabin. The rancher advanced wages so Mrs. Bean could buy groceries. The local store did not extend credit to the Beans.

Rick Bean's horse was Prince Hal, a handsome chestnut gelding, a quarter horse with elegant thoroughbred lines. Prince Hal was by far the best cattle horse on the ranch, just as Rick Bean was by far the best horseman, the only really skilled cowboy, the top hand.

A few days after the arrival of the Beans, we were to drive

six hundred head of cattle from spring to summer grazing. The cattle belonged to three or four ranchers who shared a Crown lease. I had no experience with cattle drives, and no one had time to teach me. An old, slow, fat mare was cut out, a saddle thrown on. I was given a leg up, and that was that.

To reach summer pasture, the herd had to ford the James River, a tributary of the Red Deer, milky green, chill, and silty with glacial runoff.

The cattle had been grazing in densely forested hills. Finding them was like a game of hide-and-seek. I concentrated on staying aboard the mare — her name was Buttercup — and getting my legs out of the way whenever she chose to scrape her fat sides against a tree trunk. Buttercup was slow and greedy. She kept stopping to graze and I had to jerk the reins and kick desperately with my heels to keep her moving.

We were a dozen riders advancing in a ragged line through the bush. I was thrilled, frightened, and anxious not to make a fool of myself. The strategy was to comb the hills slowly, gathering the cattle ahead of us, until we had collected the herd against a barbed-wire fence. Then we would move them down the fenceline, out through a gate, and down the road, headed for the river. Once the cows were on the road, all we had to do was keep them moving. Parked at every crossroads, women and children would keep the animals trotting in the straight line that would eventually bring them to the James. With riders keeping up the pressure, the lead animals would take to the water and the rest would follow. After fording, they would pick up the road on the other side and peacefully walk another mile or so, until a station wagon blocked the route and women carrying willow sticks waved the cows through a gate into a pasture where wind rippled waves of silver-green grass with a noise like bedsheets tearing. That was how it was supposed to happen, anyway, but of course it didn't.

The previous winter, still living with my parents and sisters in our Montreal apartment, I had obtained a list of ranchers from the Alberta Stockmen's Association. I wrote half a dozen letters begging for work. My father had no objection. I was trying to jump-start a life but he thought it was merely a question of a summer job. And he had his own lurking fascination with the West, in some ways deeper and loonier than mine.

He was born on the Isle of Wight in 1910. His mother was Anglo-Irish, his father German. When war broke out in 1914, his father was arrested and interned for four years at what was called a "concentration camp" for German husbands of British wives, at Alexandra Palace, a failed exhibition hall in north London.

My father was baptized Hermann Heinrich Lange, an uncomfortable name in wartime England. His Irish grandmother started calling him Billy. She had a son, also Billy, who had emigrated, joined the North West Mounted Police, and disappeared into the wilds of Canada.

My father left Great Britain for the first time when my grandfather was deported to Germany in 1919, after the Armistice. The family went first to a borrowed apartment in a rat-infested castle in Saxony, then to an apartment in Frankfurt, where Hermann/Billy, the Anglo-Hiberno-Teutonic schoolboy, taught himself the language of Goethe by reading and rereading the best-selling Wild West stories of author Karl May. May had not set foot outside Germany when he wrote them, and he never got farther west than Buffalo, New York, but his best characters—Winnetou, Old Shatterhand—roamed the boiled plains of Texas and the painted deserts of the Southwest, a country more passionately imagined than any Zane Grey described. May wrote of tribes, quests, warrior codes—matters close to the German heart, transposed to a different key, transferred to a North American Wild West. He was Hitler's favourite author.

In Montreal, fifty years later, my father could still hear the song May had been singing. He could imagine that he understood my longing to go west. He thought the West would toughen me. So did I—we were both German Romantics, I suppose—and one May morning I finally left home, with a friend, in a battered Ford Pinto we had picked up at a drive-away agency and promised to deliver to a used-car dealer in Calgary. My father was happy to see me go. Did he ever grasp that I was running away from him?

My bedroom at home was supposed to be the maid's room. Set apart, off the kitchen, it was the smallest room in our apartment. Pressing a button in the dining room sounded a buzzer in my room, but my parents never had a real maid to ring for, only a succession of part-time nursemaids and au pairs, and by the time my youngest sister was four, the last of the hired help was gone and I inherited the room.

The morning I left home, he handed me fifty dollars and warned me not to drive at night, when all the nuts would be out on the road. My friend and I covered six hundred miles that first day, stopping long after midnight. We got a six-dollar room in a flophouse above a tavern. Lugging our rucksacks along the corridor, we passed open doors and men sitting on their beds in dingy SRO cells, drinking rye whisky and playing cards with women who were, we imagined, whores. Pronounced *hoo-ers* in Canada. The women called out to us with scratched, boozy voices but we were too shy to answer them. It was as far from home as I had ever been.

His beautiful suits were tailored in London or Hong Kong. His shoes, handmade, were arrayed in his closet like a leather regiment, each shoe polished to radiance and rammed with a wooden shoe-tree.

We were Catholics. One of his rules was Mass on Sunday. A supplementary was jacket and tie. He selected my tweed jackets and chose every tie. On Sunday mornings when I walked up the church path, he walked beside me, throwing me frustrated, compulsive blue-eyed glances. I always tried to ignore them. My mother stood waiting for me to open the door. As I reached for the handle, he got behind me. He made his move. I felt his fingertips on my neck—he couldn't stop himself, he never could. My spine stiffened, my shoulders twitched. My father turned down the collar of my overcoat and smoothed it flat, and I shuddered, twisted, ducked into church, smouldering with resentment. Hating his touch.

I do not remember much about the Canada we crossed that spring, only its emptiness and strangeness. And the cowboy boots and lime-green jeans men wore at truck stops in southern Saskatchewan. The coolness of rubber floor mats against my bare feet. The litter of maps, torn and badly folded. My arm hung out the window, my palm cutting and planing on the seventy-mile-per-hour breeze.

We slept the last night in a field outside Medicine Hat, reached Calgary the next day, delivered the Pinto, and split up, as planned. I caught a Greyhound up to Caroline, Alberta, where I had been promised a job.

The oil boom of the mid-seventies had created a labour shortage in western Canada, otherwise no rancher would have hired someone like me. Boys raised on farms and ranches were all in Calgary earning twelve dollars an hour as union carpenters on condominium projects, or up on the Athabaska tar sands, operating backhoes the size of buildings.

It would be understatement to say that I was unprepared for the ranch. In our family there was no masculine tradition of physical labour, craftsmanship, or even general handiness. I never saw my father grasp any tools except a pen and a cigar clipper. We lived in an apartment, with a janitor to fix anything that went wrong.

I had expected a mythic landscape: stark plains, vast skies, plateaus, knobs of red rock. A singing wind. I'd seen the John Ford movies, and the West I had constructed was, of course, a spiritual condition, not a place. *Get tough. Get lonesome. Get hard.* It wasn't Alberta I was aiming for, it was independence. Separation. The freedom to make my own moves, even if they were disastrous.

I was disappointed that the foothills around Caroline were small and tight—forested demi-mountains not unlike the Laurentian hills north of Montreal, where my father rented us a farmhouse every summer. I had come two thousand miles to be a cowboy in a landscape that could have passed for Quebec without the ski resorts, without the joie de vivre.

But Caroline, it turned out, wasn't much like home after all. The foothills were blanketed with aspen and lodgepole pine, not Laurentian birch and spruce. The James River—speeding, narrow—was heart-shockingly cold, a liquefied glacier. Standing on the roof of the hay barn looking west, I could see the limestone wall that was the Rocky Mountains front range.

The foothill ranches were small and many of the ranchers were poor. The district had the classic lawless flavour of marginal hill country. On remote sections we would find dead cows on the road with their hindquarters butchered off. Any driver who hit a cow and happened to be carrying an axe or knife in his car would help himself to free beef. Sometimes it wasn't even legitimate roadkill. We'd find carcasses of animals slaughtered and hastily butchered a hundred yards inside the fencelines.

Handguns were rare, this being Canada, so people in the beer parlours felt safe to let off steam by brawling. I saw a woman walk up behind her husband, who was sitting at a table—provincial law forbade anyone to drink standing up—and crack his skull open with a bottle of Coca-Cola. There was little traffic on the section roads, which were muddy and hazardous. Cows roamed the roads at night. Firebirds and Trans Ams, driven by nineteen-year-old rig pigs back from a season of drilling on the Beaufort Sea, smashed into ditches, rolled, threw up brilliant scherzos of flame. Pickup trucks—they called them half-tons—flew off bridges and bumped downstream on the current, crunching ashore upside down on gravel bars, spilling drowned cargoes of cowboys and their underage girlfriends. I saw an old man break a horse by bucking it down the main street of Sundre, Alberta, while dragging a couple of truck tires for ballast. This was the middle of the afternoon on an ordinary weekday, and I was the only person who bothered to watch.

My father worshipped order because his early life had been a scattering, a chaos. When he and his parents crossed France in 1919, heading into Germany, into exile, their suitcases and trunks were looted by railway workers. Everything—silverware, baptismal certificates, clothes, books—was lost.

My father looked everywhere for certainty and absolute security. He could not really believe they existed, but he couldn't stop looking. He married a beautiful gambler, one of four famously gorgeous sisters, Montreal debutantes of the thirties. Raven-haired and devout, my mother had acquired a taste for cards and dice at her convent boarding school, the Pensionnat du Saint-Nom-de-Marie. She sharpened her skills by shooting dice at a *barbotte,* a Montreal gambling joint, and dealing blackjack hands with the redcaps, taxi drivers, and RAF pilots at Dorval Airport, where she had a wartime job booking VIP passengers on the trans-Atlantic bomber shuttle. Years later, kicking back a corner of the living room carpet and kneeling on the floor, she would persuade my sisters and me—we in pyjamas, she in an evening dress—to gamble our allowances, rolling dice with her before she and my father headed out to a ball, a poker game, a dinner *à deux* in the downstairs bar at Café Martin. She loved the tumbling dice, but she had married a man who would work for the same corporation for half a century. Who never bought a house because he thought real estate too risky. A man who counted the perfectly honed yellow Faber pencils arranged in the top drawer of the desk in his study and interrogated his children if one was missing.

My father quit Germany the year after Hitler came to power and arrived in Montreal on his British passport. He tried to join the Royal Canadian Navy in 1939 and was rejected for being "too damn German." His parents lived in Frankfurt throughout the war. In Montreal his business colleagues and German-speaking friends called him Bill. To my mother and her Irish-Canadian family he was Hermann, except when social circles overlapped. Then I often heard her make the shift. "Bill," she'd say, "pour me another, would you?"

I don't know why he had to be Bill to the Montreal Germans and Hermann to the Montreal Irish. I read it as a sign. People usually found my father mildly exotic, slightly misplaced, some kind of elegant foreigner. Wherever he happened to be, it was pretty clear that he was from somewhere else.

The bush was so thick and tangled that our first sweep of the hills gathered less than half the herd. Each time we pressed a group of animals up against the barbed wire, the friskiest steers jumped the fence and galloped off in all directions. This stirred the rest of the cattle the same way that a few people's restlessness or recklessness can get a crowd seething and turn a peaceful demonstration into a riot.

Cold, thick rain began. Horses slipped and skidded, thrashing in potholes so deep that they could be extracted only with ropes and winches. But forage was very thin on the winter side of the river, and the ranchers were unwilling to postpone the drive on account of poor weather, which might last for weeks.

The rain had brought the James up quickly. By the time the first steers reached the ford, even I could see that the river was running so deep and fast that the animals would have to swim or drown. The riders pushing at the rear hadn't comprehended the danger and so kept up the pressure. The lead animals were being pressed into a cold, fast current that started sweeping them downstream. I was on a flank near the front, staying as close as I could to Rick Bean, trying not to do anything to make things worse. Rick Bean spurred Prince Hal out into the river. Buttercup and I followed reluctantly. The horses struggled to keep their footing while drowning steers bumped past us. Their faces were tilted up, snorting plaintively, and their wild eyes showed how frightened they were.

The James, which had been the colour of melted pistachio ice cream, was grey and thick now, a suspension swirling with gravel, tree branches, and mud. The silty water rasped like sandpaper against my leg. The horses kept their feet, barely. Urging Prince Hal across, Rick Bean used his horse's strength to nudge one of the drowning steers to safety. He dropped a lariat over the stubby horns of another and towed him. I did nothing helpful, just hung onto my mare while the river ripped by us and more bellowing, drowning steers were swept away.

My father's politics could be liberal. He had been a refugee. He rarely fired anyone. He believed in taking care of people. He was quite capable of tenderness. I remember arriving in Montreal after driving cross-country, coming in at two or three o'clock in the morning, and finding him in his pyjamas, dressing gown and slippers, waiting up for me. And saying nothing, not a word, only hugging me fiercely, and kissing me.

He was also domineering, unable to escape his obsession with loss and his need for punctuality, control, certainty. He was ill-suited to raising children aboard an entropic planet. When he thought he was shielding us, he was blocking us. We weren't getting any light.

My sisters tried to escape the pressure by becoming best friends with girls from large, warm, tolerant, rich families. My sisters essentially got themselves adopted. We were all searching for ways to begin ourselves.

My adolescence had been a fog, but during that first hard day of the cattle drives, everything that happened registered clearly. Everything had colour and weight. Aboard an old mare, midstream in the James River, I stepped into my own life.

The drownings had spooked the herd. They were shying away from the dangerous river, turning, thrusting back up the road. The riders behind finally gave up trying to control them and got out of their way, and the cattle melted back into the bush like a successful guerrilla army.

I can remember my adolescence without being able to see myself in it. But I can see myself very clearly that afternoon: a thin boy, scared, on an old horse in a fast river. I didn't do anything brave or useful. I didn't panic either. And midstream in that noisy little river I realized something: that the world, after all, did not belong to my father. It wasn't exactly mine either, but if I could hang on, learn a few things, I probably had as much of a claim on it as anyone. At a washed-out ford, in the James River, I think I became a person, finally. Whatever happened from then on would matter. Whatever happened from then on would stick. I could start accumulating my own history.

Buttercup and I made it across, but there was nothing much to do on the other side, since no cattle had made it over except the pair of steers Rick Bean had rescued, grazing peacefully in good grass. It would take us days to collect the rest of the herd and try again. Meanwhile Rick Bean rolled two cigarettes from an Export pouch kept dry in his shirt pocket. Then we swam our horses back across and went home.

At the end of the season I went back to Montreal to start college, but for the next decade my life was focused on the West. I was never away from it for long. My life had opened up like a book fallen off a shelf, splayed on the floor. I picked it up, started reading at the open page, and went on from there. Until I was in my thirties I earned my living from manual labour. Those years had their loneliness, boredom, and frustration, but there was always the next page.

That tense warrior who was my father? Remember Max von Sydow in *Pelle the Conqueror*? People used to say that Max/Pelle was my old man in his seventies—the physical resemblance was spooky. In his last years he looked like an old eagle, tattered and fierce, with shaggy white eyebrows and wild eyes glaring out across the lives of his children.

In my late twenties I began spending winters on the coast of Maine. It was cheap and I could write there. In the spring I would drive back out to Alberta and work for seven or eight months at another harsh outdoor job where I could save up another chunk of money. One year I picked up my father in Montreal and the old man made the long drive west with me.

He was well behaved. Not too grumpy, even when his knees — ruined in a violent skiing accident in 1940, swollen with scar tissue — were bothering him. I did all the driving. It was thirty years since he had used a standard shift.

By then I had crossed the continent so many times that all the main highways bored me, so we took back roads almost all the way, across Ontario, Michigan, Minnesota, North Dakota, Montana, Saskatchewan.

Whenever my father travelled, even over the Great Plains in my beat-up car, he dressed like Prince Philip on a country weekend at Sandringham: tweed jacket, grey flannels, suede shoes, tattersall shirt. A different necktie every day.

Each evening we stopped before six so that he could fix himself a Scotch and soda in the motel room and watch Walter Cronkite. Afterwards we would go out looking for a steakhouse. He kept his temper and most of his anxiety in check, and maybe because of that, he got lucky. On our next-to-last day, driving across south Saskatchewan — west of Assiniboia, east of Maple Creek — he spied a herd of small antelope flickering like birds across that dry-spring, burnt-yellow country.

He asked me to stop the car. There was no problem pulling over; we were the only traffic for miles. He got out, opened the trunk, and lifted a pair of ancient, beautiful Zeiss eight-power military binoculars from his suitcase. They had

belonged to his father, who had once been a Prussian grena-
dier. Black metal barrels wrapped in black leather. My father
used to take them to football games.

I watched him remove his bifocals and slip them into his
shirt pocket, then raise the heavy old field glasses to his eyes.
I saw him spin the rangefinder until he got what he wanted in
focus—those tiny, hasty, delicate, finely tuned animals.

This is the picture of my father I have been given: an old
man standing on an empty highway, gazing at faraway antelope. I believe the animals are his children: the artist daughter; the daughter who died in a car wreck; the son who is
about to become a father himself. My father watches us but he
never can catch us. Wind shunts through the shortgrass, tugs
at his tweed jacket, flips his necktie, blows through the wide-
open doors of my car. Huge light of the West. The scent of
sage. The possibility of rain. His father's binoculars. His son
standing nearby. The car's engine beating softly, just below
the noise of the wind.

THE ICE STORY

Soon after I met you we took a trip. I had an appetite for mileage, for geography, and I persuaded you to leave town with me because I wanted to see what would happen. I was moving fast and you let yourself be carried along. I remember riding across a prairie landscape in eastern Washington on an afternoon between storms, and driving over a pass with ghostly elk on the highway. We slept in a Chinese motel in Vancouver, crossed the strait, traversed the island, rented the smallest of cabins on a beach miles from anywhere. It was late November, rainy, fogbound, the off-season. By then I needed you to fall in love with me. And I had to walk out every second evening to place long-distance calls to a woman waiting for me in Toronto. You knew about her but I don't remember us talking about her. Instead we walked on the beach, where the fog smelled of cedar smoke, and scavengers who lived in pearl-grey shacks helped themselves to lumber that drifted in, washed and polished by the tide.

We slept together and remained strangers, sometimes taking our walks alone. You needed time to think, you needed privacy. I wanted to stay on that beach with you forever.

As soon as we drove back into the mountains the rain changed to snow. At certain times the highway was closed and I remember motel rooms with you. I needed to savour the miles we had left and to use them sparingly because you were nearly mine while we were travelling, you almost belonged to me. Long before dark I would start scanning the outskirts of towns for motels, even when you insisted that you were prepared to drive all night, or at least another hundred miles, or just over the next pass, to the next town.

"Too dangerous," I'd say. "Too slippery." I was worried about black ice, worried about losing you. I was grateful for the storms because I wanted to keep travelling in your company, and if the weather had been clear we would have reached our town in a day and a half instead of the four days it finally took us. I relished the small rooms, the polyester sheets, every rented bed you shared with me.

In the middle of a storm somewhere in the Bitterroots, we stopped beside a broken guardrail where the air was crowded with falling snow and black, greasy smoke. We rolled down our windows, heard flames snapping. The afternoon smelled of roasting meat. We got out of the car, walked to the edge of the road, and peered down at a Swift's Sausage & Premium Hams eighteen-wheeler sprawled like a stunned animal at the bottom of a gully. Snow was falling thickly; it was a curtain blocking everything except subdued orange flames licking the sides of the trailer. Snow sizzled on blackened metal.

We started slipping down the bank. I jumped up on the running board and peered inside, expecting to see the driver's body, but he had already been taken away. Snow blew through the broken windows and rattled crisply along the vinyl dashboard. Crumbs of safety glass were scattered over the seat and the rubber floor. A pair of elk-hide gloves, stiff and sweat-stained, were wedged above the big sun visor.

Standing on the running board, gripping the big truck mirror, I looked around and saw you falling backwards, laughing, flapping your arms and making an angel in the snow, and I recognized with a kind of gasping, breathtaking pain how much had changed in ten days; how you were ruining my past, making it dim and unimportant; how I was living for nothing except you, the road, the snow, the invisible mountains. I looked up the embankment to my car: engine idling, doors flung open, taillights shining through falling grey snow. It seemed extraordinarily beautiful, hopeful, a promise of everything to come.

Trips taken by lovers who don't know each other very well can have unforeseen consequences. Attachment itself is a mystery. At some point I told you I was prepared to push everything as far as it would go. *Hope*, *faith*, and *passion* were talismanic words to me then, but when I said them to you, they only seemed to drive you in on yourself, you were silent.

When we arrived back in town, the weather was inhospitably cold, the river had seized, and hunks of ice were locked beneath the bridge. It was the middle of the morning and we ate breakfast in the café. The town was stunned under snowdrifts, our friends had vanished. We went back to my room.

I was in love, you were wary, and the inequity felt hot, something I could never swallow or digest. I kept telling you to trust me. I studied road maps while you slept. When you woke, I suggested California, Mexico. You didn't believe I was serious. I told myself that when the time was ripe I'd convince you. I went out to make a call to Toronto. I had promised to return there by Christmas, and she wanted to know exactly when I would be arriving. She knew me better than you did, though I was always lying to her, always trying to give the truth to you. She sounded anxious and I fended her off with impatient lies.

We stayed in my room for most of a week. It kept snowing, a foot of snow a day, and I believed I was winning you. To be precise, I thought you were getting weaker, that before long you'd be going anywhere with me.

Overnight, arctic air blew the sky clear. You said you needed to get out for a few hours, no matter how cold it was. We rented skis and drove a few miles out of town, my car rattling over the road on frozen tires and stiffened springs. The snow in the woods lay deep and untracked, which was why we decided to travel across the lake. The air rasped our throats and lungs. Limestone mountains glittered around the shore.

Years later I told our story to my wife after she and I had known each other for only a couple of hours. We were sitting in darkness on a beach at Cape Cod. "I heard her scream," I said. "Then I looked down and saw the snow around my skis turning blue. When I looked back, she was falling."

The beach was at approximately the same latitude as Portugal. It was midnight and we had been swimming in the white surf. She had slipped out of her clothes and dived in. It wasn't very dangerous in the waves but there was a slight riptide, an element of treachery.

I think I told her the story because I wanted her to believe that I was capable of loving someone. If she had interrupted at any point to ask what it was really about, I would have said, passion. For a long time I have been trying to attach an acceptable meaning to our story.

You slipped into the water wearing skis as narrow as bones strapped to your feet. As I lay down for you, the ice beneath my belly began to soften. I held out something to you, a stick or a ski pole, but it was ignored, and then the ice below my body began to crumble. The cold water struck my chest like the flat blade of a shovel swung hard. I could feel my lungs shrivel.

We bobbed in the hole while our lips were being sealed. I kept ducking beneath the surface, trying to detach my skis. The water in my eyes was black and burning. Breathing was difficult and noisy. When I tried to launch myself out of the hole, every piece of ice I touched crumbled in my hands. After a while it seemed less than sensible to struggle. Your breathing sounded like an engine with something severely wrong. Your hair was laced with white frost, your face was lumpy and pale, you kept looking surprised. Still we kicked, sputtered, and splashed, trying to keep apart so our skis wouldn't tangle. I already felt sorry for your family. The rest of my thinking was being lulled as the cold settled in. Water slopped back and forth, subsided, and a skin of soft new ice began forming at the rim of the hole. We would look at each other, then look away. Dying together was a little humiliating.

I told our story to another woman. We were sitting in a booth in the Chinese café last week. When I finished, she reminded me that J. Edgar Hoover kept boxes and cardboard cartons sealed with masking tape in his basement and the back of his garage. Inside were his "raw files," which he used to guard and extend his power.

"Are these your raw files?" she said.

I told her that you and I had often sat in that same booth. I pointed out items on the menu that you used to order. She said, "You have the structure of a story all set up and now you're trying to fit me into it."

She said, "Where is your wife?"

A piece of ice held and I was kicking, slowly at first, not much caring. Then with a little more will. Did you even notice? I surprised myself when I flopped up on the ice and stuck to it, sucking and gasping. All my clothes became hard, instantly. You drifted nearby; I touched the collar of your jacket, or it could have been one of your braids. Was your hat off by then? You came out on your own, pushing and kicking. You had abandoned your boots and skis in the water. You lay on the ice, making sounds.

We began crawling. The trees on the shore grew bigger, then stopped, and after a while we realized we were no longer crawling towards them. Instead we were pretending to sleep. I got up and started running and you came after me. We moved like monsters in our stiff clothes, lurching and grunting. When we reached the shore, I broke off my icy hunks of skis. We were taking in air in sore gasps. I started through the snowdrifts and you followed, shouting in pain because your feet were so tender.

We couldn't see the car for a long time, but then it appeared. The key was in the zippered pocket of your jacket. Neither of us could grasp the zipper, so I pulled the jacket off you, hooked it on the bumper, and tore the pocket open. The key dropped onto the snow. It took a long time to pick it up—it was so smooth, cold, and slender. Finally we got the door open.

I was trying to start the engine when another car chugged over the bridge. These people seemed to know what to do. They got us into their car and began driving to the hospital. I sat in the front seat and a woman tore my clothes open with a knife, pulled off her shirt, pressed her hot breasts against me. I could hear you in the back seat, suffering. The car floated into town. At the hospital they went to work on me first and left you in the hallway in a puddle of water on the floor.

Six hours later we were released and went back to my room, wearing borrowed clothes.

I called Toronto twice while heading east that Christmas. From a café in South Dakota, a motel in Michigan.

By the time I arrived she knew something was wrong. She said she had known for a long time how things would end. She was angry with me for driving all that way to tell her I was in love with someone else. The next year she met another man and married wisely, flowering with conjugal zeal. I see her whenever I'm in her city. There isn't much to say, yet I feel compelled. She would rather I didn't need to see her, but she is gracious. And I don't stay very long. A single cup of tea and I am on my way, following subway maps through the city of Toronto.

You and I had a short subsequent history. It's not important what went wrong, is it? The flaws of character and circumstance that kept us apart? I could list most of them and it would be depressing, but it wouldn't matter.

Is our story about passion, or faithlessness, or is it about an accident, a series of accidents? What seems important now is how much I remember. Your kiss in a supermarket parking lot. An argument in a basement apartment. You turning away from me at an airport while engines roared.

In the middle of that night you woke up howling. Your skin was on fire — you felt it broiling and burning and sloughing off your bones. I led you into the bathroom, shut the door, and turned on the hot water. It roared from the tap and the bathroom packed with steam. Your hair was damp, fragrant; your body reflected in the fogged mirrors; your skin was the colour of light.

COMING HOME

FIRE STORIES

Shaun Breen told fire stories. He had come to Montreal from Newfoundland with his mother. She worked in the Snow Hill Coffee Shop at the corner of Queen Mary Road and Côte-des-Neiges but was always there to pick him up after school: a blonde woman puffing a cork-tipped cigarette, a ski jacket thrown over her waitress uniform.

Shaun was the smallest boy in our class. His clothes were covered with burns. There were black charred dots on the sleeves of his shirts, scorch marks on the seat of his pants. He told the fire stories at recess or while we waited in the cold mornings for the janitor to open the school doors.

His father had been a fireman who'd broken his back falling off a ladder trying to rescue a crippled boy trapped in the attic of a house on fire.

There'd been a blaze in a movie theatre in St. John's, Newfoundland, and one hundred children had been smothered by smoke or crushed by crowds rushing for the exits, while Shaun and his mother had escaped by sliding through a trap door that dropped them into the waters of the harbour.

There was a fire at their apartment on Côte-des-Neiges Road and Shaun had awakened smelling smoke, had run downstairs and across the street, in pyjamas, to smash the delicate glass on a telephone-pole fire alarm. Water from the fire hoses broke through the windows and ripped holes in the walls. Live wires, pulled down by the ice, snapped out blue tongues of flame upon the pavement.

Our school, St. Kevin's, was in Côte-des-Neiges, a neighbourhood composed of grid streets and plain brick apartment houses that hadn't existed before the war, when there had been only fields of snow and summer melons. It was the Catholic school closest to where my parents lived. That's why I went there instead of Roslyn School or Iona, which were nearer but administered by the Protestant school board. My mother drove me to school the first day in our Buick Century. I wore a grey flannel suit with short pants, a white shirt, a red necktie, brown oxfords, thick woollen socks. My grandmother sent the grey flannel suits from England. I hated them, but whenever I outgrew one, another would arrive in a brown paper parcel tied with string.

The fire stories always ended the same way, with Shaun's escape, while around him other victims, buildings, whole towns were consumed by fire's voracious appetite.

I was at St. Kevin's for five years before being dispatched to boarding school in the Eastern Townships. I was always first in my class. The other pupils at St. Kevin's were Italians, West Indians, poor Irish. There were only a few like me who came from streets on the slope of the mountain, whose mothers spoke good English and whose fathers came to

Parents' Nights wearing business suits. Most of the parents were working people like Shaun's mother, who took whatever shifts she could get at the coffee shop and probably never attended a Parents' Night. Whenever I saw her, she was waiting for Shaun at the schoolyard fence. Even when it was below zero she was puffing a cigarette, shivering in her jacket and her half-undone, hurriedly-stepped-into snow boots. She took Shaun back to the coffee shop, where he would eat his supper at the counter, then do his homework in one of the booths until her shift was over.

Once there was a man in Newfoundland who had caught fire inside. He didn't realize it until smoke started coming out of his mouth. There was nothing anyone could do. The man was burned to a crisp.

Shaun left that school in the middle of the winter. It was the sort of district where people moved around a lot, where children were being shifted in and out of schools all the time, so it wasn't a big surprise when Shaun disappeared; half the class that had started in September wouldn't be there by June. The janitor came in and removed his desk, rearranging the others so there wouldn't be an empty space. Later a Trinidadian girl joined the class and the desks were rearranged again.

I forgot Shaun after a couple of weeks and I never saw him again. I left St. Kevin's, left all schools eventually, left the country. It was decades later that I remembered the fire stories.

My wife and I had come from California to spend Christmas with my parents. Jean had never been in Montreal, so I took her downtown on the day before Christmas to look around, to see if the streets were as I remembered them — cold, grey, crowded.

We had a bitter fight that started on a bus coming down Côte-des-Neiges Road. Jean ducked away from me at the entrance to the Guy Street Metro station and I went after her, down and down those long escalators. I waited until the train pulled out, hoping I would see her standing on the empty platform, but she had disappeared. I waited for the next train, trying to decide what to do. Finally I took the escalator back up and started walking along St. Catherine Street. It was brutally cold and people were wrapped up, hunched into the wind. I bought a copy of the *New York Times* at a newsstand. I felt like going home but I didn't want to turn up at my parents' without Jean. I didn't want them guessing we had had a fight.

The fight had actually been going on for a long time and had to do with all the pain of living together, the fact that we didn't have enough money, that Jean was unhappy with me and beginning to suspect my moods. We were living in Los Angeles, ten blocks back from Venice Beach, in a neighbourhood of drug dealers, murders, abandoned cars, sunshine. I can't remember what we thought we were trying to do there. I do remember riding the Super Shuttle from Venice out to LAX at the beginning of that Christmas trip and seeing a car, a BMW, on fire on Lincoln Boulevard—pulled over onto the median strip, flaming and casting up smoke in the December sunshine.

I went into a restaurant on St. Catherine to have a cup of coffee and read the paper. The *Times* was the only paper I could bear to read in those days. I'd been living in so many different cities that local papers didn't make sense to me. I loved the *Times* for the same reason I loved highway atlases and airports: it symbolized removal, success, escape.

I ordered coffee and toast and started reading news of the world. On the fourth page there was a feature article about parents who punished their children by forcing them to sit on hot stoves, searing their flesh with the tips of cigarettes, pressing electric irons against their buttocks.

I thought right away of Shaun Breen and the fire stories, surprised at how easily the details came back to me after twenty-five years. A tired-looking waitress kept refilling my cup. The manager was standing behind the cash, shaking hands with a customer. Everyone seemed to be in a good mood—the next day was Christmas. Montreal seemed like a cheerful small town.

I finally put on my overcoat, gloves, and scarf, left a tip on the counter, and pushed through the revolving door onto St. Catherine Street. Walking from Phillips Square to Guy Street and back again, cheeks hurting with the wind, I told myself I was searching for Jean, but I wasn't, not really. We'd always needed time to cool down after a fight. We wouldn't have had anything to say if we'd run into each other in those crowds doing last-minute shopping. I'd have ducked into a store to avoid her or crossed the street quickly against the light, and she'd have done the same.

If I'd happened to meet someone who recognized me, someone on St. Catherine Street who knew me from the old days, and if they had asked me how things were, I'd have told a fire story.

I would have described the dozens of winter bonfires that burned at night out on Venice Beach, the crowds of the homeless and crazy that gathered around the flames, and the sick smoke that hung across our neighbourhood in the morning.

I would have admitted to an obsession I had been develop-
ing about the gas stove in our kitchen: checking the valve a
dozen times a day; phoning the gas company almost every
week; worrying that the thing would blow up while we slept,
blow us from our bed, blow the whole ramshackle building
into the sky. I might have told about the flaming BMW out on
Lincoln Boulevard, how it had seared itself into my memory
while so much else that was more important was being neglected, put aside, forgotten.

In the fire stories Shaun himself was always being rescued. He was never really in danger. Dogs would awaken him
by licking his face, then lead him to safety through rooms
packed with smoke. His father would take him by the hand
and bring him to a window and, saying a Hail Mary, would
finally pitch him outside. Shaun would fall slowly, tumbling
and turning the way he had been especially trained, falling
like an acrobat through the smoke, the flames, the cinders;
bouncing on the rubbery net the men held out, bouncing so
expertly he was high up in the air again, climbing slowly,
slowly; down below they were cheering as once more he
began his descent.

It was the middle of the night in Montreal, Christmas Eve,
in the room that had been mine when I was a boy, and I was
telling my wife, after we had made love, all that I remembered of the *New York Times* article and Shaun Breen. I was
describing the pattern of concentric black rings that could
only have been scorched onto the seat of his pants by an electric stove burner. Jean was so upset that she finally got out of
bed and went to find a phone directory. She brought it back
to the bedroom and started searching to see if a Shaun Breen

was listed. She wanted me to find him, to telephone him in the morning. *Shaun, are you alive? Did you survive?*

Luckily there were no Breens in the Montreal phone book. Then I remembered the reason Shaun had left St. Kevin's was that he and his mother were returning to Newfoundland. The rest of us learned where Newfoundland was by looking at a map of Canada the teacher unrolled over the blackboard. She described the long journey Shaun and his mother faced, by train, by bus, by ferry across the Cabot Strait in midwinter.

Everyone else in the house was asleep. After a while Jean slept, but she awoke after an hour, disturbed by my restlessness. Finally she switched on the light and started to read a Henry James novel that she'd picked up at the bookstore on the Venice boardwalk, near the café where we sometimes ate breakfast on Sundays, when the winter sky was clear and California sunlight sparked on the waves.

I got out of bed, telling her I was going downstairs to make some tea. We could read all night if we wanted to. We could sleep all the next day, which was Christmas.

I heard my father snoring as I passed my parents' bedroom. I went downstairs and into the kitchen, where I filled a kettle and set it on the stove. A full moon shone through the windows and there was no need to switch on any lights. After a couple of minutes the steam ripped out a high-pitched whistle and I recalled Shaun's oval, darkened face; his hair, cropped short by blunt scissors; his tense, nail-biting expression.

My parents' house smelled clean, dusted, polished, at peace, and I stood with my feet bare on linoleum while upstairs my wife waited for me, my parents slept, and Shaun repeated stories that possessed a terrifying power and were fixed, like dreams, with perfect detail. I was thinking of our marriage, our apartment in California, the Pacific Ocean, what it meant to have come this far and to be bending around now, falling backwards, returning.

FIONA THE EMIGRANT

Alun did himself in with an overdose. Fiona always knew exactly what her father would say—"What'd you expect, getting involved with a fellow like that?" She didn't have an answer.

A few weeks later she quit Aberdeen University and her mother, who ran a bank branch, met her at a tearoom and gave her cash for a plane ticket to Canada and said, "You have to get away from this country."

Fiona's parents had been emigrants. Fiona was born on Vancouver Island but her family had returned to Scotland when she was two. As a teenager she often dreamed of a deep green tossing sea and her father said this was a memory of the Pacific Coast, where he had endured a collapsed partnership and six different sales agent's jobs, hating them all, before swallowing his defeat and booking their passage home.

"Don't tell your father I gave you the money," Fiona's mother declared.

Fiona flew from Prestwick to wintery Toronto, where her aunt and uncle met her at the airport and took her to their suburban home. Their living room looked over a golf course buried under snow. During the first couple of weeks in Toronto it snowed constantly, and the sidewalks in front of the house were scraped by a little diesel plow, pushing through the drifts while snow was still falling. Fiona fell into a pattern, rising early and helping her aunt get the older children ready for school, doing housework and minding the baby while her aunt went out shopping. There was a lot of shopping, a lot of eating. In Scotland she'd been a vegetarian. Here she wolfed it all down: hamburgers with ketchup for supper, cheese sandwiches for lunch, chocolate cereal in the morning, liquid diets from a tin, bowls of popcorn while watching films on television. The sidewalk plows with their scuttling engines and steel blades worked at night, scoring the concrete. Their noise made Fiona feel protected inside the house, cocooned.

Her aunt kept urging her to go downtown to see the sights. And one afternoon she set out, intending to take the subway to Queen Street, in the heart of the city, but she got no farther than the neighbourhood shopping strip a half-mile from her aunt's house. She was frozen; her feet felt raw; she had never been so cold. Instead of crossing the street to the subway station, she ducked into a café and ordered a cup of coffee. It was eleven o'clock in the morning and the café was empty. Her toes ached, she could barely move her fingers, and she was starting to hate Canada with a deep, active, personal resentment. As if the country were a stranger who'd crept up on her. It was like being knifed or beaten.

The white walls of the café was decorated with woven

shawls in electric neon colours, and travel posters of jungle and beaches. The dark-haired man behind the cash register filled her cup and watched her sipping coffee. It was black and bitter. She'd been in Toronto for two weeks without once venturing from the suburb, but the day before she'd seen a flyer for a Jamaican dance club on Queen Street. Her aunt had never been that far downtown. Her uncle said Queen Street was where the gays lived.

Gays, Jamaicans — life. Fiona thought she might look for work down there. A waitressing job. A place of her own.

The dark man approached with the coffee pot. This wasn't downtown Toronto; this was still North York, and he wasn't Jamaican, but he did look somewhat dark, up here in the suburban snows.

"More coffee?"

"I've a buzz on already," Fiona told him. "I don't think I could take another."

His tight Calvin Klein jeans had been ironed and he wore a tightly fitted turtleneck sweater, baby blue.

"It's good coffee," Fiona said.

"You think?"

He took a stained Xeroxed menu from the next table, where it was wedged between the salt and pepper and the paper napkin dispenser. He handed it to Fiona.

"Not hungry. Sorry."

Most of the dishes — *pupusas*, black beans, tamales — were under ten dollars. The menu was in Spanish and English.

"No, no, but the menu, the style — what do you think? Okay, yes?"

"It looks very good."

"Businessman's lunch, you see? Good idea?"

"Probably." She stood up. Buttoning her jacket she felt dizzy. Central heating forced stale air through steel ducts, and the taste, the flavour, of metal was everywhere in Canada, a metal country, hard and cold and buried deep. She stood gripping the back of a flimsy chair. She'd never seen anyone faint but knew she was about to.

He offered her a matchbook printed *Café Roberto Salvadoran Specialty.*

"I am Roberto. Would you meet my family?" He gestured towards the kitchen. She could hear a baby crying.

She didn't want to go downtown. She felt weak, chilled, without hope. She looked down at her boots, stained with salt from the mush on the sidewalks, then shut her eyes. She felt an impulse to undress. Strip off her pea jacket, pull off the woollen muffler and turtleneck jumper, kick free of her boots, step out of her too-tight jeans, and lie on the restaurant floor on her pile of clothes. Her white body padded with fat from all the junk food. Writhing on the floor while the restaurant owner watched, helpless, awed, disgusted.

Instead she followed him numbly to the kitchen. It was warm. Inside every room in Toronto there was a current of dried stuporous heat that made the Canadian wind seem demented when you had to face it. They scattered tons of gritty, salty sand on their roads, their days stank of sodium chloride.

Roberto, swarthy, smelled of aftershave. She disliked scent on men. Alun had smelled clean though he wore the same clothes from week to week. Liked to take hot showers but couldn't, not often, not in the Glasgow squat or the borrowed rooms in Aberdeen. He enjoyed shaving. A clean, soapy scent, like a baby fresh out of its bath, was one of the many innocences about him.

Two women and a baby in the kitchen. A television tuned to her aunt's favorite daytime show, *Wheel of Fortune*. Roberto introduced his teenaged sister, Isabel, wearing bright pink sweatpants and mopping the floor.

His mother barely nodded when Fiona was introduced. She spoke sharply to Roberto in Spanish, irritated about something.

No one was watching TV. Roberto found Fiona a stool, poured her another coffee. Another teenager, a boy, came in from the cold-storage locker carrying a crate of stubby green bananas.

"My brother, Franco."

Roberto sent Franco out to the dining room to prep tables for lunch.

"The people — humans — are why I am in business," Roberto said. "The exchange. I like to talk. I am fond of it. You believe this is a good locale for the restaurant business?"

"Don't ask me."

"In Salvador I was teacher, then taxi driver and owner of garage. My ambition is, to be a dealer."

"What sort of dealer?"

"Toyota!" He smiled. "I will earn a franchise. First a small garage, body shop. But I will be a big car dealer. You'll see."

The baby was asleep in its cradle on the counter. Roberto rocked back on his wooden stool, a confident entrepreneur. He lit a Player's cigarette and blew smoke to the ceiling. Maybe the family had suffered in Central America, maybe he was a refugee, or maybe he was a retired policeman or soldier, even a war criminal. Why had he brought her in here? Clearly the women, mother and sister, believed that she was beneath their Roberto. He took the cigarette from his lips.

"The autos, they are the secrets of my success."

His mother, recognizing the passion in her son's voice, smiled. The baby began crying. Isabel took him in her arms and started to jiggle him.

"What's the baby's name?"

"Miguel. The father, he is dead."

Isabel was ignoring them and the baby was howling and Fiona suddenly knew if she were not present Isabel would be unbuttoning her blouse and nursing her son.

"What do I owe for coffee?"

"No, no, you are my guest."

Roberto held open the swinging door and followed her out into the dining room. Franco was setting candles in coloured glass jars on every table. There were no customers. People in this suburban neighbourhood probably never went out for lunch, they stayed at home like Fiona's aunt, with the TV on, and made themselves grilled cheese sandwiches. Fiona wrapped her muffler around her neck and pulled her woollen watch cap down over her ears. Roberto grabbed a snow shovel and held open the plate-glass door then followed her outside, where all the warmth was sucked from her body within a moment or two, and she felt withered and aimless and frightened.

"Goodbye," he called.

Despite the cold he was hatless and coatless. He started to scrape and hack at veins of snow and ice on the sidewalk.

The bright sound of chopping and shovelling rang through the bitter air and followed her down the street and she knew it was, in some way, directed at her — he was celebrating her with the noise, teasing her, needing her attention.

Alun took the needle under his tongue. That was the quickest. He'd been telling everyone he was getting his act together and moving south to London to be a designer. No one believed him except the dealers he knew, who all had similar fantasies.

Alun's history. Father an army officer, shot dead in Belfast. Left school at sixteen, working as a ticket seller at British Rail, a job he got through an uncle. Quit and travelled overland to Turkey. A year on the beach at Goa in India, losing thirty pounds and nearly dying of dysentery. Return to Aberdeen. Drinking and fights in pubs. Mother remarried and moved to California. Older sister married to a scientist.

What did you expect?

Her father's question, with its neurotic calculus of love and death, came back to Fiona while she lay in bed in her aunt's house, boiling with midwinter flu. Her father's life had been a failure. Not so dramatic a failure as Alun's, not quite such a blowtorch of despair. Not at first, not on the surface. A religious family. A sober education. A position at the bank, where he met Fiona's mother. Then marriage and imigration to Canada, followed by three unsatisfactory years in Victoria, British Columbia, where he had finally disappeared into a hospital suffering what they called a "breakdown." What they called "nerves." They'd sailed home to Scotland afterwards and he'd never held a job again. At fifty he looked seventy, white-haired in his armchair, staring at news programs, World War II documentaries.

Her suitcase was underneath the bed. Inside was a manila envelope. Inside the envelope, negatives, contact sheets, photographs. Do-it-yourself porn, Alun called it. She'd let him persuade her. He could talk her into anything. No one else could.

Needing money for his heroin, he had already sold his TV, CD player, and VCR, most of her books, and all his clothes except the jeans and the leather jacket he was going to be buried in a couple of weeks after the pictures were taken.

The photographer had turned up at the funeral, sans camera. He and Alun had been mates at school, played Dinky cars together. He'd paid Alun fifty quid in advance hoping to sell the photos to a Dutch magazine. On the road outside the cemetery he took the manila envelope from his car and handed it to her. "That's the lot, burn it or keep it, it's all yours."

What did you expect?

Fiona found Roberto inspecting avocados at a fruit-and-vegetable store on Dufferin Street. He wore a pile-lined Levi's jacket with the collar turned up. When he saw her he seemed happy.

"I hoped I will see you again!"

"How's the restaurant?"

Fiona held a paper sack of oily banana chips. She was wearing a German military parka and snow boots.

He shrugged. "I am car guy, not restaurant guy."

She waited behind him at the checkout while a young Chinese clerk sorted rapidly through his piles of vegetables and fruit.

"I am seeking a good buy, a good used car," Roberto told her while the clerk's nimble fingers tapped at the electronic cash register. "I would like you to come along. Tomorrow. With me. To look for the car."

Fiona handed over her sack of banana chips to be weighed. She'd put on eight pounds since coming to Toronto. She was addicted to banana chips.

"I'd be no use," she said. "I don't know about cars."

They left the shop headed in the same direction, into the scathing wind. She wished she could duck behind him, get some protection. Most pedestrians were going the other way, moving fast with the wind at their backs, the wind that had churned the sky clear, a glimmering violet sky. She noticed for the first time the hawkiness of his profile, his strident chin, beaked nose, and glittering eyes. Three pink scars were notched into his throat. He must have shaved a few hours earlier, but a shadow of dense black beard was already sprouting. She wondered why he didn't grow his beard to hide the scars. Perhaps he was proud of them. Maybe they were a mark of honour in the country that he came from. Or perhaps a beard wouldn't grow on the damaged seams of skin.

Three taxicabs stood in a rank at the corner, motors idling, white exhaust spitting from tailpipes. Three forlorn women stood in the middle of the road on the streetcar island. They wore skirts and stockings and stood apart, each with her back to the wind. They looked brittle, in agony. The wind was attacking from the north; Fiona heard a rattling, banging sound as a steel garbage can lid flew down the street and was crushed beneath the tires of an express van. The wind spat grains of sand and ice like diamonds.

"Auto body, good business," Roberto shouted to her.

She never thought about sex or money. Or the future. Her aunt was happy to have her stay for as long as she wanted.

"Taxi," Roberto said.

"Not for me," she said, grimacing. It was painful to speak in the Canadian wind, useless to speak at all in this climate.

He glanced sideways at her. "Come."

"Where?"

"To assist me to buy a car."

"I know nothing about cars," she said. "I wouldn't be any use to you."

"Tomorrow, ten o'clock?"

"I don't want to."

He stopped at the first taxi in the rank. "I shall meet you at York Mills subway station, tomorrow morning, ten o'clock."

Tears were scratching her eyes and she realized that she was crying. She told herself she did not trust him: spoiled and domineering, a raptor, his life catered by women.

The taxi's trunk lid flew open and the Sikh driver got out from behind the wheel to help Roberto load his plastic bags of groceries. The Sikh wore a tie and a pale blue sports coat and no gloves.

"Will you accept a ride?" Roberto asked Fiona as she stood raising first one snow boot, then the other, off the freezing pavement, where snow had hardened in blue-grey moraines.

"No."

The Sikh slammed the trunk lid and a chunk of hard slush fell off the car. The Sikh got back behind the wheel.

"No matter, I will take you," Roberto insisted.

In his flimsy shoes, thin clothes, smiling, Roberto stood holding open the taxi door until she gave up and threw herself inside.

When they reached her aunt's house across from the golf course, she agreed to meet him Saturday at ten o'clock at the subway station.

Alun had owned a car once. A rusted Cortina without a back seat. It had run out of gas and they'd left it under the motorway in Leith and forgotten about it.

They met in a suburban subway station on Saturday morning. Toronto a city of silent crowds and restraint, the only savagery was weather. Roberto found her a seat and rode clutching a strap, studying his list of used-car buys culled from classifieds in the Toronto Star. The train shunted evenly from station to station. Muffled passengers waited on clean platforms. At each stop the crowd allowed riders to exit before boarding the train. Soon the subway car was packed and hot, but no one spoke.

Fiona asked about Isabel's husband. He had been assassinated by Communists. The Communists had accused him of stealing a truck full of liquor, but Roberto insisted his brother-in-law was not, had never been a criminal. "No, no. In Salvador the criminals are the Communists! Or the police."

She couldn't tell if the other passengers, faces set in the grim appetites of cold, were listening.

"He was very good. A good man. Now I, I am the father," declared Roberto. "But maybe in the summer she can meet another. Someone else from the Salvador."

Fiona sat crushed between two drab women with large paper shopping bags. Roberto swayed in front of her in his belted leather overcoat with fur collar, grey flannels with permanent crease, black boots with zippers and hideous two-inch heels. His gloves were very new.

The train slid south, mostly underground but sometimes out in the open, through one of the snowy ravines.

I have a past, but it doesn't interest me anymore, thought Fiona. I have a future just because I haven't the courage to kill myself.

The first car they inspected was a rusty Subaru in a driveway on Palmerston Avenue. Roberto walked carefully around the car while the seller, a young Portuguese man in a bomber jacket, watched him warily. Roberto kicked the tires politely, but she knew from his chilly smile that he wasn't going to buy.

The next car was a massive yellow station wagon parked behind a house on Euclid Avenue owned by some kind of sect. She could see pale white women in saris, puffy down vests, and snow boots playing in the yard with white children who wore little turbans.

The seller wore a white turban, narrow cotton trousers, and a down vest. He had freckles, blue eyes, and a fringe of orange beard, and his accent was relaxed, American. "Not so great on gas but real steady," he told them. He sounded like an American university student. Fiona watched Roberto prowl around the car like a predator sizing up its prey. He had brought a rubber sheet with him and a flashlight. After spreading the sheet on the frozen slush, he crawled beneath the car and remained for a couple of minutes. "Ball joints no good," he called softly.

"Fifteen hundred bucks," the American boy in the turban said. "Those tires are like new."

Roberto slid out slowly from underneath the car. He shook his head and smiled. "No. It is not the one I want."

They walked down Harbord Avenue to a bakery café, where he bought her a cup of coffee.

"You are very secret," Roberto said, sipping his coffee. They were at a little round table. There were pools of water on the floor, damp sawdust, melted snow from boots. The plate-glass window was steamed up. Fiona could barely see the traffic outside.

When she didn't say anything, he sighed and took another sip of his coffee. She had been about to ask him about the scars chipped into his neck, but she decided she did not want to know that story. She looked at the Canadians in the room, students, the university was nearby. Such healthy faces, glowing, blooming. Husky college boys with lank hair. Pretty, honey-coloured girls with silver rings in their eyebrows.

"It's unreal," said Fiona.

"Perhaps I am in love with you," said Roberto.

"Oh, bother me not," she said angrily.

He looked wounded. She felt a sense of drift and helplessness. They finished their coffee and went back outside. She had spent her life in climates that were assaults. The steady rain of Scotland where male bodies smelled of must, neglect, coldness.

They crept along the sidewalk, bodies bent, faces white and creased by the ferocious wind.

In neighbourhoods from the Danforth to Kensington Market to Dufferin the used cars they saw that afternoon were huge, rusty, forlorn, the cars of immigrants.

They were inspecting a thirty-year-old Cadillac convertible with a damaged roof when Fiona told him that her boyfriend had died in Scotland.

Roberto had been trying without success to start the Cadillac. He listened calmly, gazing at something through the cracked windshield, shaking his head, then patting her hand, his glove to her mitten, saying nothing.

It was getting dark and they toured through cramped used-car lots on College Street. The shiny cars were packed in under strings of lights and the skinny salesmen—Italian, Portuguese, Asian—were impatient, and probably freezing, and eager to get home. Red and yellow streetcars grinding along College Street were crowded, the shops beginning to close.

"I will find the one I want. It always takes a little time."

Roberto was not discouraged.

They went into another café, in Kensington Market, and he bought two cups of Cuban coffee and a sweet roll, which they shared.

"For you to come with me is a wonderful thing I appreciate," he said.

Perhaps it's some form of mental hysterectomy, Fiona thought. I've been spayed, emotionally.

She had taken off her mittens to eat the roll. He took her raw pink hands and started massaging them. She watched his face. She didn't want to hear stories of what he had done, why he had come to Canada, or what had happened in his home country. Immigrant stories were all the same. If Alun were in Toronto what would he be doing? Sitting on a radiator keeping warm his skinny arse and firing heroin under his tongue? Had he died in Toronto, how would they have got him into the ground, when the ground was like iron?

"I think you are very beautiful," Roberto said.

He finally released her fingers and she crammed a piece of sweet roll into her mouth then pulled off another piece and fed it to him. She licked the sugar and the flakes of crust from her fingers.

"It is all right," he sighed happily. He looked tired but seemed confident again. "Say nothing. It is all right."

Then there was a thaw. Patches of yellow grass opened in the snow. There was an afternoon of sombre rain. But the following morning it was sunny once more and getting colder—the satellite weatherman warned of a high-pressure front from the west—and she was sitting in her aunt's big, soft car, waiting for her aunt to finish shopping at the discount drugstore. She noticed Franco across the street, in the alley behind Café Roberto, unloading supplies from a rented truck, wearing a T-shirt and work boots with the laces untied and tongues flopping out. She got out of the car, crossed the street, went into the alley behind the truck. Franco told her Roberto had gone to Buffalo with friends to go shopping. When she followed Franco into the storeroom, he seized the belt of her jeans and made a taunting, tearing gesture as if he were trying to tug the jeans down, tear them off her. She kicked him hard in the shins and he yelped. She punched the side of his neck using plenty of knuckle, then fled outside, down the alley and across the street to her aunt's car. The motor was idling, the heater gushing warm air, and the door locks snapped shut with the touch of a button.

On Tuesday night Fiona stood at the picture window in her aunt's living room, watching the sky darkening. It went purple as a bruise, then black. She put on her parka, snow boots, elk-hide mittens and watch cap, and went outside. The air was sour in her nostrils, a tang of pickling salt, cold and withering. In *National Geographic* she'd seen photos of long-lost Arctic explorers in long-lost Arctic graves, flesh leathery and black.

She followed a ski trail over the golf course, turning off onto another, narrower track that switchbacked into the woods before braiding into side trails and animal tracks through underbrush. With the thaw no skiers had been out for days. She soon lost her sense of direction. Her boots rattled on the crusty snow. Maples, tamarack, and silver birches made tortured noises. Fiona peered between the gaunt trees, trying to identify street light. She clapped her hands and decided to keep going in one direction, orienting by the moon. Certainly much less than a half-mile away were restaurants, shops, churches, petrol stations.

Deep within the woods a pack of dogs began barking with full, delirious throats. Fiona slipped, her feet skidding out from under her, and fell over backwards, cracking her head on the hard-packed snow. She lay on her back and fought down terror. The fierce music of the dogs rose to a howl. They were after something. They were chasing something through the woods. She scrambled to her feet and looked about for a weapon. As she seized a stick, she thought of her boyfriend Alun smashing into a parked car on a dripping, freezing night in Scotland. A muffled crack after he swung the brick, and clumps of safety glass hanging in gluey strands from the window frame, and Alun reaching in and snatching someone's handbag off the front seat.

The trail switched down the side of the ravine. Clutching her stick she began to hike, treading warily. She could hear animals behind her, eager and sinewy, paws scratching on the icy marl of snow and mud. When she reached the bottom of the ravine, there was a clearly marked trail through a glade of rough-barked trees. The woods ended abruptly at an open fairway sprawled under the moon. She saw street lamps. The dogs' barking faded away.

Roberto called on Thursday and invited her to the restaurant for dinner the following night, with her aunt and uncle and her young cousins.

"All of us? Are you sure?"

"Of course."

When Fiona arrived at Café Roberto with her family, little candle jars were burning brightly on each table. Her uncle wore his tweed jacket and brown tie, her aunt wore a fussy peach-coloured dress, and Fiona wore a short skirt. There were only six customers when they came in. Isabel, pale and plump in a tight black dress, stood near the cash register, self-conscious, gripping menus. Fiona introduced her aunt and uncle and cousins. Isabel nervously shook hands with everyone.

"Where's Roberto?" Fiona asked.

"Trouble."

"Is something wrong?"

"Franco."

"What is it?" Fiona stood up. "I'll go back and see."

She pushed open the door of the kitchen. Roberto and his mother were beside Franco, who slouched on a stool at the sink. The tap was running and his mother was cleaning Franco's face. Roberto turned and saw Fiona. Franco leered at her. The front of his shirt was spotted with blood. One of his eyes was dark and swollen shut.

"Salvadors at the mall...Stupid Franco, he get in a fight." Roberto cuffed Franco on the side of the head. The scars on Roberto's throat, wrinkled and pink, looked like deep clawings.

Franco defended himself in Spanish, sounding indignant while pulling on his coat. Roberto began pushing Franco and his mother out the back door. When they were gone he flung the wet washcloth he was holding into the sink and stepped up to Fiona, wiping his hands on his jeans. He placed one hand on her shoulder and kissed her on the cheek.

She stepped back, but he stayed with her. The floor was wet. The kitchen smelled of steam and cilantro and coffee.

There was a pile of chopped cilantro and knife on the counter. Roberto took Fiona's arm in a hard grip above the elbow and kissed her forcefully. As his tongue tried to probe her lips he forced his pelvis against her and backed her against the refrigerator, still trying to work his tongue inside her mouth. She felt nothing.

Finally he had to let her go. He was smiling but she could tell he was confused. She could have picked up the chopping knife and slashed him. The thin, strong reek of cilantro scented the room.

Instead she turned and went out through the swinging doors and sat down with her family. A few minutes later Roberto served the meal. He was relaxed and dignified, the perfect host, and her aunt and uncle were impressed. They hadn't eaten out since they'd come to Toronto. Now they ate *pupusas*, seafood *sopa*, and plantains. They ate *yuca frita*. They had Pilsner beer and Salvadoran coffee. Her uncle smoked his pipe with the coffee. Her aunt spooned ice cream.

She next saw Roberto in the neighbourhood branch of the Toronto Library. He was sitting at a wooden table in the room where foreign newspapers clipped to sticks hung like flags in lifeless air. He was studying *Auto Trader*. He sprang out of his chair and followed her downstairs to the vending machines, where she bought a cup of sour coffee. She felt no fear though they were alone. The basement was lit with dim green fluorescence. The air smelled of photocopy chemicals.

He asked her to come with him while he continued his search for the right automobile. That was all he wanted. He would not force himself upon her, he had acted that way only to help her, help her learn what she wanted.

She was barely listening. He moved closer as he spoke. She sipped coffee and watched him. She felt no fear. What were those claw marks on his throat, and what was he saying?

The car was a Taurus station wagon, ten years old. The seller, a middle-aged Chinese man, was eager for them to take a test drive. He hurried into his house and came out in a grey overcoat and a pearl-grey fedora with a tiny feather roosted in the band. He sat poised and erect in the centre of the back seat while Roberto backed out carefully from the driveway, cutting the wheels hard to swing into the narrow street of Toronto immigrant houses, crumbling brick with steep gables, patches of dead garden heaped with husks of snow, concrete saints' grottos.

They drove west on Danforth until the Chinese man directed Roberto onto the Don Valley Parkway heading north.

On the highway Roberto relaxed, and she saw how confident he felt behind the wheel. After the first coagulation of traffic at the Eglinton Avenue exit, he pressed harder on the accelerator and she felt the engine open up, breathing. She guessed what he was feeling: that a car was as powerful as a man. That once he had a car, this car, there'd be no stopping him. That everything he desired must sooner or later be his— blood and earth and unlimited power. Around him a jungle of opportunities, possibilities, loyalties, and obligations would soon snake and climb, growing dense and luxuriant. A car was as powerful as a man, that's what he was thinking, and a man was as powerful as what he wanted.

He had pulled into her aunt's driveway, honking proudly. Now they were parked around the corner from a theatre showing a Mexican movie. He had just asked her to lend him money. Registration and car insurance were more expensive than he'd expected, he said. He was temporarily short of cash and if he didn't pay the rent on time the Korean landlord—always looking for an excuse break the lease—would throw them out of Café Roberto and give the space to his nephew to open a Korean grocery store.

The child-carrier bought in Buffalo was established in the backseat. An air freshener in the shape of an evergreen tree dangled from the station wagon's rearview mirror.

"How much do you need?" She already knew she wasn't going to lend him money.

"Eight hundred dollar. One thousand."

"Can't help you. Sorry."

He ignored her then. He got out of the car and locked his door and she got out and followed him across the dirty sidewalk towards the box office, where he paid for two tickets, then seized her elbow and led her past the usher collecting ticket stubs and into the old warm velvet theatre.

She couldn't follow the dialogue but the story was simple. There was a bad man, there was a brother and sister, good triumphed over evil, and many unnecessary people were killed. As they sat there he put his hand on her thigh, calmly. She was wearing jeans. He began to stroke her thigh through the

material. After a few minutes of stroking her thigh and staring at the screen, where the colour of the images was washed
out and faded, with browns and pinks predominating, and
close-ups of insects on the flesh of dead men, and the vil-
lain drinking whisky sloppily, then being shot down by the
brother, he moved his hand higher and worked it between her
legs. But she felt no excitement, no stirring, no warmth, and
after he had been rubbing her and stroking her for almost a
minute, she roughly pushed his hand away.

She waited another minute, then stood up abruptly and
seized her jacket from the seat in front. It took him a moment
or two to react and before he could stop her she was hurrying
up the aisle and across the rotting lobby and out to the sidewalk and the shadowless municipal light. She buttoned her
parka as she ran for a few blocks along College Street, then
walked, then ran again.

Fiona and her aunt sat in the little sewing room off the
kitchen, where the biggest television was. It was one o'clock
in the morning; everyone else in the house was asleep. The
neighbourhood was comatose, its streets stained by a residue
of road salt; out on the bare highways no one moved.

Roberto would come by, she knew, sooner or later. But she
wouldn't see him. And if he refused to leave she would ask her
aunt to call the police. He would be wary of the police, and
the threat would be enough to get rid of him forever.

Satellite imagery swirled on TV, winter storms drenching
the west coast. Fiona's aunt was reminiscing about her youth
in Scotland and Fiona felt herself mentally drifting in the dull,

crackling light coming off the TV. She felt herself floating in the beam of light until she was back in the room in Aberdeen with her boyfriend Alun on top of her, panting and almost weeping, and she felt as though for the first time the passion, the frailty, the delicacy of his ardent body.

IN MONTREAL

Downtown they struggled against winter but in Saint-Henri they let the snow fall without fighting it. All the buses had stopped running and Mike had to walk home from his last class at McGill. There was no traffic, only driving snow, and light from the windows of ground-floor flats.

The little depanneur at the corner of their street was open. The shop window was steamed up but he could see Monsieur Thibault inside, spreading sawdust on the floor. A bell jingled when Mike opened the door, and the storekeeper set down his bucket of sawdust and moved behind the counter. A television was on somewhere in the back of the shop: hysterical applause and a screaming announcer. It sounded like a game show in French.

Mike asked for cigarettes. "Has Nora been in at all today?"

"*Non,*" said Thibault, sliding a pack of Export As across the counter. "*Pas aujourd'hui.*"

Mike paid and headed for the door.

"Anything wrong?" said Thibault.

"It's a bad night out."

Thibault nodded and Mike pushed open the door. Tucking his chin into his collar, he hurried up the street.

He and his wife, Nora, lived in the top-floor flat in a building Thibault owned. The storekeeper's elderly mother lived immediately below them. Mike and Nora had settled in the Saint-Henri *quartier* because it was close to downtown and rents were so cheap that she could afford a separate studio in the district. Nora was a painter and Mike an assistant professor.

He planned to spend the evening correcting papers. With any luck, classes would be cancelled the next day and he wouldn't have to teach.

An iron staircase rose from the sidewalk to their front door. Mike climbed the icy steps one at a time. His fingers were so cold it was hard to grasp the key, but he was finally able to shove it into the lock and press the door open.

The apartment was dark. He called her name and the sound hung in the hallway. Light shone in through the door glass, and ice dripping from his beard made little stains on the floor. He placed his briefcase on a table and hurried back down the stairs.

Thibault was counting cash when Mike entered the shop.

"Is my wife here?" Mike demanded.

Without waiting for a reply he walked around the counter, pushed apart the curtains, and stepped into the back room, where old Mme Thibault was dozing in an armchair in front of the television, with a cat in her lap. On top of the set was a container of holy water in the shape of a statue of the Virgin Mary.

"Where is Nora?" Mike demanded. *"Où est-elle?"*

The cat leapt to the floor and Mme Thibault looked up.

"Pas ici," she said. *"Elle est allée à l'église."*

Thibault squeezed into the room behind Mike. "You have to go," the storekeeper said. "Go find your wife."

Mike left the store. The street was lined with buried cars. At the next corner a truck went by, with workmen shovelling sand in graceful arcs down onto the road, and Mike hurried along Rue Notre-Dame.

Before they moved to Montreal Nora's work had been included in group shows at galleries in Toronto, and dealers were interested in her. After they had been in Saint-Henri a month she learned she was pregnant; a few days later one of the Toronto dealers phoned and offered her a solo show in the spring, in Toronto. It would mean a lot of work over the winter. The dealer wanted her to produce twelve new paintings at least. She didn't tell him she was pregnant.

"What happens now?" Mike asked.

"Don't you want to have this baby?"

"It's not me that's going to have the baby."

Nora looked at him and rubbed her belly. "Don't know if I can do this," she said.

Nora was sick every morning for a month. Meanwhile Mike collected pamphlets on pregnancy and read a book on home-birthing and composed lists of names, scribbling them in the margins of his typed lecture outlines. For the first time he began to think about saving money. He began to think about investing. He started bringing his lunch to school instead of buying it. Sometimes he felt oppressed at the idea of becoming a father. Sometimes the feeling was helplessness, as if he were falling in deep soft snow, but it was a joyful feeling.

One morning she told him she was afraid the baby was being poisoned by the fumes in her studio. They were in the kitchen, getting ready to go to work, and he was feeling deeply unprepared for the lecture he had to give.

"Okay, maybe you shouldn't have the baby," he said sharply.

Nora swallowed a glass of grapefruit juice, put the glass in the sink, and left the kitchen without a word. He heard her put on her coat and boots by the front door. Her studio was ten minutes away, in an old tobacco factory near the Lachine Canal.

"Wait a sec," he called.

As he started down the hallway she ducked outside. When he reached the front door he put on shoes and stepped out on the icy porch. He peered down the street but she had already disappeared around the corner.

She seemed okay that evening. His lecture had gone all right. They went to dinner with a couple from the department at a Greek restaurant on Duluth Street. They rode home in a taxi and didn't talk about the baby. She seemed fine all week, but on Thursday night when he came home late after teaching his evening class Mme Thibault was sitting in the chair by the bookcase in the living room, with a pile of knitting. When she saw him she dropped her needles and whispered, *"Pauvre madame! Pauvre madame!"* then pointed down the hallway.

Mike went into their bedroom and found Nora lying in bed with her face turned against the wall.

She'd had the abortion at a clinic in the Town of Mount Royal. She said she hadn't told him because she hadn't wanted to discuss it with him because whatever he said, whether he wanted her to keep the baby or not keep the baby, she would have hated him for saying, and she didn't want to hate him.

The taxi had cost twenty-four dollars each way.

"Do you hate me?" she said. "Tell me the truth."

Mike took her hands and kissed them. He stroked her hair for a long time. "Baby, what's the old woman doing here? Did you tell her?"

"She was sweeping the steps when I came home. I told her I was sick."

He lay down beside her until he thought she was asleep. When it was dark, he went out and found Mme Thibault still sitting by the bookcase, needles clacking. Mike took ten dollars from his wallet and gave it to the old woman. He tried to remember the French word for cramps.

"Thank you for staying with her," he said. *"Merci beaucoup."*

Nora went to work the next day but it didn't go well, and that evening she told him she had decided to give herself a few days off. After that Nora gradually stopped going to her studio. Soon she didn't want to leave the apartment for any reason. By then it was winter. She said it was too cold outside. The Montreal winter was savage, brutal, violent, worse than anything she had imagined.

Mike made the appointment for her to see a therapist.

There was a three-week wait, but after the first session Nora seemed more like her old self. The next day she went to the studio—she still had her solo show to get ready for. She told him she had begun two new paintings. Mike felt relieved.

Nora started going to the studio every day. They'd walk as far as the corner together. He'd wait for his bus and she would head down Workman Street towards the canal. Sometimes when he came home after teaching an evening class, he found her asleep in the bedroom with the blinds pulled down and Mme Thibault dozing in the living room. The old woman always got up and left when he came in. Sometimes there was food—soup, meat pies, a roast chicken—on the stove. Nora said the old woman was lonely. He paid Mme Thibault for the food and always gave her something extra.

Her opening was scheduled for late April. They would stay two nights at a fancy hotel in Toronto. Mike started teasing Nora, asking when he could visit the studio, see the work. He knew she disliked showing any work in progress.

A small silver box dropped out of Nora's pocket one day when he was hanging her jacket in the closet. He picked it up and opened it. Inside was a set of black rosary beads.

"It's the old woman!" Mike said. "She knows what happened! She's got her claws into you!"

He hurried past Nora and down the outside stairs. He pounded on the old woman's door until it opened. He pushed the rosary beads through the crack and shouted, "Stay away! *Elle est malade!*"

Nora started seeing the therapist twice a week. He sent her to psychiatrist, who prescribed medication. When she was home, she moved around the apartment with her shoulders stiff and her neck very straight, as though she were balancing something precious on top of her head. Mike did all the cooking, all the shopping, all the laundry. Nora was working very hard but would not allow him to visit the studio. She said she had to paint for her own eyes and no one else's.

Then Mike found a registered letter crumpled up and crammed into a kitchen drawer. It was from the owner of the old factory where her studio was located. The landlord was threatening to padlock the studio until the rent was paid. Nora had always paid the studio rent from her own bank account. When he confronted her with the letter, she admitted that she hadn't been inside the studio for months.

"What about the work?" he said.

"Sometimes I go to church with Madame."

"If you don't go to the studio, where do you work?"

"I'm done with all of that. It's so useless."

Mike mailed a cheque to cover the rent arrears, but Nora refused to go back to the studio. Now, instead of getting up and pretending to go to work, she stayed in bed, except certain mornings when she would bustle around the kitchen making crazily elaborate breakfasts Mike hadn't time to eat. He took the rolls and fruit tarts and sausages and fried mushrooms and wrapped them in paper napkins that he stuffed into his pocket and dropped in a garbage can on his way to school.

He decided they should leave the Saint-Henri district, which was poor and depressing. But all apartment leases in Montreal ran until May. They'd have to wait for spring. When he saw Nora's therapist, the therapist said they probably should remain in the neighbourhood for now.

"No big changes," the therapist said. "Geography's no solution. Let her work through this in her own time."

Mike kept paying the rent on her studio. One Saturday in March he found Nora's key and went to the studio alone. Squirrels had gotten in through a broken window and made a nest beneath the worktable. He repaired the window, cleaned out the nest, and scrubbed the floor. He dusted the shelves and washed all the windows. He collected a few tubes of paint and brushes and carried them home, but she dumped everything in the kitchen trash.

"I'm done with it," she said.

The March wind was cruel along Notre-Dame and the broad steps outside the church were blown free of snow. The oak door was hard to open, and when Mike finally slipped inside, it slammed thickly behind him.

It was dim inside the church—a glow of electric light in the vaulted ceiling, a throb from the sacristy lamp, waxy specks from prayer candles. The altar was dim and bare, with a stark wooden cross planted on it. He saw Nora kneeling in the front pew. He started down the aisle. A scent of waxed wood rose up from the pews. His steps seemed to crash and echo against the stone floor.

He slipped into the pew beside his young wife, and after a few moments she looked up at him and nodded. She kissed the rosary and slipped the beads into her pocket. She stood up and followed him down the aisle. While he struggled with the massive door, she dipped her fingers into a font of holy water. He pretended not to see her crossing herself. He turned away and shoved at the door.

When they got home, Mike cooked the meal, washed the dishes, and put them away. When the counters were bare and clean, he made a pot of coffee and went into his study to work on his stack of papers. Sometime after midnight he went to bed. Instead of disturbing her, he made up a bed for himself on the sofa in his study. The coffee kept him awake, and he lay there wondering whose fault their sorrow was. There was enough street light reflected from the snow that the outlines of everything in the room rose up clear. He had grown up in a world where, if something went wrong, there was usually something or someone to blame, and it was usually pretty clear exactly who or what. But he knew he could not blame her. And he couldn't blame himself, so who else was there? The Toronto dealer? The old woman living downstairs? The endless Montreal winter? He had always assumed that every-thing—career, love, marriage—would work out for the best, but now he knew that Nora was going to be the first person he really lost in his life—he could see it coming—and he wondered how he would feel when it happened, and how he would feel after.

OUTREMONT

Kathleen draped the table with a linen cloth and set four places, using her wedding china and the silver she'd been collecting since her eighth birthday, when an aunt had started her with the gift of a spoon. Except for the more exotic pieces—fish knives, fruit spoons—her pattern was complete.

It was a warm August evening. She took her bath as soon as the table was ready. She was making the salad when John got home, and immediately sent him out to the corner depanneur to pick up a bag of ice. At seven o'clock Pierre and Anna arrived. They all had a drink, a couple of drinks, and now Anna stood with her in the narrow kitchen while Kathleen opened the oven and peered inside.

"What do you think?"

"Oh, I'm no good at all, don't ask me," said Anna. "But it looks done, doesn't it."

"Here goes." Kathleen slid out the pan and set it on a cork counter-pad.

Anna took a sip of wine. "Oh, it's perfect! It looks wonderful!"

"Sole is really easy; you might try it sometime."

"I should, I really should," said Anna. "I'm dreadful, you know, but I'm so tired when I get home from work. We end up going out for dinner lots. But I love this apartment, this little *quartier* of yours. *C'est charmant.*"

Anna was a notary in her family's old-fashioned law firm. They handled mostly wills and family trusts, and Anna was related to a lot of her clients. She had grown up in rather a grand house on rather a grand street in upper Outremont, and Kathleen sometimes found her Marie-Antoinette manner tiresome.

In their more modest part of Outremont, the section below Côte-Sainte-Catherine Road, the shady streets were lined with terrace houses and pleasant pre-war flats, nothing grand. There were at least three different sects of Hasidic Jews living in the neighbourhood, but most of the neighbours Kathleen had spoken to were Québécois professionals or artists.

She began arranging food on the plates. She'd grown up in a remote town, a camp really, on the Labrador iron range, daughter of a geologist.

"But Pierre is quite a chef, you know," said Anna.

"Is he?"

"*Mais oui!* He makes lovely things. He does *coq au vin* he learned from my grandmother's cook."

"Really? Carry out the salad, would you."

Kathleen picked up the dinner plates and followed Anna to the table. John and Pierre were watching the local news on television.

"I can't get over it," Pierre was saying. "Not one single bloody word about the nomination!"

John switched off the set.

"What's he talking about?" said Kathleen. "Please, everyone, come and sit down."

They took seats at the table and John uncorked the wine. "As if there's any power left in government. You guys, or your clients, already own the power."

"Are you going into politics, Pierre?" said Kathleen. "Federal or provincial?"

"It's okay to be ambitious," said John, "but you're not supposed to show it."

"Where did you get this lovely bread?" said Anna.

"The philosopher's *boulangerie* way out on Laurier. Pierre, please tell me what's going on."

"Well," said Pierre, "there's a group of us—"

"Eager beavers," said John. "Up-and-coming masters of the universe."

"You know most of them, Kathleen," said Pierre. "Remember Peter Languedoc from McGill? He was in Ottawa for a couple of years at the Prime Minister's Office. Louis Desbaillets, who made partner at our firm last year. I was telling John we've been meeting informally for almost a year now. Call it a study group if you want to. Every now and then we had a visitor down from Ottawa."

"This sounds exciting," Kathleen said.

"The bottom line is we wanted Peter Languedoc to run in the next federal election and we wanted a reasonably safe seat, preferably on the island of Montreal."

"Have you got it?"

Pierre sipped his wine. "As of today. A bunch of old-timers controlled the riding association. There was a squabble, which actually isn't a bad thing—opens up the whole procedure, gets people out for the candidate. But the goddamn media, I am learning, have zero interest in nomination fights in ridings."

"What about you?" said Kathleen. "You were always smarter than poor Peter Languedoc. How come you're not running?"

"I guess you could call me his campaign manager."

"If he wins, you'll go to Ottawa?"

"Who knows? Not immediately. And Peter's got to start by winning the seat."

When Kathleen was growing up, there'd been no roads in Labrador extending beyond the settlements. When her family left for their summer holidays, their car was shipped by rail to Port-Cartier, on the St. Lawrence. From there it was five hundred miles by road to Montreal.

Sometimes they got out by plane. Her parents had taken her to Disneyland when she was eleven and sent her to boarding school at thirteen. She had been just starting her PhD at McGill when she met John, who was just starting his residency as an orthopedic surgeon. Pierre was best man at their wedding and found them the apartment in Outremont.

Earlier in the summer, after Pierre had won a partnership at his firm, there had been a plan for the four of them to go out for dinner to celebrate. Pierre arrived at the Outremont apartment with a bottle of champagne, but without Anna.

"Where's your date?" Katherine asked.

"It was a boring party and she was so happy there I decided to leave her. Where's Dr. John? Let's open the champagne."

"Still at the hospital. He'll be home soon. Come on outside."

She got glasses in the kitchen and led him out to the balcony. Pierre opened the wine. He poured them each a glass and drank his own immediately. His necktie was stuffed into his pocket. Two buttons had been ripped from his shirt.

"Were you in a fight?"

"They tried to throw me into the swimming pool. Lawyers are fraternity boys. Assholes. Look, *ma chère*, pour me another glass, would you?"

"Well, you're one of them now."

"*Bien oui.*"

"Where did you get the champagne?"

"Took it from the party."

It was peaceful out on the balcony. Kathleen loved the view across the tops of the trees that shrouded the neighbourhood. She loved the calm of the apartment. John planned to teach as well as practise. They'd leave Montreal eventually and probably buy their first house in another city with a top-notch medical school and an art museum, Toronto or Vancouver, Houston or San Francisco. In the meantime the apartment was perfect. Outremont was perfect.

"You should be proud," she told Pierre. "You've done amazingly well amazingly quickly. You're a rocket."

He poured himself a third glass of champagne, spilling some on his pants. "All the senior senior partners were there this afternoon. We were all sucking up to them like crazy."

"Is that when they tried to throw you in the pool?"

The phone rang and Kathleen went inside to answer it.

"Are they there already?" John asked.

"Anna's not."

"Hold the fort. I'm due in the O.R. in two minutes; the boss needs me to assist. If it's routine I'll get a taxi, be home in an hour. If not, I'll catch you at the restaurant."

When she went back out onto the porch, Pierre grabbed her hand. She laughed and gave his a squeeze, but instead of letting go, he tried to stand. He stumbled and pulled her close to him, roughly. She felt his body heat and smelled his sweat and his heavy breath. He kissed her below the ear, then tried to kiss her on the lips, but she pulled away.

"Come on, Pierre. You don't want to ruin everything." Without looking at him she went inside and put on a linen jacket. When she came back, he had put on his jacket and was drinking the last of the champagne. He started telling her what was wrong with the province of Quebec, a litany he must have recited before when he was being wined and dined by all the powerful firms that had wanted him.

And now it was late summer. Still green, but cool at night. In the cool breeze from the northwest, the rustling of leaves had a different sound, crisper.

"I think we might have coffee in the living room," Kathleen said. "It's cooler in there. We can open the French doors."

"I love these streets," said Anna. "I don't mind the Hasidim, they add some colour, though it's mostly black. Two of my mother's maiden sisters, Tante Madeleine and Tante Louise, lived on Rue Querbes."

"Great dinner," said Pierre. "Compliments to the chef, Kathleen."

"I don't know how you do it," said Anna. "Your little apartment looks so lovely, you're always so busy with your dissertation, you are so chic—I don't know how you do it."

When the coffee was ready, Kathleen brought the things in on a tray. The doors in the living room were open to the balcony. She liked hearing the northwest wind rustle the old trees. Pierre was sitting in the chair in the corner and John had sunk into the sofa beside Anna, his legs stretched in front of him. Kathleen poured coffee and handed around the cups.

John leaned back, cradling the demitasse in his hands, and sighed. "Thirty-six hours not on call. I feel purposeless already."

Kathleen smiled. She stood before the window, looking out. The old iron lamps on Querbes Street were shaded by the maple trees.

"Kathleen," said Pierre, "do you remember Tom Katsiaficas?"

"Sure I do," she said, without turning around.

"She was going out with him when she met me," John said. "He started two years ahead of me but didn't make it."

"I spoke to him last week," said Pierre.

"I haven't thought of Tom for a long time," said Kathleen.

"I've a list of alumni with addresses in our riding," Pierre said. "I've been cold-calling, hitting up people for campaign contributions. One of the names on the list was Thomas Katsiaficas and it rang a bell. Then I remembered you used to go out with him."

"How is he? Where's he working?"

"That's the point," said Pierre. "He's on the list as Dr. Thomas Katsiaficas, so I say, 'What about you, what kind of practice are you in?'"

"I think he wanted internal medicine," said John. "His father owned a Greek restaurant in Laval."

"Well, he didn't get internal medicine. He's a veterinarian in Sainte-Anne-de-Bellevue."

"Poor Tom," said Kathleen.

"Oh, I don't know," said John. "Better a great vet than a lousy surgeon. The whole point is, be good at what you do."

"I can't see you as a veterinarian, Johnny," said Pierre.

"Why not?" John sat up on the sofa, rattling his cup and saucer. "Those people make excellent money if they're good. We'd be outside the city on a farm somewhere, a nice old farmhouse, big garden. I'd be driving a brand-new pickup truck instead of taking the Ninety bus."

"Oh, I can see you enjoying all that. You're no Albert Schweitzer."

"What is it, then?" said Kathleen.

"Mainly," said Pierre, "it's you. You would never have married a man who flunked out of med school."

Kathleen shut the doors. "You're right," she said. "I married John, didn't I."

"Top of his class, rookie of the year, hot-shot surgical resident. You would not have settled for a prosperous animal doc."

"I think she made an excellent choice," said John. "I ought to take her to the races some time — she can really pick a comer."

"You're being very silly," said Anna. "It doesn't work like that at all."

"Doesn't it?" said Pierre. "I know it's not supposed to, but I wonder sometimes."

Kathleen turned around and smiled, framing herself against the French doors.

"Look at her," said Pierre. "She knows us; she can tell you."

"I love you just the way you are," Kathleen said.

Pierre gazed at her. "You're incredible."

Anna laughed. "She's a wonderful cook, you needn't tell me that."

Cool night outside, dry rustling of leaves, pale street light.

"A drink," said John. "Can I get anyone another drink? More wine? Drop of brandy?"

WANDA

We arrived at Newark sometime after midnight. Jane was carrying her briefcase on a shoulder strap as we came off the plane, and I held a copy of my book, *Chaos and Dexterity: Conflict Management in Regional International Systems*. We'd met while working on a U.S. Navy–sponsored dyadic analysis of Syrian–Israeli air battles of the 1973 war, and after some weeks of desultory academic flirtation I had married her, hoping to banish Wanda from my dreams.

There were two Port Authority policemen standing in front of a poster for the Gerhard Richter show at MOMA. One of the cops had a hold on a girl, who was trying to wriggle free. We tried to get as close as possible. Someone told us she had been turning tricks during the flight and had drawn a plastic knife on a passenger in the first-class lavatory. The girl was young—eighteen, nineteen—and didn't look different from any ordinary passenger. She could have been a college kid on spring break. When the cop took handcuffs from his belt, she started screaming as if she was being attacked. The cop tugged her arms behind her back, then slipped on the plastic cuffs, which made a plasticky clicking noise as they closed around her wrists.

We had come to New York to meet with Hermillo Kruger, who had been Jane's thesis adviser at Columbia and was now a United States senator. We were scheduled to lunch with H.K. the following day, somewhere uptown. Jane was eager to maintain and strengthen their relationship. Washington connections are most essential in our field.

We reached our hotel at Gramercy Park after a racketing cab ride through the tunnel. Jane immediately drew a bath. While she was in the tub I checked the Manhattan directory for Wanda's number. I wanted to call her but was afraid I would not be able to control the excitement in my voice, and that Jane would overhear. I had always told her Wanda was a fling, a flirtation. Jane always laughed and said she didn't believe me, that I was still in love with Wanda even if I'd not seen her since New Orleans.

She lived in the east Fifties. I found what ought to be the correct number, but instead of dialling it immediately I dropped the directory back in the drawer and began hanging clothes in the closet. I promised myself that I would find Wanda in the morning. She wasn't expecting to see me in New York.

Jane came out of the bathroom wearing the hotel terry cloth robe, towelling her hair, and we went to bed.

Jane was prone to insomnia, and the prospect of seeing Wanda made it hard for me to find sleep, but sleep we did. However, in the middle of the night I awoke with a feeling that I was drowning. Water was surging and foaming all around me and I could taste brine at my lips. Then I realized Jane was on top of me and we were in a hotel room in New York City, making love. The windows were open, a breeze was tossing the sheer curtains, and I could hear traffic down on Lexington Avenue. A few seconds later Jane came violently, and I found myself climaxing. We did not speak. After another moment she rolled off me and we rested, tangled, dead, until first light.

Wanda was a cousin of Joe Crozier, who had served with me in the First Air Cavalry Division in Vietnam in 1970. Joe had problems after the war and I'd always tried to help him by lending him money and giving him a place to stay whenever he was in California. Six months earlier, Joe's father had phoned from New Orleans to say Joe had been killed in an explosion on a drilling rig out in the Gulf of Mexico. The Coast Guard had searched for a week without finding his body. They concluded that sharks had eaten him.

From the way the old man spoke, I could tell he expected me to drop everything and come to the memorial service at St. Augustine's Church in New Orleans. I was the only non-African-American there. Afterwards there was a wake at a tavern in Marrero, across the river. People were hugging each other, dancing, howling. I stepped up to the bar, and it was there I met Wanda. She was tall as a sunflower. She told me she had a good job taking care of a rich old man in New York City. While she spoke she touched my wrist. Her fingers were dry and cool. She told me she never came home to Louisiana except when relatives got killed or married.

We danced and I bought drinks. When she offered me a ride back to the French Quarter, we headed out to the parking lot and found her car, a big Lincoln Town Car with New York plates. She asked if I would drive. When we were on the highway, she turned to me and said, "Do you believe the dead stay dead, or do they come back to cause trouble?"

She had lowered the passenger window and the thick Louisiana night was pouring in, smelling of rot. In the moonlight her skin was almost blue. I took my hand from the wheel and touched her knee. She didn't object and I moved my hand higher. I told her that of all the dead I'd seen, not one had ever caused trouble, unless he'd been booby-trapped. She moaned and slid down on the seat and I pushed farther and rubbed between her legs. She was already wet. We were barrelling along an expressway, crossing the river, re-entering the city proper. It was almost three o'clock in the morning and there were no other cars on that highway. She was almost on the floor, with her skirt pulled up around her hips and her right hand out, planing in the rush of sweet, muddy air.

I took the first exit after the bridge and drove through the French Quarter to my hotel. We left the Lincoln in the hotel garage and took an elevator to my room on the ninth floor. She asked if Joe had ever spoken of her, and I said I couldn't remember him doing so. During the war, she told me, she had gone to church every week, lighting candles for her cousin. His parents and sisters hated her—for family reasons, she said. They wrote Joe with all kinds of lies about her. When she moved to New York City, they told him she had gone off to marry an old white man, and when Joe got out of the army, he would not come near her or answer her letters. But she never stopped loving him.

When she said this, she was wearing a sheet wrapped

around herself and staring down at me like a Yoruba princess. I believed her, and envied Joe. I'd always thought of his life after the war as a series of ridiculous escapades, but now I saw that there was grandness in what he had been denied. He had been in and out of jail on assault charges and petty larceny, had slipped from one questionable job to the next. Yet every week, Wanda told me, she stepped around the corner to St. Patrick's Cathedral and lit a candle for him.

When I awakened in the morning, she was dressed and standing at the foot of the bed, her lips open in a kind of smile, showing ivory teeth. Before I could sit up in bed the door had clicked shut behind her. I ran to open it but she had already disappeared down the corridor. I hurried back to the room and the French doors, twisting the latch and stepping out onto a narrow wrought-iron balcony. A few moments later I watched the big green Lincoln pulling out from the hotel garage and moving down St. Charles Street.

I was flushed with such despair that I thought I'd died and my soul had passed from my body. I grasped the iron rail, covered with a film of soot that I could feel soiling my hands. I stared down at the cobblestones until I could identify the colouring and texture of individual blocks. I was in the grip of some natural law, inviolable and direct as gravity, and was prepared to vault that iron railing with no more thought than I would have given to stepping out for a carton of milk or a newspaper.

Then some internal thermostat opened up and cooled me. I felt light-headed and there was pressure ringing in my ears. I stepped back inside the room, closed and latched the French doors. I remember turning on the television and sitting on the edge of the bed watching a morning news program: a blonde woman asking questions, then rough footage of tanks moving down a street. I passed out.

When I woke up, it was noon. I felt well. Sunlight poured in the window and New Orleans lay sprawling and yellow beneath a light river haze. I felt I had been cured of something. Dropping to the carpet, I did a brisk thirty push-ups. Then I got dressed, and after a room-service meal I took a cab to the airport and made my flight to California.

It was raining in Manhattan when Jane and I were awakened by a phone call confirming our lunch with Senator Kruger. He would meet us at his favourite Austrian restaurant in Yorkville at one o'clock.

As Jane and I sat in the glassed-in sidewalk café having breakfast, I studied the people out on Lexington Avenue while she scanned the *Times*. I was distracted by Wanda's presence in the city and feared to recognize her in the sidewalk crowds. I hardly glanced at the paper and absent-mindedly dropped a cufflink into a pot of Scotch marmalade. Jane asked if I was feeling jet-lagged.

By then she had her diary out and was planning her day around Hermillo. I reminded her that I'd be busy all morning with meetings of my own but promised to be at Le Vieux Kitzbühel by one. Jane scribbled the address from memory and handed it to me. I knew she'd had an affair with the old man while he was her thesis adviser, and I was morbidly curious to meet him. But before anything else I needed to see Wanda.

Jane left. In Marrero, Wanda had told me that the old man she took care of was nearly ninety, and bedridden. He'd been in the diamond trade in Antwerp and the Nazis had murdered his family. He was always accusing Wanda of stealing from him and not caring about his food. He fired her almost every week and then would plead with her not to abandon him and promise to leave her all his money.

I walked uptown. Wanda and the old man lived on a quiet block of East 51st Street, in a building with an awning and a doorman. Buildings in California don't have doormen. If there had been a doorman where I used to live, I would have been able to turn away Joe Crozier when he used to come begging. Joe was good in the war, but I used to cringe whenever I heard his voice over the lobby intercom, and often used to dream of packing up and moving away, leaving no trace, just so I'd never have to deal with him again.

The doorman at Wanda's building buzzed upstairs, then allowed me to pass through the lobby. I felt a moment of liquid fear as I stepped into the elevator and punched the button. When the doors opened to the fifth floor, I found her waiting in the hallway. She wore a crisp white nurse's uniform.

"What do you want? What you doing here?"

The elevator door began to close and I had to hit the hold button.

"I got no time for you," she said. "Get out of here."

"I thought we could have coffee," I told her. I stood there in my raincoat feeling like some glib cheap detective. "There's a café I like up near the museum. Or we could go to look at the paintings—"

"Shut up, shut up," she said, but she moved back and allowed me to step out of the elevator. She kept backing away and at the end of the hallway she turned, opened the door of an apartment, and stepped inside. I expected her to shut the door in my face but she held it open until we were both inside, then let it click shut and leaned against it, as though to stop others who might try to break in.

We were in the foyer of a gleaming modernist apartment that smelled of Jewish cooking.

"Old man died five minutes ago," she said.

"What?"

Wanda grabbed my hand and pulled me down a passage-way into a large bedroom filled with sunlight. There was a chrome-railed hospital bed in one corner, and on it the body of a withered old man, head resting on a fat pillow. His eyes were wide open and he looked surprised.

"I feed him his Jell-O an hour ago, then I come in here to see if he wants his shave and he's lying there dead."

"Have you called 911?"

"Not yet. No sense now." She touched the old man's cheek. "Maybe I ought to shave him now. He always hated whiskers."

"I got into town just last night. I had to see you again." I clasped her, kissing her throat just above the crisp white collar of the nurse's blouse.

"Every time I see you someone's died."

"Oh, Wanda!"

"Gives me a bad feeling."

I released her and stepped away. "It isn't my fault the old man died. Or Joe either. Wanda, you can't blame me. Be reasonable."

"Joe told me he saved your life plenty of times over there. He comes to you, all you give him is a handout."

Joe Crozier used to come to my place—the spotless East Bay co-op where I lived before marrying Jane—to drink my liquor and steal my clothes. He always became enraged when I wouldn't give him more money. He'd wrecked my Italian motorcycle and my Porsche. He used to go looking for fights in Berkeley, Fremont, Gilroy. The cops would pick him up on some petty charge and he'd come whining to me for bail money and a character reference.

She smiled when I reminded her of all that. "Why'd you do that, let him walk all over you? That's what got him so mad. You should've shown him more respect."

"It wasn't my fault, Wanda." I could hear a quaver in my voice and felt near tears. The old man on the bed, the way she was looking at me, her passion for a dead soldier...I'd walked inside another world. Yet everything outside, everything safe and comfortable, everything paid for and arranged, now looked like a hollow purchase. This was the real world.

"Okay, okay," she said. "I'll see you tonight. Not till late, though. Eleven o'clock."

I tried to kiss her but she turned away and touched the old man's face. "I'm a rich woman now; I can do what I like. You better get out of here. You don't want to be here when the police come."

I left the room. In case I had somehow accidentally touched the corpse, I went into a small bathroom off the foyer and washed my hands. As I stepped out into the hallway I heard a noise from the bedroom—a moan rising to a howl. She was keening.

I hurried to the elevator. On the way down I tried telling myself it would be a mistake to become further involved
with a woman like Wanda. Her colour reminded me of purple
smoke grenades. She smelled of the war. I told myself I should
have let go after Joe died, I should have closed that chapter.

As I crossed the lobby the doorman nodded politely and
held open the door. A brisk wind had opened up the sky.
Sharp shafts of sunlight reminded me of tracer and the smell
of tracer, and as I turned the corner onto First Avenue I saw
a black man flagging a taxi. He wore a long grey overcoat,
and while I waited to cross on the light he glared at me. The
eyes above cruel cheekbones were streaked red and he had a
wide, leopard's mouth. The face was a version of that face I'd
known so well. A cab pulled over and he leapt inside.

The dead live on in your imagination for a while. I had
already seen Joe five or six times in California, coming
towards me on an empty street, sometimes carrying a knife. I
had twice seen his face pressed against the passenger window
of a passing car on the 880 freeway. I was teaching myself not
to get upset each time this happened. The dead stay with you,
like a reflex. Doctors say it's normal.

I walked the thirty blocks to Yorkville, dawdling in the sunshine. Somewhere in the sixties I went into a bar and ordered
Irish coffee. I spent half an hour in a furniture store and very
nearly bought a buttoned leather ottoman. I was brooding,
trying to analyze the situation dispassionately, but I soon
gave up. After all, passion was its essence. Love and war
are much the same. When you start to believe you're seeing

things perfectly clearly you've fallen for the most dangerous illusion of all.

I ended up arriving half an hour late at Le Vieux Kitzbühel. As soon as I entered I saw Jane sitting on a corner banquette beside an old man with salt-and-pepper hair. At the next table three husky young men in nearly identical navy-blue suits were watching me.

Jane and the old man were so engrossed they didn't notice me at first. I thought they were holding hands beneath the table, and it wasn't until I was standing directly in front of them that I saw Kruger was in fact clutching a small, shiny pistol that was half concealed by the drape of the tablecloth.

Jane glanced up and saw me. Kruger looked up slowly, then dropped the little gun onto his bread plate, where it made a clink. Jane immediately picked it up and shoved it into her briefcase.

"Professor's become very security conscious," she said quickly. "He thinks I need to have something for protection."

The old man rose to shake hands. "Where I live now, in Washington, I see trouble everywhere," he said in a trembling voice. "I'm just an unhappy old man."

He had been appointed to the Senate the year before, after his predecessor committed suicide by throwing himself under a train at the Falls Church Metro station. Kruger was pre-eminent in our field, one of the great war theoreticians. Apart from his academic career he had been Kennedy's man in Argentina and one of the professors who strongly supported the Gulf of Tonkin resolution. Reagan considered appointing him ambassador to the USSR but inexplicably passed him over. No one knew for certain what madness or secrets had driven his predecessor to kill himself, although the usual rumours were aired by the media.

"I wish you'd never gone west," Kruger said, turning to Jane. "Life in California coarsens and insulates."

Jane smiled, then threw a glance at me. Her eyes are green and she doesn't blink as often as other people do. Hers are like deer's eyes: calm, quick, calculating. She has always been extraordinarily responsive to danger.

When Jane first told me about her aged lover, I had imagined a distinguished figure, a man of the world, tall, silver, erect. I had seen photographs of Hermillo Kruger in newspapers and magazines, usually flanked by men even more renowned—presidential advisers, Wall Street princes—and he always looked forceful, masculine, saturnine. But in the flesh he reminded me of a flotilla of mothballed destroyers on the Hudson that I was taken to see when I was a little boy. Kruger pulsed with the same greyness, the same atmosphere of decay. His cheeks sagged, his pale eyes were bloodshot, and his collar was loose at his scrawny neck. His manicured fingernails were thick and yellow, dead looking, as though his manicurist were a funeral director.

I thought of Warrant Officer Joe Crozier, so precise and delicate, so ferocious and so quick, flying terrible, joyful, violent missions out of Radcliff and Toughie, Belcher and Becky, and all the other forward base camps and fire bases whose stew of crazy monikers I can't seem to forget. W-1 Crozier, a cool, efficient, superbly trained twenty-year-old, in repose at the controls of his gunship.

One thing you can say about war, it is an affair of youth.

The waiter arrived with three bowls of red goulash.

Kruger immediately started in on his. A moment later Jane, beside me, gave a little start. Glancing down, I saw Kruger's hand on her knee. She pushed it away, but a few moments later, when I checked again, it was there, and this time she let it stay.

The three young men at the nearby table had an air of having spent too much time in each other's company. Every now and then I caught one of them staring at me or at Jane, as if they were trying to transcribe us directly into their computer files.

Kruger had insisted on ordering the entire meal — Jane told me this was an old habit of his. The waiter arrived with plates of dried beef, noodles, Wiener schnitzel. As we ate he recited what must have been one of his old Columbia lectures. Jane had told me that Kruger was very sensitive to the fact that his theoretical contributions to the field had never been as widely cited as his infamous area studies. Afterwards plum cakes were ordered for us, and *kaffee verkehrt*. We were sipping plum brandy when Kruger began begging Jane to go with him to the apartment he still kept near Columbia. He said he wanted to give her some books and hear her opinion of an op-ed piece his staff had been working up. He was very disappointed when she said she had an unbreakable appointment downtown. I noticed a dribble of saliva on his chin, which Jane, reaching over, deftly wiped with her napkin. In seemed to me that Kruger had aged at least six years between the goulash and the last, bitter drop of fruit brandy.

Jane was supporting his elbow as we left the table. The navy suits rose from theirs and followed. At the checkroom

Jane and I were introduced hurriedly and capriciously, as though to servants or graduate students. The young men took over, two of them helping Kruger retrieve his overcoat and hat while the third went to summon a taxi.

Out on the sidewalk, Kruger hugged Jane. It was apparent that he didn't want to let her go. A young man was holding open the door of a cab.

"*Te quiero,*" Kruger croaked as the young men bundled him gently into the cab. Two flanked him in the back seat, the third sat with the driver. Jane and I stood watching as the cab pulled out into the stream of traffic. Then she furtively slipped the little pistol from her purse and dropped it into a trash container.

A few minutes later we were in a cab racketing south on Second Avenue. Jane's elegant face was pressed against the greasy window while blocks of restaurants and bars slid by. "He said if I wouldn't sleep with him he'd shoot himself," she remarked. "But I don't believe he was serious. He's always operated that way."

The traffic thickened in the seventies and our driver lost the rhythm of the lights, stopping for the first red in thirteen blocks. There was something sexual in this battle of traffic, cars and trucks and buses lurching forward, drivers competing to gain a few seconds on the lights. I began kissing Jane's neck. Our cab broke free from the pack and raced south before sinking into another cloud of traffic below 66th Street. There is powerful desire connected with cab rides in Manhattan, with plane trips, with people thrusting through sidewalk crowds. On our flight home in 1970 a couple of sergeants smuggled a girl onto the plane and offered her at ten dollars a throw all the way to Oakland. I understand why businessmen on coast-to-coast flights are on the lookout for girls.

In the fifties I began scanning the sidewalks, searching for dark faces. It's not hard to get preoccupied with the doings of the dead. But what had I done that was so terrible? Gotten drunk the night of his memorial service, taken Wanda to my hotel, tasted her, smelled her scent on me for months afterward?

There had always been in-country stories, stories the troops never brought home. At Fire Support Base Toughie there had been a mortar platoon with a famous sergeant, Sergeant Kyle, a Kentucky woodsman who was killed one afternoon when a round blew up in his mortar tube. This was early in the war, before our time. They had him in a bag waiting for evac when the perimeter was breached and a portion of the fire base was overrun, including the hooch where they stacked the bodies. Afterwards everything got blown up or torched and they never recovered their sergeant.

Three years later, when Joe and I were regularly flying in and out of FSB Toughie, Sergeant Kyle was still a fact of life in that mortar platoon, though most of the troops at the base had still been in high school when he'd gotten zapped. But the way they told it, Sergeant Kyle was still out beyond their last perimeter, sniffing the ground, keeping an eye on things. Patrols sometimes found VC corpses with their throats cut, out there just beyond the wire.

We used to pray to Sergeant Kyle before flying a mission out of Toughie. We all did. There was a shrine in one corner of the mess tent. No one was ashamed.

Jane's afternoon appointments were a fiction. We let the

cab take us back to Gramercy Park, and as soon as we were back in our room she insisted we make love. When I kissed her, I could taste fruit brandy on her lips. Page proofs of her article that was to be published in *Foreign Affairs* were spread out beneath us on the bed, and I could see my book on the night table, lying open at a page she had wanted to memorize.

Jane liked to sleep in a pile of blankets; she felt protected that way, an animal in a burrow. Sometimes the thick, acrid silence of hotel rooms makes me wonder if I am dead. Is it the drapes blocking noise and light, the noxious chemical traces left by frequent and vigorous cleaning, the lifeless aroma of nylon carpet? When it was dark, I crept from our room, carrying my shoes, and ate dinner alone in a noisy place downtown that seemed to specialize in tiny drinks and food portions too large for anyone to consume. As I was sipping my thimbleful of Scotch, a filthy bearded individual entered the place and hurried among the tables, snatching food from plates. Diners were too frightened, perhaps too startled, to react, and the manager, a blond youth in flannel shirt and corduroys, did nothing while the derelict stalked up and down grabbing steaks, sandwiches, and handfuls of salad, stuffing everything into his pockets. After he stalked out the door I watched him pacing on the sidewalk in tight, obsessive circles, cramming our food into his mouth.

When Joe died, it had been a relief, not just for me but also for everyone who'd known him. For Joe himself, probably. That's why his memorial service had felt like a celebration.

I took a cab uptown. The doorman of Wanda's building admitted me without question. When I knocked lightly at her door, it cracked open a few inches and Wanda peered at me.

Neither of us spoke, and after a few moments she unhitched the chain, opened the door wider, and pulled me inside.

The apartment was so dark I couldn't see, but it smelled of fear, the way my slick would smell when it was crammed with pure-blooded nineteen-year-olds I was ferrying to some hot LZ.

"I told you not to come till eleven," she said.

Gradually my eyes were adjusting and I could make out pricks of light from candles she had lit and placed throughout the apartment. As soon as I saw the candles I asked if Joe had been visiting.

"He tried to come up here this afternoon," she admitted. "Doorman says, 'Wanda, there's a gentleman to see you.'

"'See me? You mean like the rabbi, the lawyer?'

"Doorman says, 'Noooo, ain't no rabbi. It's a black man. Want me to send him up or not?'

"Then I feel it: I know it's Joseph. I say, 'No, no, you send him on his way, tell him don't come round bothering me.'"

"Why?" I asked. "I thought you loved him. Anyway, are you certain it was Joe? Couldn't it have been the UPS man or something?"

She wrapped one arm around my neck and kissed me, piercing my mouth with her tongue, pressing her body into mine, curling and twisting like a snake.

"He walks," she said. "And tonight, just now, I can feel he's real angry."

She took my hand and led me into the kitchen. In the candlelight I saw what looked like jewels and blocks of money piled on the countertop.

"Old man keep stuff in the icebox." She picked up a diamond ring and handed it to me. "Feel how cold that is."

"I thought I saw Joe this morning," I told her.

She did not seem surprised. "You're like brothers, what Joe used to say. I could tell when I saw you that night—you are Joe beneath the skin. Same as him, no different. That's maybe why he is after you. He wants to come back inside. And he wants me, same as you do."

She gave a little shudder, though I wasn't convinced she really was afraid. Then she began shoving jewels and shrink-wrapped packages of currency into what looked like a pillow-case. "You ride with me. We take the Lincoln."

Thirty minutes later we were on the other side of the tunnel. Wanda was at the wheel, smiling, teeth glowing in the green light from the instrument panel. I told her about Jane and the senator and my fear that the old man was planning to murder me. I don't know if Wanda was listening. She licked her lips and switched on the radio, setting it so the tuner leapt from station to station in ten-second bursts.

I saw her glance at the rear-view mirror and for a moment I felt Joe Crozier rising, quiet as a cat, from his hiding place in the back seat. My brother in arms. Wanda drew breath sharply and let go the wheel for an instant, and the big car swerved towards the concrete divider. But she recovered fast, and in another moment we were back in the smooth, almost liquid flow of the passing lane, doing an effortless seventy. I looked around. The back seat was empty.

We did not speak. What was there to say? We were on our way to—where exactly? Philadelphia? I stared at gas flares on the refineries. Across the river, the ribald lights of Wall Street were winking and making money, and on all twelve lanes of the magnificent highway, on access ramps and bridges, the glittering flow of thousands of headlights surrounded us, embracing us. I could feel my sinews beginning to relax. We were safe; we had gotten away with everything. We were safe at home in our beautiful country.

CUP OF TEA

The river is frozen, I can see that. As the airplane taxis to
the terminal I notice a pack of wolves frolicking on the run-
way, animals down from the north, famished. Welcome to
Montreal, ferocious town. Welcome home. I am in from foreign parts and it is the third week of January. They said that
my father is dying, that I must come quickly. But I hate winter.

He's in a private room in the Ross Pavilion of the Royal
Victoria Hospital, and I aim to turn his last hours into a piece
of writing; literature is to be my brilliant career, although
it hasn't yet started and never does. All I ever am is the
wary child of a great white, grizzled sea captain, the last
Edwardian, at this moment snoozing in a hospital he isn't
ever going to leave.

This city is grey, not charming, not *vivant*. Steep streets
nasty with ice. Just inside the hospital's main door the Queen-
Empress sits heavily on her throne, rings on her fingers, eyes
blank as stone. The hospital so warped and warrened by over-
lapping reconstructions that first- and second-year medical

students study maps while steering themselves from one era
to another. It's Montreal, January, early 1980s. No acrobats in
town, not yet; no Euro-clowns; months' worth of festivals as
yet uninvented; and what I feel here, baby, is the cold.

He stirs, recognizes me, and insists that I check to see that
his seabag is undisturbed in the closet. It is, and he orders me
to start packing, for he has been in hospital long enough; he's
bored and prepared to ship out. Sliding open the drawer in
his bedside table, he displays a sheaf of passports along with
his favourite chronometer. We can go anywhere, he declares,
and there is plenty of time.

I live in a town on the beachy central coast of California,
my own anti-Montreal. An excellent surfing break, sharks
offshore, black cod, halibut, a shortage of safe anchorages,
and no deepwater harbour. Oranges, Meyer lemons, and avocados fester in the backyards. I sail a pickup truck into a dusty
zone beneath the freeway, and labourers scamper onboard
and ride back to the house to eagerly gut the bathroom, lay
sod, pick oranges, do anything asked, in return for meagre
wages. This is horrid, I agree. Yes, this is exploitation. Not
very Canadian at all. But I have never liked winter and won't
pretend otherwise.

If we can't leave here in a taxi, he says, why, let's at least
step down the hall and find ourselves a cup of tea, which he
calls "tay," an Irish pronunciation borrowed from the French.
My father is—let's keep him in the present tense for the time
being—a mariner. An old captain, a bucko seaman who has
known many a storm and carried many a passport and now
finds himself dying, just like everyone else, which is something of a surprise to both of us. He swings his lovely legs

out of bed, for the first time in a week, his nurse admits. My father groans and whistles while I slide red leather slippers onto horny feet and help him into his seersucker dressing gown. He clutches my arm with some ferocity as we exit the death chamber and start tottering down the corridor to the solarium, where afternoon tea is being served. We can smell the buttered toast. How nice.

The sheaf of passports? My old man has travelled too far, past the point where he could ever return to good old Ireland, England, Germany, or even Brooklyn. Pack ice has closed in on my papa, snapped his vessel to splinters; he's another Franklin who has gotten hopelessly lost searching for the Northwest Passage, for the cheap route to China. Way back in November he was already eating his sled dogs, and they told me he would be chewing his boots in the waiting room at the radiation clinic, every second Thursday.

The dying man's voice is missing here. What about it, Dad? Do you hear wolves barking? Are you seeing everything? Are you snow-blind?

What I feel here, baby, is the cold. The father's dying stops the callow son the way missing an elevator does. It's nothing at all like getting on a plane and flying back to California. It's not like coming home to the sun.

TRAVELLING LIGHT

Leaving Montreal, driving south for the border, he crosses the St. Lawrence on the Victoria Bridge. The convertible roof is down, the windows rolled up. It's night; it's August 1946. The war in Europe has been over for fifteen months.

He can smell the river, its salts and stinks. Irish navvies and Mohawks built this bridge in the 1860s. The Irish working low—dredging, ballast work—and the Indians working high—iron men, riveters. Looking up, he scans for ghosts walking the fretwork of iron beams.

The car chases the splash of its headlights. Tires sing on steel decking.

Driving south to see a woman. He is married, but she isn't his wife.

Anticipation, lust—he wouldn't be feeling such things if he were dead. No sense of speed if he were dead. No sense of time.

Only that morning he had decided to buy himself a car. His father had given him a cheque a week before. One thousand dollars. His weekly salary at the firm was seventy-five bucks.

"Buy a car. Do something lively! Take your wife to New York! Make her happy! And let me make a few telephone calls. It's August, almost too late, but still there's time. I have a few strings to pull, you know."

Ever since he'd come back from the war, his father, Louis-Philippe Taschereau, KC, had been urging him to apply to the McGill law school, meanwhile paying him a salary to sit in the file room of his law office, proofreading documents.

"I don't understand you. You're not getting any younger. You're no kid!" When annoyed or impatient, Louis-Philippe tended to jump back and forth between languages. Having started in English, he now switched to French. "When I was your age, *mon dieu*, I'd won some great cases! I'd argued before the Privy Council in London! I put vicious gangsters in jail—remember Buck Cohen? I sent men like that to their executions!"

"I remember you saying you admired Buck Cohen."

Louis-Philippe raised extravagant eyebrows. "Not precisely."

"At the dinner table. I remember, it was a Sunday night. They'd hung him at Bordeaux Jail the night before, just after the hockey game—Maroons versus the Canadiens. He had money riding on the game and you let him listen to it on the warden's radio."

"He was a dangerous criminal, but he had certain qualities. A civilized man, meticulous even. And he understood very well the practice of affairs. In another realm he might have been a truly significant figure."

Johnny tapped a cigarette on his wrist. "He *was* guilty, right?"

Louis-Philippe smiled. "I do believe you ought to have been one of those Jesuits. We began by discussing the difficulty you seem to be having settling down to a serious life; now we interrogate the condition of my soul. You would make a very effective lawyer." He paused. "In any case, consider my profession. As Crown prosecutor, I sent men to their deaths. You might say I functioned as a professional killer. So, perhaps, did you."

Louis-Philippe had never enquired about his war experiences. No one had. The war now seemed like a movie he'd watched with his nose five inches from the screen. He'd killed, participated in killings, but hadn't thought of killing Germans as killing people, except once or twice.

"I wish to reorient our little talk," Louis-Philippe said. "Is anything wrong with you, physically? Did you acquire any disease during the war?"

"What do you mean?"

"You are able to enjoy your wife?"

"Papa, you didn't used to talk such *merde*. Jesus. If you've got something to say, say it plain."

Louis-Philippe nodded, then briskly proceeded to lay out his case. "Stop being a superior, snotty-nosed little Jesuitical bastard looking down at the rest of us because we were not fighting by your side for the liberation of Europe. Accept that you are a grown man, that you live in this city, have a wife and child, and it is your obligation to make a successful life. Submit yourself to learning the law—McGill or Laval, it doesn't matter to me—and training your mind. Otherwise you might as well drive a taxi. That's all you'll be good for. You're no Buck Cohen; you haven't his gifts. Am I plain enough? Are you hearing me, *mon fils*? *Tu comprends?*"

"Loud and clear."

"*Tiens.*"

That would have been the moment to lay the cheque down on the desk and walk out of the office for good. Instead he'd deposited the money, though without mentioning it to Margo, and kept walking to work every morning.

Until this morning. When he'd made up his mind. To buy a car.

Just that. Nothing more than that.

"If you're looking for a new machine, you're out of luck."

They sat in Ed Doyle's small beige office at Doyle Motors in Verdun, chatting about men they'd known at Loyola, where they had never been close pals. Ed's buxom red-haired secretary brought coffee. Then Ed got down to business.

"None of us dealers have new machines available at the moment. We'll be getting inventory any day now, but here's the catch: it's already spoken for. My dad's had customers on a waiting list since nineteen forty. So I won't have anything for you for maybe three, four months. By then we'll probably be in another depression. What sort of machine were you looking for?"

"Convertible."

"You need it right away?"

"That's what I was thinking."

"Our used cars are clean and solid; we don't deal in junk. Interested?"

"I suppose so. If that's all there is."

"I'd be moving twenty, thirty new cars a week if I could get my hands on them. Let's see what's on the lot. We'll find something to suit you, Johnny. How much you willing to spend?"

"Depends."

"Uh-huh. Well, let's have a look around, pal."

They had graduated in the class of 1939 at Loyola, earning BAs from the Jesuits and commissions through the officer training corps. Johnny had gone active with the Régiment de Maisonneuve, Ed Doyle with the Black Watch.

A few days after landing in France, Johnny had been leading his company through a wheat field when he'd come across a dozen Black Watch corpses laid out in a neat row, probably caught by a single machine-gun traverse. The wheat had been ripe, dusty, waist-high. Weapons, rations, and pieces of equipment had been picked over and were strewn about, another sign that the Germans in Normandy were running out of ammunition and food. The Black Watch, like the Maisonneuves, were a Montreal militia regiment, but he hadn't recognized any of the dead. He hadn't looked too closely, though, before detailing two of his men to fix bayonets on the rifles and plant them along the road, where a Graves Registration party would see them.

Ed led him out to the lot. Placards with snappy sayings were on all the windshields. STEAL THIS BABY! ONLY $499!

"Ignore that bullshit, it's embarrassing." Ed Doyle took a handkerchief from his pocket, hunkered down, rubbed the inside of the tailpipe, then displayed the handkerchief to Johnny. "A little grey smudge—that's fine, that's what you want. If it comes up with black grease, soot, means she's burning oil, the rings are gone, probably the engine's cooked. If your hanky comes up clean, the seller has been shining her up and hoping for a sucker. Light grey is fine. All things in moderation, eh? Let's take a recce under the hood."

The hood opened with a groan. "V-8," Ed said approvingly. "Battery looks almost new. We'll put in a couple of new hoses." Unscrewing the radiator cap, Ed poked his finger inside, sniffed the fluid, then rubbed the moisture between his thumb and forefinger. "Clean. You don't want oil in the rad, or something's cracked. Have a look underneath, Johnny. See if there's any drips. She's been sitting here a week at least."

Johnny got down on hands and knees and peered underneath the engine. "I don't see anything."

"The rubber looks pretty darn good. She must have been stored for the duration. Why don't you slide in, see how she feels."

Before the war, he and his sister had shared a white Studebaker coupe. The engine block froze and cracked sometime during the war, after Lucie had entered the convent at Sault-aux-Recollets. Their father still drove a stately black Packard he had bought from the bishop of Trois-Rivières.

The Buick's seats were red Naugahyde. The rubber floor mats had been swept. There was room to stretch his legs, and the clutch pedal felt firm when he pressed it. He gripped the wheel and cupped the gearshift in his fist. "Who owned it before?"

"I'd have to check. We might have picked it up at auction. What's the mileage?"

Johnny read it off the odometer. "Eleven thousand, five hundred, and forty."

Ed gave a low whistle. "And I'll tell you one thing: my old man's probably the only dealer in town who never turns back a clock. For five hundred bucks, Johnny, this really is a steal. We're making no money. It sounds like bullshit, I know, but if you don't buy it somebody else will, and pay six hundred bucks at least. You're getting a Fifth Brigade special here."

"Where's the key?"

"Never let the customer cold-crank a car. If they ask, I say I left the keys in the office. We walk back and one of the mechanics sneaks out to turn her over. Any machine'll run better when it's warmed up. But go ahead, do your worst. Under the floor mat, passenger side."

He turned the key and pressed the starter pedal with his foot. The engine instantly kicked into life. Ed gave a thumbs-up.

The car, trembling slightly, felt solid and alive.

Ed leaned in at the window. "Well, what do you think?"

"I really want something a little newer."

"Johnny, for four hundred bucks you're looking a gift horse in the mouth. Now you want to kick it in the ass?"

"All right. Four hundred."

He'd been overseas nearly three years. Margo had given up their apartment and was living at her parents' home in Westmount.

When he wanted to make love, in the bedroom that had been hers as a girl, she didn't resist, but she didn't respond with much feeling either, or so it seemed to him. After thirty-six hours he was convinced that he didn't love his wife and

never had. As far as his daughter, Barbara, was concerned, he
had hardly any feelings, except impatience when she cried.

Margo had found them an apartment in lower Westmount
by the second week. Most of their furniture had been a wedding present from her parents and had spent the past two
years in storage; it was unfamiliar to him.

A cleaning lady came in two mornings a week. They
lived in the apartment like a couple of old people. Their new-
found privacy only made the distance between them even
more obvious. He bought two suits and walked to work at
his father's law office, five days a week. He came home, sat in
an armchair in the living room, and tried to read the *Star*. But
the only pages he could bear to look at were the sports and
weather.

They ate alone together after Barbara was put to bed.
Margo lit candles, set out their wedding silver, and used the
good china, even if they were eating at the little table in the
kitchen. Her manners, her style were perhaps some version of
love. Maybe that would have been enough for him before, but
now it plainly wasn't.

"Do we love each other, Margo?"

He'd been a little drunk. Maybe she was too. He'd mixed
martinis, then gimlets, then opened a bottle of wine from the
case Louis-Philippe had presented to them.

"You tell me."

I married you, he thought, *for those cold green eyes, that chin,
that Irish toughness.*

"I know you're unhappy," she said.

"How about you? I don't feel your happiness. I don't feel it
in the air of this place."

"I'm trying to adjust to having you home. Looking forward to it for so long somehow makes it harder."

"I wish you'd let me fuck you on the kitchen floor."

"Why do you have to talk that way?"

"Don't you think it's important?"

"You're just trying to sound like a soldier."

"If you're buying a car you must have a job." Ed Doyle spoke without looking up from the paperwork on his desk. They were back in the beige office.

"I'm doing a little work for my old man," Johnny replied.

He lit a cigarette. The chairs in the sales office were red leather with chrome armrests. He liked them. They could have been car seats, or bucket seats in a bomber. Montreal was full of old-fashioned crap, dark and heavy.

"Nice to be home," Ed said.

The Black Watch had been a strong outfit, though they'd had their bad days. Of course the Maisonneuves had had their bad days too.

"Ed?"

The car dealer looked up.

"Are you married?" Johnny asked.

"Not yet. What about you?"

"I married in forty-one."

"Oh yeah. One of the O'Brien girls, right? Frankie?"

"Margo."

"If she's anything like Frankie, she's a peach. I dated Frankie once or twice. Their old man still around?"

"He is."

"He's a tough nut. Have any kids?"

"One, a girl."

"The world needs kids."

"I find I don't know her at all. My wife."

Ed didn't respond at first, and Johnny thought he was pretending he hadn't heard.

Then Ed looked up from the paperwork. "Sure, I can understand that. Hell, it's got to take a while—it was a long fucking war. Sign there and there." He pushed papers across the desk. "I took Frankie O'Brien to a dance at Victoria Hall. Remember after those dances, the girls always taking off their shoes and stockings and wading in the pool under the fountain, holding up their dresses? I used to think they looked like swans."

Life before the war seemed like something you were looking at through the wrong end of a telescope.

"How are you going to pay me?"

"Will you take a cheque?"

"Sure. You're an officer and a gentlemen, aren't you."

It was just a car, not even a new car—a new old car. He'd had a notion of taking his wife north for a drive in the country, a swim at the lake. Really. That had been the plan.

Instead of going downtown to the law office he turned left on Sherbrooke Street, headed into Westmount, parked on their quiet little street.

They could leave the little girl with one of Margo's sisters for the afternoon.

Each little flat in the Edwardian terrace had its own front door. As soon as he opened theirs he could hear the electric clock on the kitchen stove and smell the floor wax and furniture polish, and he knew the apartment was empty. The cleaning lady had gone home and Margo had probably taken Barbara to the park or up the hill to her grandparents' house.

He walked through the empty rooms, smoking a cigarette. In the spotless kitchen he tapped his ashes carefully into the sink, then wheeled and walked back out to the living room, where he stood at the front window, staring out at his car. The bulbous grey fenders were the colour of gunmetal, the seats were red, and the soft top was cream, the colour of a woman's healthy skin.

Going into the bedroom, he began lifting shirts and underwear from a drawer and packing them into his old army kit bag.

Back in July, in Maine, Margo had been sitting in a striped canvas beach chair, scribbling on a yellow legal pad. "There!" she said, drawing a brisk underline stroke on the page. "Done."

"Done what?" He lay on a beach towel, groggy, abstracted by the sun's desirous heat. They were staying with his parents at their cottage on Kennebunk Beach. Southern Maine was crowded with Canadians, for the first time since 1939. They overheard plenty of French in cafés and gas stations and along the beach, and fresh copies of the *Star* and *La Presse* were stocked at the local stores, along with Canadian cigarette brands — Sweet Caps, Player's, Export A.

"A weekly budget. I've written down everything we spend money on. You can check it and tell me if there's anything I've forgotten." She held out the pad but he didn't take it. "I'm trying to figure out exactly what we need to live on while you're at law school. It comes to forty-three dollars per week if we cut Mrs. Moodie to one day and your father pays your tuition."

"I am not going to law school, Margo. I've already told you."

"You haven't said what you're going to do instead." After a few moments she continued. "You have to do something, Johnny. You can't keep clerking for your father. You're not a clerk. Summer's over in a little while."

He lay with his eyes shut, wishing he were back in the army and still looking forward to the end of the war. He heard her rummage in her beach bag for a cigarette, scrape a match, light up.

"You're not the man I married. You're like a bloody stranger."

The flat aroma of tobacco smoke reached his nostrils. He wanted a smoke but he didn't want to sit up, open his eyes, didn't want to look at her.

"I don't know what's gotten into you," Margo said. "I know you can't be the same as you used to be. I just wish you could be someone more likeable. It's hard to have any respect for you at all."

"Does your mother respect your father, do you think?"

Once or twice a year, Margo's stern, puritanical old man would disappear on crazy binges. One of the children would be dispatched to New York City to retrieve him from whichever hotel he'd holed up in—the Waldorf, the Plaza, or the Biltmore—and bring him home on the train, whisky-soaked and tremulous. Johnny had twice accompanied Margo on those trips. All the O'Brien girls were fanatically loyal to their father.

"I'm going inside." Margo stubbed her cigarette in the sand.

"Look, Margo—"

"No, thank you." Standing up, she grabbed the beach bag and walked off.

He'd stayed on his towel as a fog began rolling in, slowly driving people from the beach. The tide was falling. He could feel a heavy surf thumping the sand. He knew he was alive for no good reason. It was a matter of inches and split seconds, of choosing to take a step this way instead of that way. It wasn't hard to imagine having made different choices, in which case he'd now be parked in one of the soldier cemeteries in Europe.

He rose and walked down to the hard-packed wet sand. When he was a child, he had stood with the cold Atlantic biting at his feet, calling across the waves to his grandmother in Ireland. Ireland was actually a long way to the north. Kennebunk lay along the same latitude as Bayonne, France. He had checked it out in the dog-eared, summer-thumbed atlas at the cottage.

Wading through hissing surf, he shoved his body beyond the first breaker, then dove in and swam strongly out beyond the break. The water was fizzing and chill, but he kept heading offshore.

After swimming for ten or fifteen minutes, he was at the peak of a swell when he heard a metallic clanging: the red buoy marking the mouth of the Kennebunk River navigation channel. He realized he was in some danger of being run over by a vessel making for the river. A skipper at the helm of a fishing boat or a sardine carrier would be unlikely to notice a swimmer.

The tide was pulling offshore and he let himself swim along with it, wishing to get clear from any boat traffic as quickly as possible. At the bottom of a swell he could see nothing except grey-green sea. He had felt a grain of fear then, and swam even harder.

After ten more minutes of powerful swimming, he could feel his head leaking heat. At the top of a swell he looked around and felt another chill of fear: he couldn't see the shore. He started swimming against the pull of tide, hoping that he was heading for the beach and not the river channel. He'd lost his sense of time, his stroke was getting weaker, and he could feel his thoughts slowing and thickening, like a gearbox overfilled with oil.

He forced himself to swim another forty strokes. His right shoulder, dislocated in a Jeep accident, was throbbing. His stroke was losing all efficiency; he wasn't getting the torque his body needed to screw itself through the water. Feeling the drag of his swim trunks, he shucked them. The rising tide beat like a hammer against his head and shoulders.

The bright, bitter taste of gasoline startled him. Swallowing a mouthful, he sputtered and coughed. Then he saw the lobster boat, fifty yards off, heaving up and down on the swell. There was a figure at the helm, another in front of the red triangle of stern sail. He knew right away that they'd seen him—the boat was circling—but he didn't notice them throwing the life preserver until it plopped near enough for him to reach out and drag it over his head, then wriggle until it was lodged under his arms. It was a drill they'd practised many times in England.

As he was towed through the water, the snarl of exhaust

grew louder and the stink of bait and gasoline more intense. He came alongside the boat, slithering against the hull planking, and was hoisted and swung aboard on the block used for hauling traps.

"My God, he's buck naked!"

Someone wrapped a blanket around him, helped him to the shelter of the wheelhouse, and sat him down on an overturned bucket. A little boy was staring at him.

The skipper opened up the throttle and turned his bow into the swell. "What the hell happened to you?" he shouted. "Is anyone else in the water? Where's your boat?"

Johnny shook his head.

"No? You sure?"

He nodded.

"Pour him some coffee outta my Thermos," the skipper said to the deckhand, who was coiling the lifeline.

The skipper turned back to Johnny. "Where'd you go down? Can you give me a heading?"

Men had died of cold along the Scheldt even before there was snow on the ground. They'd died in their foxholes after four days of Dutch rain. He knew he must catch hold of his senses, which had somehow slipped out of gear, like a burnt-out transmission.

The deckhand was handing him a tin cup of steaming coffee. Johnny was shaking and it was hard to hold the cup, but he made himself sip the hot liquid, burning his lips. Swallowing, he felt it scorching down inside. But he wasn't getting any warmer; he could feel his body still leaking heat.

"I'm very cold," he said, his voice whispery and weak.

"What?" the skipper shouted.

Johnny tried raising his voice above the hammering engine. "I have to get warm."

"We'll be on the wharf in ten minutes." The skipper opened the throttle. "You want a smoke?" As the engine roar increased, the bow lifted out of the water. "Hey, Polly! Give the guy a smoke."

"He doesn't need a smoke. He needs you to strip down and get under the blanket with him and give him your body heat."

Johnny saw that the deckhand was a young woman with a white, thin face and dark hair.

"He'll die if you don't, Leo! Go on, I'll take the wheel."

"No fuckin' way."

"Then I will." She began unbuttoning her mackinaw. "I'm going to hang my coat over your head, mister," she told Johnny.

He couldn't see anything with the jacket draped over his head. It was warm and heavy and stank of wool. But he heard her pulling off rubber boots, unzipping her dungarees.

"Jesus, Polly."

"Okay, open up, mister. Let me in."

He held the blanket open and she sat down quickly on his lap, pulling the blanket around them both, then lifting the coat off his head so he could see.

"Leo, he's shivering so bad. He's really cold."

The skipper was at the wheel, staring straight ahead. She wrapped her arms around Johnny, pressing herself against him. He could hear his teeth chattering uncontrollably. The sound was frightening, but he couldn't stop it.

"Come here, Jackie." She was reaching out to the little boy, who was staring at them balefully with his thumb in his mouth. "Come inside with Mama, where it's nice and warm. Leo, he could use more coffee."

The skipper filled the cup and handed it to her. She drew the little boy under the blanket with them; Johnny could feel the boy's feet stepping on his toes. The woman draped her arm around Johnny's neck while she held the tin cup to his lips. "Swallow this, it'll help."

He could feel the liquid burning down into his core. She hugged him for a long time, and he began to feel the heat radiating from her breasts and her arms. By the time the boat entered the Kennebunk River his head was clearing and the shivering had subsided.

"Look at the seals, Jackie." The woman pointed to harbour seals basking on a breakwater.

The skipper said, "You sure there's no one else out there, pal?"

"I was alone. I was swimming off the beach."

"You were heading for the fuckin' Azores when we saw you. Polly, get some clothes on before we tie up."

"We ought to take him to the hospital maybe."

"No," Johnny said. "I'll be all right now."

"You sure?" She looked at him doubtfully.

"Ask me my name."

"Huh?"

"Taschereau, Jacques Taschereau. From Montreal. Staying at my parents' cottage, Beach Avenue, Kennebunk Beach. It's Friday, July twenty-first. No, twenty-second. Harry Truman is president and Mackenzie King's prime minister."

"Yeah?" She seemed amused.

"It's how to tell if a man's losing heat—ask questions. See

if he's thinking straight. You can see I'm oriented. I'll be fine."

"I'm going to cover you up again," the woman said.

She hung the woollen mackinaw over his head and he listened to her getting dressed, zipping up her dungarees. When she lifted away the jacket, he blinked in the garish light. They were approaching the wharf that the lobstermen used; the skipper cut back the throttle.

"Leo, you got some clothes he can wear?"

Something in her speech was familiar but Johnny couldn't quite place it.

"Look in the seabag."

She was pulling dungarees and a blue shirt from a canvas duffle when something fell onto the deck with a clunk. She picked it up and he recognized a Colt .45 automatic, the weapon American officers and MPs carried as a sidearm. She dropped the pistol back into the seabag and handed Johnny the clothes. "Here, put these on."

He felt dizzy as he stood up. The skipper saw it and reached out, steadying him. "Sure you don't want a corpsman, pal?"

"No, no, I'll be fine." The chambray shirt and dungarees were daubed with crusts of red-lead bottom paint. The shirt had USN stencilled on the chest. He began pulling on the clothes.

"Polly, take the truck, drop him off up the beach, then come back for me. I got a few things to take care of on the boat."

As they approached the dock she stood amidships, dock line in hand. They had hung a couple of auto tires over the side as fenders. The skipper laid up neatly alongside the float, and she jumped off and quickly cleated dock lines fore and aft.

The skipper lifted the little boy over the side, then turned to Johnny. "Need a hand, pal?"

"No, I'm fine." He reached out and shook hands with the skipper. "Thanks."

"Anytime."

As soon as Johnny had stepped onto the dock, Polly threw the lines aboard. He read the name freshly painted on the transom, *Marie Claire,* as the old boat began chugging back out to a mooring.

"Watch out, mister, with your bare feet—there's broken glass. The truck's over here. C'mon, Jackie, let's take this man home."

"I'm Jacques Taschereau," he said, extending his hand.

"Yeah, I got that." Her hand was small and strong. "Polly Beausoleil."

Bo-so-leel. It explained the dark hair, the familiar lilt in her speech.

"*Vous êtes canadienne?*"

"My *mémère*'s from Canada." She grabbed the little boy's hand and they started towards the parking lot, where a dozen rusting pickups stood in awkward stances, like men with bad knees.

"*Parlez-vous francais?*"

"Not really, not anymore." She opened the door of a green pickup as battered and rusty as all the other trucks. "Come on, Jackie, climb aboard. Your mama's going to drive this thing."

Johnny climbed in on the passenger side. Polly lifted the boy in, then climbed in herself and shut her door. "I hate this old truck, the brakes are shot." She found a key in the ashtray, switched on the ignition, and ground the starter pedal with her heel. The starter whined a few times before the motor caught, and the truck began shuddering and smoking. She shoved it into gear and steered out of the lot, and they were immediately caught up in the heavy tourist traffic inching through Dock Square. She kept shifting into neutral and gunning the motor so it wouldn't stall.

The little boy had climbed onto Johnny's lap and was gazing out at the cars and tourists. Polly patted the seat beside her. "Hey, Jackie, sit."

"He's fine here."

"He loves trucks. And boats. Wait'll he sees an airplane."

"Is your husband fishing full-time?"

"Leo's my brother."

"Oh."

"He says he's never crossing the Piscataqua Bridge again, never leaving Maine. He bought that tub when he got back from the war. He's going to put in a new engine, he says. He wants to lobster, but it's hard when you're not born to it. They don't like outsiders around here, especially Frenchies from Biddeford. They been cutting his traps, trying to scare him off."

He watched people in bright clothes licking ice cream cones on the balcony of the River View Café. On the other side of the road, tourists waited in line to order lobster rolls and fried clams at the window of Gooch's takeout shack.

"Lot of tourists," he said.

"Oh, yeah. In this town they're back to making money."

They finally made it over the little drawbridge. She drove up to the junction and turned left onto the road following the river out to Kennebunk Beach.

"You live in the 'Port?" he asked.

"Biddeford."

A textile town, five miles up the coast. The mill was on Main Street, one red-brick wall rising sheer from the sidewalk, with rows of tiny windows and iron shutters. When he was a kid he thought it was a jail, not a factory. It used to scare him. He used to dream about it.

"They don't like outsiders in the 'Port, especially from Biddeford. Leo, they cut his gear, and now sometimes he finds bullets they put on the front seat. But he won't give up. He's a crazy Frenchman."

"Were you lobstering today?"

"Not on Sunday. He just took us for a ride. Jackie loves going on the boat with Uncle Leo, don't you, sweetie?"

"Where's Jackie's father?"

"Killed in the war."

The old truck's motor was nearly as loud as the boat. The road bent to follow the beach. The fog had blown off, the light was clear and detailed, and people were walking on the shining wet sand.

"It's nice out here," Polly said. A salt breeze was blowing, snapping flags on whitewashed poles. "I wouldn't mind living out here all summer. It gets awful muggy up in Biddeford."

"What do you do?"

"I was at Hôpital Notre-Dame, sort of a bookkeeper for the nuns, but I got pretty tired of it. Now I'm working at a garage, keeping track of the bills. It's tough in Biddeford with the boys back from the war—Pepperell's are letting people go. But the garage is good. *C'est une bonne job.* My *mémère,* she minds Jackie. Where's your parents' house? Is it one of these?"

"Up around the point. You can't see it yet."

"You don't sound so French."

"My father's French, my mother's English. I grew up in both languages."

She braked to allow two women in sundresses, pushing strollers, to cross the road. "Does everyone speak French up there?"

"Most people. But there's English too."

"We were going to live in California after the war. Jeff did his pursuit training at Santa Barbara. He fell in love with California and I was going to go out. A bunch of the pilots brought their wives out, only I was pregnant, and pretty sick for a while, then his group got orders for the South Pacific. He said after seeing California he never wanted to live anyplace else. He sent us boxes of oranges for Christmas. We were all going to move out there after the war, his parents, brothers and sisters, *mémère*, everyone. Was Canada in the war?"

"Yes, two years before the States."

"You don't hear much about Canada. My *mémère* grew up in Tingwick—know where that is?"

"Arthabaska County. It's what they call the *bois francs*, hardwood country. It's near where my father's family is from."

"You should meet my *mémère*. She came down here when she was twelve. Got off the train and went right to work at Pepperell's. Her back's all crooked from bending over the loom. She talks about going up to Canada, but she never will."

There were swimmers in the water, and kids playing in the waves.

"Sorry about your husband."

"Yeah." She pumped the clutch and downshifted. "I'm a little tired of all the 'sorry' stuff, to tell the truth." She was gripping the wobbling wheel with both hands. "I never was on a boat before the *Marie Claire*. It's nice being your own boss, but I don't know if I'd be willing to fight off the whole town just to spend ten hours a day hauling traps and the rest of the time on my back working on an engine. You were in the war, right?"

"Yes."

"When I go a few hours without thinking about Jeff, it feels like I'm committing a sin. Even Leo said—" She caught herself. "Okay, that's enough. *Ferme ta gueule.*"

The boy bounced happily on Johnny's knee. They were coming up to Lord's Point. Past the Point it was only a couple of hundred yards to the cottage.

Polly suddenly veered the truck across the road and brought it to an abrupt stop beside the seawall. Switching off the engine, she shook out a cigarette from a pack of Chesterfields, then offered him one. She lit them both with a match. Inhaling, she leaned back until her head touched the rear window. She wore her dark hair tied back. Her neck was long and slender. She might have been an Indian.

"You need to get home," she said, "but let me finish this. I can't smoke and drive. Holding this machine on the road takes all my concentration."

"A few minutes won't make a difference."

"Jeff's father has a funeral home—Salon Funéraire Beausoleil. They wanted Jeff to be a priest but he ended up going to the Suffolk School of Law in Boston. He finished just when the Marines were looking for pilots. He could have been a navy lawyer, but flying was something he always wanted to try. He thought he'd be good at it."

Reaching across, she touched her son's curls. "My life is

like someone else is living it, not me. What everyone wants is for me to marry Ray. He owns the shop where I work—Ray Prudhomme, Jeff's cousin. Not right away, but maybe in six months. That's what they're hoping will happen. 'Ray'll give her a good home, make a good papa for Gérard's boy,' that's what they say. Gérard, that was Jeff's Canadian name."

"Is that what you're going to do?"

"Oh, Christ. Maybe I will."

She flipped her cigarette out the window and was leaning forward to turn the key when he placed the palm of his hand on her back and, leaning forward, kissed her.

The first kiss landed on the side of her mouth, but she turned to him, and the next kiss was full on her lips. Her soft, dry lips tasted bitter from the cigarette.

They broke apart. The little boy was still perched on Johnny's lap. Without a word, Polly pressed the starter with her heel, then shoved the truck into gear. Glancing over her shoulder, she steered back out at the road.

"How long are you staying?" she said.

"We're driving back to Montreal tomorrow."

"Oh God, you're married."

"Yes."

"Where's your cottage? Is it one of these?"

"Keep driving, forget the cottage. Just keep going."

"Which one is yours?"

"That one." He pointed.

She stopped the truck just past the garden gate, and he could smell the rancid sweetness of the *Rosa rugosa* his mother had planted so many summers before.

"Your wife will be worried sick."

"Forget about her."

Both hands on the wheel, she stared straight ahead. "I don't know who the hell you think you are, but you better get out now."

He shifted the little boy onto the seat, then opened the door and climbed out. She gunned the motor and started off before he'd even closed the door, which clanged shut on its own as he watched the old truck rocking down the road.

Reaching for the *Rosa rugosa*, he pinched one of the prickly stems between his fingers, then leaned down and breathed the musk without trying to pluck the ragged little pink flower. There was a dab of dark blood, almost purple, on his fingertip. He touched it with his tongue, tasting salt. No sense of taste if he were dead.

Now it's night, he's in the new-old Buick on the iron bridge above the St. Lawrence, and he isn't thinking about his wife or his daughter, or even Polly Beausoleil. He's thinking of the long-since dead, the Irish navvies with their dredges and barrows, the Mohawks in their moccasins cat-walking iron beams two hundred feet above the river.

Then, all of a sudden he's across. The Buick floats down the bridge ramp almost by itself, he barely needs touch the wheel. Commissioned or demobbed, lost or found, dead or alive, he's on the South Shore. The powerful scent of farm country rises up, cattle, manure, late-summer, hay and he feels the big car bending itself south onto the highway for New England.

AUTHOR'S NOTE

The oldest story here ("In Montreal") appeared in *Best Canadian Stories 1977*; the newest ("Civil Wars") was written last week, provoked by the experience—occasionally painful—of rereading the others. Most were published in a 1987 collection, *Night Driving*. I have revised the older stories, but tried to avoid rewriting. I approached them more in the spirit of a translator.

I have arranged the stories (roughly) by geography, which seems to correlate (roughly) with tone, theme, and the ages of the main characters. The first stories are mostly set in Montreal. The characters or voices are boys or very young men. The next bunch is set on the road or in the West, and the protagonists are usually lost souls in their twenties. The last group of stories is set in cities, with characters edging towards their thirties—which doesn't, of course, seem so old anymore. At the very end is a pair of stories that came up when I was trying to write my way into an extended family story that is the subject of my first two novels, *The Law of Dreams* and *The O'Briens*, and is the story I am still writing in my third novel. "Cup of Tea" and "Travelling Light" are approaches to that family story.

I grew up in an apartment on a hillside in Montreal, within a reasonably affectionate middle-class Canadian family. There was a good deal to be explored there but I did not notice it at the time, or only caught it in glimpses. I got the title of the original collection from my gentle father, whose final piece of advice when I was eighteen and leaving home for the first time — heading out west in an old car — was, "Never drive at night. That's when all the nuts are out on the road." Leaving home, going out west, spinning down the night road, was very much the spirit behind the original collection.

The young man who wanted to be a writer and who self-consciously rackets through many of these stories was a Dylan-obsessed boy eager to quit the staid Montreal apartment, to leave the hillside and the impeccably middle-class family. There are thousands of versions of that boy, or that girl, throughout history. Later on, writing screenplays in California and not doing very well at it, I began to see that my real subject as a writer might be everything I'd been trying to escape, but the stories here — most of them — are still about the voyage out. Their dynamic is night driving, night drives. They seem to be heading for the wonderful, scary place that people in Maine, where I live now, call "away."

But even as I was assembling *Night Driving*, my gravitational curve was bending towards home. "The Servants' Way" and "Yellow Dress," both from *Night Driving*, aren't road stories at all. In one, a boy leaves home but the story's about the home. Both are grounded in an urban, middle-class childhood in a specific time and place. I've not lived in Montreal for decades but that city still seems radiant to me.

These stories now seem to be mostly about growing up. A young person is in love with language and syntax but is not very wise and owns little first-hand experience. He's often not writing what he knows. He doesn't know what he knows. He doesn't grasp that experience counts for a lot, that wisdom exists, that silence is—sometimes—golden. He's trying to claim a life for himself. Sometimes he's trying to fake it. He does, however, believe in the world.

In my first novel the protagonist reminded himself *An animal is all you are. And the world's just ground and light.* A writer's corollary to this might be: *Well, then, pay attention.* That is what the young man who wrote these stories was trying to do.

ACKNOWLEDGEMENTS

Many of these stories were published, in slightly different versions, in *Night Driving* (Macmillan of Canada, 1987.) Stories not in that book first appeared in the following publications: "Smell of Smoke," *The Walrus*; "To the Dead Girl," *Rubicon*; "Father's Son," *Brick*; "The Ice Story," *Saturday Night*; "Fire Stories," *Translation*; "Fiona the Emigrant," *Fiction*; "Cup of Tea," *Globe and Mail*. "Mermaids Too" was published as "The Dream of Tenderness" in *Matrix*.

PHOTO: RYAN GOODRICH

PETER BEHRENS is the Governor General's Literary Award–winning author of *The Law of Dreams* and *The O'Briens*, published around the world to wide acclaim. His short stories and essays have appeared in *Atlantic Monthly*, *Tin House*, *Saturday Night*, and the *National Post*. He was born in Montreal and lives on the coast of Maine with his wife and son.